Marcia Willett's early life was devoted to the ballet, but her dreams of becoming a ballerina ended when she grew out of the classical proportions required. She had always loved books, and a family crisis made her take up a new career as a novelist – a decision she has never regretted. She lives in a beautiful and wild part of Devon.

Find out more about Marcia Willett and her novels at www.marciawillett.co.uk

www.rbooks.co.uk

THE SUMMER HOUSE

MARCIA WILLETT

CORGI BOOKS

TRANSWORLD PUBLISHERS
61–63 Uxbridge Road, London W5 5SA
A Random House Group Company
www.randomhouse.co.uk

THE SUMMER HOUSE
A CORGI BOOK: 9780552158480

First published in Great Britain
in 2010 by Bantam Press
an imprint of Transworld Publishers
Corgi edition published 2011

Addresses for Random House Group Ltd companies outside the UK
can be found at: www.randomhouse.co.uk
The Random House Group Ltd Reg. No. 954009

The Random House Group Limited supports The Forest Stewardship
Council (FSC®), the leading international forest certification organisation.
Our books carrying the FSC label are printed on FSC® certified paper.
FSC is the only forest certification scheme endorsed by the leading
environmental organisations, including Greenpeace. Our
paper procurement policy can be found at
www.randomhouse.co.uk/environment

Typeset in 11½/15½pt Garamond Book by
Kestrel Data, Exeter, Devon
Printed and bound in Great Britain by Clays Ltd, St Ives PLC

4 6 8 10 9 7 5 3

To Rufus

THE SUMMER HOUSE

PART ONE

CHAPTER ONE

The photographs were in a packet at the bottom of the rosewood box. He flicked through them, surprised to see that each one of them was of him – a photographic record spanning thirty years – and then tucked the packet back into the box. Solid, square, with pretty gold inlay, the box carried not only his mother's small treasures but a whole cargo of family history. It had belonged to his father's mother and therefore held a special link with the man whom he could barely recall. His memories of this shadowy figure had been jealously guarded, eked out and plumped up with a dozen tiny scraps of information dropped from the conversations of friends and family.

'Of course, *you* can't remember him,' he'd say to his small sister, Imogen. '*You* were just a baby when Daddy died.'

She didn't care; Im was blessed with a happy,

confident nature that made it nearly impossible for him ever to feel superior. She'd shake her head cheerfully, quite content for him to be the one who knew. She didn't care about the box either. The small treasures he was allowed – under his mother's surveillance – to put into the delicately scented interior were too fragile for her tiny, destructive fingers: a perfect shell, a frail crimson leaf, a shiny unblemished conker.

'Shall we put it in the box, Mummy?' he'd shout, running to bring her these gifts, and he'd watch whilst the little ceremony was performed: the box lifted from its shelf, the key produced and inserted into the gold lock and the lid opened. Eagerly he'd bend to look in, to see the familiar contents. If his hands were clean he'd be allowed to unfold his grandmother's small silk handkerchief kept in the embroidered, soft suede pochette that smelled of lavender; to take out the letter his father had written to him all the way from Afghanistan, and to look at the photograph that had been enclosed. The letter, which his mother would read to him, made him feel proud and strong; his father told him to be a good boy, to look after his mother and little sister, and then they would look at the photograph: his father smiling at them, standing in a dry, dusty, arid place. The biggest treat was to play with the carved and painted wooden cat which, like a Russian doll, separated into two halves to reveal yet another smaller cat, and then another, until the final, delightful surprise: a tiny mouse. Each cat had a wickedly mischievous expression and even the mouse appeared to be content with his lot, his painted whiskers curling jauntily, one eye closed in a wink.

As he grew older the enchantment gradually faded until he forgot the box altogether except as one of the familiar objects that moved with them from the small house in Finchley to the big, ground-floor flat in Blackheath, and finally to his mother's room at the nursing home.

Now the box and its contents were his; the packet of photographs probably collected together and added very recently. Matt sighed and pushed the box and photographs away. It was odd, and perhaps would be hurtful to her, that there were none of Imogen, but she needn't know. Their mother had been distanced from them for so long, first with her gradual descent into depression and alcoholism, and then with the onset of liver disease, that it was unlikely that Imogen would be upset: they were both too used to their mother's mercurial moods and irrational behaviour to attach much emotional importance to her actions. Even so, he wouldn't tell Im.

Matt took the packet out of the box again and flipped through the photographs. There was something odd about them but he couldn't quite decide what it was and he was too restless and preoccupied to study them more closely. The prospect of his next book, unwritten and unformed, pressed on his consciousness. Each new promising idea proved dull, each putative plot stale. And Im's phone call had unsettled him.

'We're having such a great time,' she'd said. 'I can't believe we're living down here on Exmoor at last, even if it is in a holiday let and we still don't know where we'll go at Easter. Jules is a bit twitchy but it's utter heaven being a few miles away from Milo and Lottie. Why don't you come down for a few days? They'd love to see you and so would we.'

Matt stood up, wandered to the window and stared down into the dismal late winter afternoon. The city street was damp with misting rain; the roofs of the parked cars glistened with chill moisture. In his mind's eye he saw the rosy sandstone house, standing beneath the high bare shoulder of Hurlstone Point, looking over the village of Bossington towards Dunkery Hill and westwards across Porlock Vale to the sea, and he felt a childish longing to be there with them all.

'What would we have done,' Im had once asked him, 'without Milo and Lottie?'

'The odd couple,' he'd said lightly, not wanting to admit how important those two people were to him.

'They're our real family,' she'd said, 'aren't they? They saved our lives and kept us normal.'

Now, Matt glanced at his watch: twenty past three. If he got a move on he could be there by suppertime: in the galley kitchen at the High House, Milo – tall, thin, elegant – would be stooping over a saucepan of delicious soup or some exotic sauce that simmered on the Aga. He'd be calling through the archway to Lottie in the breakfast room, who'd be sitting at the long, narrow table that was always piled with books and newspapers, and reading some article or letter aloud to him. He'd call a response and they'd both roar with laughter.

Matt felt another stab of longing for the familiar scene. He picked up his mobile and scrolled down the names until he reached Lottie's. Half an hour later he was on his way.

Lottie tracked Milo down in the garden room, sitting in an old cane chair in a warm splash of February sunshine. His beaky eagle's profile was fierce with concentration as he frowned at the newspaper he was reading; his long thin legs were stretched out and crossed at the ankles showing a glimpse of red sock. A golden-brown spaniel was curled under his knees.

'Matt's on his way,' she said. 'Isn't that fun? He'll be with us in time for supper.'

Milo put down the newspaper. 'Now that *is* good news. How is he?'

Lottie made a face; wrinkled her nose. 'Can't quite tell. A bit mere. I daren't mention the new book, of course.'

Milo shook his head. 'Poor old boy. He's paying for all that early success. An international bestseller and a Hollywood film with your first book is a very difficult act to follow. Everyone sitting round waiting for the next one to be a disaster.'

'He says his mind is quite blank with the terror of it. He thinks it was just a fluke and he'll never write anything again. At least he's financially secure, and I'm sure it will happen in time. I'm just making some tea. Shall I bring it out here? Now who's that?'

She stepped forward to the window, shielding her eyes from the low slanting sun, staring down the long drive which wound up from the village between unfenced fields. The car slowed to allow several ewes to amble across the track and then came on, bumping over the cattle grid and disappearing round the end of the house.

'It's Venetia,' Lottie said, resigned. 'I'll go and meet her.'

Milo showed no especial delight at the advent of his mistress. 'Don't let her see the cake,' he advised. 'You know her. There won't be a crumb left. Never known a woman who could pack in the carbohydrates like Venetia.'

'And still remains as thin as a pin,' said Lottie enviously. 'Sickening, isn't it?'

She went out into the warren of rooms that led through to the hall and met Venetia coming in from the little back porch. Elegant and gaunt as an old greyhound, she bent to embrace Lottie, lightly touching a perfectly *maquillée* cheek to Lottie's unadorned one.

'The snowdrops are simply amazing, Lottie,' she said. 'Not only here at the High House but everywhere. And the daffodils are just beginning. So heartening, isn't it?'

Lottie smiled. 'Spring is coming,' she agreed. 'We were just going to have some tea. Would you like some? Milo is in the garden room. I'll bring it through.'

'Darling, that would be very sweet of you. No cake, I suppose? Or a choccy bic? I'm simply ravenous.

Why do good works make one so hungry? I've just been visiting poor old Clara. She's simply gaga now, I'm afraid, and I'm quite exhausted with answering the same question over and over, and today she couldn't remember who I am. She was such a pretty girl. Oh, Lottie, it's all so bloody depressing, isn't it?'

At the back of the still-beautiful, deeply shadowed violet eyes, Lottie saw the flicker of fear and horror.

'But spring is coming,' she reminded the older woman, 'and there's cake for tea.'

'Oh, darling.' Venetia's voice was full of gratitude. 'You are such a comfort. Honestly.'

'Go and find Milo,' said Lottie. 'Matt's coming down for a few days so he's feeling very cheerful.'

Venetia wandered away and Lottie heard her greet the spaniel that came to meet her. Presently he appeared in the kitchen. He was a pretty fellow; the result of a mating between a cocker and a Sussex spaniel. He had a very sweet nature – though, as Milo unkindly observed, he was as thick as two short planks. His coat was the colour of sticky toffee pudding, one of Milo's favourites, and he'd called the charmingly roly-poly puppy 'Pud'.

'All these new crossbreeds,' Milo had said to her. 'Labradoodles, sprollies and sprockers. Well, if a cross between a springer spaniel and a cocker is

18

a sprocker, then a cross between a Sussex and a cocker is a sucker. Which just about sums up Pud nicely.'

He sat now, looking hopefully at Lottie as she prepared the tea.

'You heard the word "cake",' she told him, 'but you won't get any.'

She thought about Matt arriving later and was seized with a mixture of delight and anxiety. Ever since his mother had died a few weeks earlier she'd had a strong feeling that something momentous was about to happen: but what could it be? Imogen and Matt had long since ceased to depend on Helen, and her death had not been in the least unexpected. Her life had been a sad one, widowed so young and with two small children to bring up, but it was by no means unusual; other women had managed in the same situation without relying so heavily on drink. Of course she'd been devastated by the way Tom had died, caught in cross-fighting between factions in Afghanistan whilst reporting on the war, but her depression had begun before then.

Lottie could remember trying to talk to Tom about it once. It was some while after the little family had returned from Afghanistan the first time around, but he'd been evasive, not wanting to discuss it, hinting at a miscarriage that had badly upset Helen when they were out in Kabul and from which she'd never quite recovered. Lottie hadn't pressed him; by then she'd begun to love them all, Tom, Helen and the children, but Tom most of all. He'd never guessed; never, in all those hours they'd spent together over the editing of his book on the war in the Belgian Congo, had he suspected how much she'd loved him.

Lottie made the tea, assembled plates and forks and the cake, and, with Pud at her heels, she carried the tray into the garden room. At the door she hesitated. Venetia had pulled her chair close to Milo's and sat with her knee touching his, her frail, thin hand cradled between his two large warm ones. Her eyes were closed.

'Poor old Clara. It's so desperate, Milo, isn't it?' she was saying.

He watched her. His expression was tender, thoughtful, and Lottie knew that he was remembering the young, beautiful Venetia as he'd seen her on that very first occasion: the wife of his senior officer, Bernard – 'Bunny' – Warren at a ball at Sandhurst. Just for a moment Lottie could see them, too: Venetia, glamorous and sexy in her ball gown; Milo, tall and gorgeous in his mess dress. She saw their handclasp, the exchanged dynamic glance, and heard the murmuring of laughter and voices all about them, the chink of glasses and the distant sound of music.

'Old age is not for cissies, sweetie,' Milo said now, breaking the spell. He glanced round at Lottie, gave her a tiny wink. 'Here's the tea.'

Venetia opened her eyes and Lottie put the tray on the round glass-topped table. She wondered if Milo would ask Venetia to stay for supper. Lottie knew that Matt wouldn't mind. Though he valued and guarded his isolation and privacy when he was working, yet he loved the open-house atmosphere at the High House when he was relaxing – and he liked Venetia. Lottie had tried to be sensitive to the older woman's occasional moments of over-whelming loneliness and depression since she had been widowed, though Milo had all the instinctive wariness of the male lurking beneath his genuine affection for her.

'Can't be too soft-hearted,' he'd say when Lottie showed signs of giving in to one of Venetia's hints. 'She'll be living with us if you're not careful now dear old Bunny's gone. She's a tough cookie – Venetia. She knows what she wants and she goes for it.'

'So Matt's coming down,' Venetia was saying. 'You are so lucky to have your young close at hand. Imogen and Julian just across the Vale with that darling baby. And Matt popping down so often.

21

They keep all these ghastly things in proportion, don't they? I never see mine these days . . .'

Lottie, pouring the tea, caught Milo's eye. He raised an eyebrow: she nodded.

'Stay to supper,' he suggested. 'Would you like to?'

Venetia looked hopefully at Lottie. 'Would I be in the way? Would Matt mind, d'you think?'

Lottie shook her head. 'Of course he wouldn't. Do stay.'

'Aaah,' Venetia expelled a breath, as if released from some anxiety or fear; she relaxed back into her chair. 'I'd love it.'

After tea, Lottie left them together and went out into the garden to pick snowdrops. The early evening sunshine cast long shadows across the lawn; around the roots of the ancient beech trees rings of crocus flowered in circles of fiery gold and inky purple. A blackbird swooped low, his stuttering cry of warning shattering the silence. There were ghosts in the garden; the ghosts of people and of dogs but she had no fear of them. She knew them all and could sense when they were nearby: that great cloud of witness, some of whom seemed as close to her as the two she'd left in the garden room. She couldn't remember a time when she hadn't been aware of the pressing in of other worlds. As a child, in an attempt to rationalize it, she'd invented stories in her head: fragments of make-believe twined in with actual events with which she'd entertain – and even frighten – her school friends. Once, when she was seven, a school friend's father had accused her of telling lies to his daughter. Shocked and surprised, she'd been unable to show him the fine line between the absolute truth and the realities of the imagination – and something more: some sixth sense. Later, comic or dramatic embellishments, added to fairly ordinary encounters, amused her friends, entertained her workmates and distracted from this ability 'to see further through a brick wall than most', as Tom had once described it. Nevertheless, a reputation grew up around her rather like the thicket around the Sleeping Beauty; it fascinated yet held others at arm's length.

Only Tom had penetrated it. It was odd that it should be Tom, who dealt with facts and the tough journalistic world, who had truly understood her; but Tom was a black-browed Celt with a grandmother who had the Sight. It was as if he'd recognized her at a profoundly spiritual level and she'd experienced a great relief in being acknowledged; as if she'd become visible at last. For the first time in her life she hadn't been lonely. Working on his book with him, enjoying occasional lunches, they'd shared a great deal; quickly, they'd arrived at a deep level of understanding which had filled her with happiness, and given him comfort.

Milo, on the other hand, had accepted her in a different way. She was simply little Charlotte, the much younger sister of his ex-wife, and his attitude was fraternal and uncomplicated and reassuring. It was he who had given her the nickname 'Lottie'.

She'd loved Milo from the very first moment that Sara had brought him home to be introduced. Sara had already warned her not to make a nuisance of herself but she'd been too fascinated by Milo's height and his happy, infectious roar of laughter to obey. His warmth drew her to him, Sara's warning scowl lost its power, and he'd been sweet to her despite the thirteen-year gap between them.

Very quickly she'd been aware of the discordant vibrations between Milo and Sara.

'Why are you going to marry him?' she'd asked, confused by the outward and visible demonstrations of affection and the silent tensions that quivered in the air around them. Sara had stared at her with an angry contempt.

'Suppose you mind your own business?' she'd snapped smartly.

Any sibling relationship seemed out of the

question. Sara was determined to blame Lottie's birth for the death of their mother six months later ('She was never the same once you'd been born!') and it didn't help that Milo's parents preferred the engaging little sister to the prickly, possessive and outspoken older one. Milo's mother 'adopted' the ten-year-old Lottie; she was invited to stay at the High House during part of her school holidays and very soon was given her own room. Her elderly and distant father had been clearly relieved; Sara had been irritated and contemptuous. She called it 'sucking up' but this new joy in finding genuine love and a sense of family was too great for Lottie to abandon simply in order to appease the volatile Sara, who now lived with Milo in married quarters near Warminster.

When their father died it seemed a natural transition for Lottie to make her home permanently at the High House. She loved it when Milo and Sara and baby Nicholas came to visit and, ashamed though she was to admit it, she loved it even more after the inevitable divorce had taken place and Milo came alone or with Nick. By the time Milo inherited the High House, Lottie was so much a part of it all that it seemed quite natural for them to continue to make their home together. Milo was a newly retired brigadier and Lottie was weekending from her publishing work in London, and it was then that Imogen and Matt became regular visitors, too.

Now, walking in the garden with her hands full of snowdrops, Lottie thought about Matt. He was uncannily like his father; a glance from his narrow brown eyes, the way his thick black hair was pushed into peaks by his restless fingers, these things could translate her back thirty years to remind her of that odd blend of happiness and heartache that belonged only to Tom. How hard it had been when he died not to be able to mourn openly; to be expected, instead, to comfort and support Helen whilst never showing for a moment the real pain of her own loss. The children had grown to depend on her as Helen had slipped further into despair and denial and silence. Lottie had brought the two of them down to the High House as often as she could to give Helen a respite from their demands and to allow Matt and Imogen freedom to run and shout and play, and she was deeply grateful to Milo for the all-embracing affection he showed these two little newcomers. Even Nick had enjoyed their visits, whilst trying to remain alert to his mother's warnings that these usurpers might steal his inheritance or worm their way into his father's affections.

Lottie turned back towards the house. She was worrying about Matt, still feeling that something cataclysmic was about to happen; yet she had no premonition of actual disaster, not that real dread she'd experienced when Tom had returned to Afghanistan. Matt had been a difficult child, prone to nightmares, terrified of being left alone. When his father died there had been an increase in his terrors, which took her own and Helen's combined efforts to overcome. That's when Helen had sold the house in Finchley and moved to the garden flat in Blackheath with Lottie as a lodger. It worked well for a while but even she had been unable to keep Helen balanced or protect her from the despair that tormented her. At least she'd been able to comfort Matt and settle him into his first school, and take care to ensure that Imogen was not infected by the overactive imagination that disturbed his sleep.

As he'd got older he'd managed his private demons with a stoic bravery that tore at Lottie's heart. One of his methods was to write little stories; these were generally about a child who was lost, or who had been abandoned, and was required to defend himself against a monster or an animal or a wicked magician. Behind the child stood an alter ego: a spirit child who protected the hero. These stories were odd and disturbing, and Matt's teachers were alternately impressed and anxious; none of them was surprised when he began to collect prizes for

27

his essays or, later, got a scholarship to Oxford. He'd managed a first and gone straight into a publishing house and then, a year or two later, he'd begun the long slow work on his novel of fantasy fiction that had won him such acclaim. It wasn't really surprising, either, that he should be suffering from writer's block after such a huge success and Lottie was puzzled that she should be feeling this level of anxiety for him now that he had achieved so much. Yet experience refused to allow her to shrug it off. Perhaps when she saw him and talked to him she would have a better idea of the cause of it.

CHAPTER TWO

Driving round the Chiswick roundabout, heading
west on the M4, Matt too was remembering those
early stories and how his writing career had begun
out of a need to come to terms with the death of his
father and the odd, painful sense of incompleteness.
Yet the inner restlessness and a terrible loneliness
still pursued him.

'That's why we write,' a fellow author had once
said to him. 'We create out of our emptiness; it's because we lack something essential that we need to
invent alternative worlds.'

As he left Slough and Reading behind him, glad
to be ahead of the rush-hour traffic, Matt wondered
if this were true for all creative writers; he felt
truly alive only when he was putting words down,
arranging them and rearranging them. He needed
the buzz of city life to get the ideas flowing; watching
people hurrying by or sitting at café tables or in

pubs. He'd never adapted to country life as Imogen had. Oh, he loved to go down to the High House but even as a child he'd never engaged in the riding and hunting and the passion for dogs that Im had so readily taken to herself. When she'd left school she'd worked with horses and it was so utterly fitting that she'd fallen in love with a veterinary surgeon and married him.

Matt liked Jules. He was a straightforward, uncomplicated fellow and it was clear that he and Im were ideally suited; even the baby was a placid child. Yet the sight of his sister's domestic happiness engendered no envy on his own part. He was fearful of such a commitment, aware that his demons might make life intolerable for someone else. Immediately he thought of Annabel. He'd sent her a text – a cowardly move – telling her that he would be away for a few days; he hadn't wanted to hear the disappointment in her voice. After all, they weren't at that stage yet where he was obliged to include her in his plans; the relationship was still on a fairly casual footing. He knew very well, however, that she would like it to be much more than that and that they were heading for some kind of showdown any time now.

These few days away would give him a chance to think things through carefully, he told himself – and then snorted contemptuously at his speciousness. The point was that though Annabel was pretty and fun and – being a publicity assistant in a big publishing house – well enough aware of his own status to be rather flatteringly in awe of his success, yet he could feel none of the passion and longing that he believed should be part of falling in love.

'You're too detached,' his mates told him. 'Too analytical. You think too much. Have a few drinks, let yourself go and she'll do the rest.'

Perhaps they were right and he was expecting too much; perhaps he should go along with Annabel's desires and maybe love would follow. Then again, maybe it wouldn't . . . and what then?

He pulled off at Leigh Delamere for a Costa coffee; the café was busy but he found a corner table and prepared to people-watch. There was a middle-aged couple talking earnestly to each other, their faces serious. A young woman checking her text messages glanced at him, half smiled, and looked away again. Beyond her a man was almost hidden by the newspaper he was reading. Matt could make a little history for each of them, but, before he could begin, the middle-aged woman extended her hands in a dramatic gesture of despair.

'But what shall we *do*?' he heard her say, and saw her companion sit back in his chair, biting his lip.

Matt drank some coffee whilst his mind invented various scenarios: perhaps they were lovers meeting clandestinely and she was growing tired of the secrecy, hoping to push him into some kind of resolution. He looked at them again. Neither of them was dressed smartly, nor did they seem to have made any special effort with their appearances: perhaps not lovers then. It might be that they had a grown-up child going through a difficult time, a divorce, say, and there would be grandchildren to worry about; or it might be that there was an elderly parent involved, needing special care. Immediately he thought about his own mother and the sadness that had blighted her whole life. It seemed impossible to believe that she was dead; and yet her life had been steeped in such hopelessness that she'd hardly ever really been alive. Sometimes he'd felt guilty that he was capable of joy and laughter whilst she was wrapped in such melancholy.

'But why should we feel guilty?' Im would demand. 'I was much too young to remember Daddy properly and you were only four when he died. It's not reasonable that we should spend our lives being miserable. The way that Lottie talks about him I know he'd want us to be enjoying every minute of them. If only Mum would stop using drink to dull the pain she'd be able to see that.'

Matt knew that Im was right but he wasn't capable of being tough when he was with his mother. His own loneliness gave him an insight into her misery and he'd often sat with her in long periods of silence, especially when she'd become ill.

'Why?' he'd asked Lottie when he was growing up. 'Why doesn't Mum talk any more? Really talk, I mean.'

She'd shaken her head and he could see that she was puzzled too; that grief should take the form of enforced silence, as if his mother were frightened to speak lest she should say things she might regret. He'd been glad in the end to get away, to leave his mother to Lottie, though he felt guilty about that too. How he envied Im's insouciance.

'Lottie doesn't have to stay,' she'd say. 'She has a choice. She says she's quite happy with things as they are and she can always go down to Milo. Stop *worrying*, Matt.'

The middle-aged couple were getting up to go. Matt finished his coffee and went out to the car. The drizzle had stopped. In the west the sky was still brilliant with golden light but soon it would be dark. For the rest of the journey he kept the radio on, distracting his thoughts, keeping his mind occupied.

It was nearly eight o'clock when finally he turned

off the A39 into Allerford and drove along the long narrow lane into Bossington. As he crossed the tiny Aller Brook and jolted over the cattle grid at the bottom of the drive he could see the lights shining from the windows of the High House on the hill above him.

'That was Lottie phoning to say that Matt's arrived,' announced Imogen, appearing in the doorway of the sitting room. 'I'm glad I phoned him now. I honestly didn't think he'd just get in the car and come straight away, though. He's brooding too much. It'll do him good to have a change. Lottie says he looks great. Venetia's staying for supper. Oh, I wish we were there too, don't you?'

'No,' said Julian. He finished stacking logs in the big open hearth, followed her across the narrow hall into the kitchen and washed his hands at the sink. 'I'm tired and hungry and I want to watch *Life on Mars*. It's not that I don't love them all but tonight I can live without them. Thank God I'm not on duty tonight and I can have a drink. Do you want one, Im?'

He held the wine bottle up and she nodded. He handed her a glass and filled one for himself. 'Nothing new on the house front?'

'Nothing we can really afford.' She dished out

pasta on to hot plates and put them on the wide pine counter that separated the galley-kitchen from the rest of the big, light room. 'I can't decide whether we ought to be panicking. I wish we could stay here but Piers says he's got bookings from Easter. To be honest, I thought that there would be a bit more money from Mum's estate. I had no idea how expensive all that nursing care was. It's a bit of a shock, actually.'

'It doesn't matter.' He carried the plates to the table. 'There's the cottage at Exford that would be OK if we're really stuck. I know it isn't exactly our dream house but Exmoor is where we really wanted to be, isn't it? That's the important thing. There have to be compromises sometimes. And there's always the barn at Goat Hill. That's very handy for Simonsbath; barely a ten-minute drive to the practice and you'd have the village shop in Challacombe, as well as the one at Exford. Billy Webster says we can rent it once his son's house is ready to move in to, which is any minute by the look of it. Poor old Billy is fed up with holiday letting and he'd love a long-term let.'

'I know that.' She sat opposite. 'I must go and have a look at it, if his son doesn't mind. But I'd rather buy if we can.'

'House prices are falling.' Julian helped himself to pesto. 'It might be sensible to wait a bit but I want to be as near the practice as possible. Being on call four nights a week is bad enough from here. I wouldn't want to be any further away.'

Imogen pushed her fair hair behind her ears and rested her chin in her hands. 'It would be good to be nearer to Simonsbath.' She grinned at him. 'We are just so lucky. And it was sweet of Milo to let us store our odd bits of stuff at the High House. It takes the pressure off, doesn't it?'

Julian was overwhelmed by a huge wave of love for her: her energy and warmth made him feel anything was possible as long as she was there with him. She was watching him, smiling a little.

'So what about the puppies?'

He began to laugh. 'Are you really serious? Look, we're in a furnished let with a nine-month-old baby and we have no idea where we'll be in a few weeks' time . . .'

'There are always good reasons for not doing things. I've spoken to Piers about it and he says—'

'Spoken to Piers?' he interrupted her. 'Honestly, Im . . .'

'Well, I had to, didn't I? It's his cottage. I'm not totally irresponsible, Jules. He told me that he lived here when he was a little boy, before they went to Michaelgarth, and then again when he was first married. He says there have always been dogs here

36

and that one more puppy won't make a difference. I just love Piers, he is utter heaven.'

Julian rolled his eyes and sighed. 'So that's that then.'

'I'm afraid so. Will you ask the farmer if I can go and see the puppies?'

'I suppose so.'

'You said you like them. You said that they were really pretty and sweet.'

'I know I did. More fool me. Remember, we have no idea what the father is.'

'That's OK. A collie cross is ideal. Intelligent, no finicky stomachs or overbreeding. I can't wait to see them. Rosie and I could go tomorrow. Matt might want to come.'

'OK. I'll phone them from the surgery in the morning and let you know.'

She beamed at him. 'Want some apple crumble?' She got up and collected the plates. 'Oh, and did I say? I love you, too.'

He laughed. 'Puppy love,' he said, and she laughed as well.

'Just a bit. A very tiny bit.'

He caught her as she passed his chair. 'It'll be OK, won't it, Im?'

She looked down at him, puzzled. 'How d'you mean? The puppy?'

'No. Well, yes. Everything, really. Having a baby and a puppy and nowhere to live. Easter's only a few weeks away, after all.'

She put the plates down and put her arms round him, rocking him as if he were Rosie.

'If it comes to it we can go to the High House; that's why I'm not panicking. Milo and Lottie are OK about it. There's enough room. No, I know you don't want to, and neither do I. I love them but living there could be tricky, I know that. But it does mean that we shan't be homeless. If it were just for a few weeks we'd manage, wouldn't we? And then there's the barn. Something will turn up. Don't worry. We'll be fine.'

Julian took a deep breath. As assistant to the owner in a very small but expanding veterinary practice his job was a big one and really important for him. He needed to be able to concentrate on it: the demands, from both small-pet owners and farmers alike, were very exacting and the pressure was high – as was the suicide rate for vets. A friend of his, with whom he'd trained, had killed himself only a few months ago with a dose of Euthatal. However, with Im's arms around him all Jules' natural confidence and courage returned.

He kissed her. 'I know,' he said casually. 'What's

the time? I don't want to miss *Life on Mars* but I'd like some crumble. Is there any custard?'

She was right: something would turn up.

Imogen stacked the dishwasher and made some coffee. In the sitting room Julian had lit the fire and was standing with the television remote in his hand, channel-hopping.

'Aren't you coming to watch?' he asked, as she stood his mug of coffee on the small table at the end of the big, comfortable sofa.

'Just going to check on Rosie.'

She ran up the stairs and paused at the door of the smallest bedroom. In the light from the landing she could see that Rosie was peacefully asleep, utterly relaxed. Imogen stood silently, seized with the familiar mix of love and terror that the sight of her daughter evoked. She knew that the fragile vulnerability of this tiny person could be disguised by a steely determination to get her own way that could render her parents frustrated and exhausted, but generally she was a placid baby. Imogen hoped that the child would not be heir to the restlessness that drove her uncle Matt and gave him nightmares, or to Jules' tendency to worry, but had inherited, along with the fair hair and blue eyes, her own cheerful disposition.

Since her marriage, and the birth of her baby, she'd longed for Matt to know such riches: the joy of being with someone he could trust, of sharing his life with someone special. She'd said as much to Lottie.

'But does Matt actually want that?' Lottie had asked her. 'His idea of fulfilment might not be the same as yours.'

She'd had to think about that. 'But even all this wonderful success hasn't bought him real peace of mind, has it?' she'd argued. 'So what *does* he want?'

Lottie had shaken her head. 'You know how complex he is; those nightmares he has. There's something he's searching for though I'm not sure what it is. But I have a feeling that we might know soon . . .'

And then her gaze had widened, drifted; her eyes focusing on something visible only to her. It was as if she'd entered another dimension, a different world: a familiar habit of hers but one that even after all these years made Imogen feel slightly uneasy.

'What is it?' she'd asked almost fearfully – but Lottie had smiled reassuringly and refused to answer.

Now, Imogen left her sleeping daughter and went downstairs. Julian was sprawled comfortably on the sofa and she sat beside him, folding her legs beneath her, resting her cheek against his shoulder.

His solidity and warmth reassured her and renewed her natural resilience.

'OK?' he asked without taking his eyes from the screen.

'Definitely OK,' she answered.

CHAPTER THREE

Matt slept late the next morning. Lottie made porridge and sat at the table finishing yesterday's *Telegraph* crossword but found it difficult to concentrate. Presently she would drive into Porlock to do some shopping; she began to make a list on the block of paper that was kept on the bookcase beside the table for this purpose, along with a small clay pot full of pens and pencils. Imogen had made the pot at school when she was eight. 'Tea,' Lottie wrote. 'Dog food. Chemist.' Milo came into the room. He raised his eyebrows, gave a little smiling nod, which was the extent of his social capabilities before he'd drunk two cups of coffee, and acknowledged Pud's greeting by bending to pat him in a rather perfunctory fashion. Pud resumed his position at Lottie's feet and Milo passed through the arch into the kitchen, pushed the kettle on to the hotplate and glanced back in her direction.

'Yes, please,' said Lottie automatically, but continued with her shopping list: 'Vegetables. Fairy Liquid. Butcher.' Milo would want to give her his own instructions regarding the meat.

He came to peer over her shoulder. 'Cheese,' he muttered. She added it to the list.

'Jolly nice supper last night,' she said.

Milo raised his chin and pursed his lips, as though acknowledging the compliment, and Lottie began to chuckle.

'Honestly, though,' she said. 'Poor Venetia. She was longing to be asked to stay the night. Matt thought it was so unkind of you to send her off all on her own in the dark.'

Milo had his back to her, making the coffee, but he hunched a shoulder defensively and Lottie laughed aloud. Venetia had enjoyed her evening; she adored Matt and when supper was over she'd hovered reluctantly, clearly hoping for an invitation to stay on.

'Whatever is the time?' she'd asked, peering at her tiny wristwatch. 'It's been such a lovely evening. Goodness, is it that late?'

'Not late at all,' Milo had answered bracingly, finding her coat and helping her unwilling arms into its sleeves. 'Home in no time.'

He'd gone out with her to the car. Matt had

watched the little scene, clearly feeling rather sorry for Venetia.

'Will she be all right driving round the lanes?' he'd asked rather diffidently. 'She drank quite a bit, didn't she?'

'Not that much, and we have to be a bit tough,' she'd defended Milo. 'Venetia's here quite a lot since Bunny died.'

Matt frowned. 'It's odd really, given that they've been . . . well, so close.' She'd noticed with amusement that he'd balked at the word 'lovers'. 'After all, Milo's been so good to all of us. He's such a pussycat.' A little pause. 'Isn't he?' he'd added doubtfully.

'Pussycats don't get to be brigadiers,' she'd answered lightly.

Now, Milo put some coffee beside her notepad and sat at the end of the table. There was silence for a while. Milo poured a second cup of coffee.

'The boy's looking well,' he observed.

Lottie, who had reverted to the crossword, laid down her pencil. She'd had the oddest impression that when Matt had come into the house last evening he hadn't been alone. So strong had the sensation been that she'd looked past him as they'd embraced, peering over his shoulder, so that he'd glanced behind him, saying, 'What is it?' and she'd been obliged to cover her confusion by making some foolish observation about Pud running out into the garden. It was almost as if the spirit alter ego that Matt had given his fictional protagonist had become a reality.

'He does look well,' she answered now. 'I half expected him to be all gaunt and anxious but he looks great. I'll ask him if he wants to come into Porlock with me. We could go and see Imogen and Rosie.'

'Bring them back to lunch,' suggested Milo. 'Have they found anywhere to live yet?'

Lottie shook her head. 'They'd like to be near Simonsbath but even very small cottages are quite expensive within the National Park. Im's hoping to have a garden because of Rosie, but there's not much around at the moment. They'd get better value for their money in the towns, of course – Minehead or Barnstaple – but Im keeps hoping for a miracle.'

'I was wondering about the Summer House. I told you the Moretons are going out on Lady Day. Moving back up country to be nearer to their children and grandchildren.'

Lottie looked surprised. 'D'you mean they could rent it for a while? Well, I suppose they could. Im would be thrilled; she's always adored the Summer

House, it's such a pretty little house, but I think they want to buy.'

'I know they do. But why shouldn't they buy the Summer House?'

'Are you crazy? Firstly, they couldn't possibly afford it, and secondly, even if they could, Sara would be furious. She was incandescent when you told her that I was to be allowed to stay on here if you died before I did.'

'That provision still stands. Nick's fine with it.'

'I know.' She smiled at him. 'Let's not talk about it.'

'I know that you're not really happy with the plan. That's why I was thinking about Im and Jules buying the Summer House. If anything happened to me maybe you could move in with them.'

'My dear Milo, it would be hell for all of us. Anyway, I don't want to live with Im and Jules in the Summer House. And I still think that it would be much too expensive for Im to buy at its proper value, and you can't simply give it to them. Look, Matt might come in at any moment. Let's talk about it another time. But you mustn't do anything foolish. You've done enough for us all already. Forget it for the moment and tell me what else should be on this shopping list.'

*　　*　　*

Up in his high attic bedroom, Matt kneeled at the low dormer window. Across the vale the slopes of Dunkery Hill were washed with sunshine and patched with wintry colours: red-rust bracken and pale stones; bleached brown grass and the cold white flash of water. Away to the west, low cloud lay along the Severn Sea, dense as a thick grey curtain drawn across the Channel. Sheep, pretty Exmoor Hornies, strayed across the drive and grazed beneath the great beeches. Leafless, as they were now, it was almost impossible for him to identify the beech dragon in the tree nearest to his window. As a small boy he'd first noticed it: the branch extending like a leafy, flexible neck; the head formed by an oblong bunch of leaves, whilst two twigs, set at right angles on the skull, made the ears, and the small gap, through which he could see the darkness of the trunk of the tree, looked just like a round, fierce eye. The jaws snapped and gaped when the wind blew, and one long slender twig, bright with leaves, looked exactly like a tongue of fire.

He'd used the image in his childhood stories and, later, in his book. The beech dragon had become such a familiar friend of his childhood that he'd been unable to make his dragon an enemy of his child hero but instead had made him the boy's champion, whistled up by the spirit alter ego, whom he'd called 'David'.

'Why "David"?' his mother had demanded almost angrily. He'd been surprised by her reaction until he'd reminded himself that his father's second name had been David and that, anyway, most of her reactions were unreasonable and exaggerated.

'Why not?' he'd answered calmly. 'It just came to me that that was his name.'

She'd shaken her head, her face twitching with that old distressing tic that tore at his heart.

'You said that he was a spirit,' she'd mumbled. 'Such a silly name for a spirit.'

There had been many such conversations, always critical and negative, and he wished that she could have been truly proud of him. His unhappy relationship with her had taught him to be wary of giving away too much of himself to the girls to whom he was attracted; part of him, instinctively expecting the same reactions from them, made him too cautious. He turned away from the window, pulling a jersey over his head, turning his thoughts to the day ahead. Perhaps Imogen was already on her way over. He switched on his mobile to see if there was a message from her.

There wasn't, but there was one from Annabel.

'Sounds gt. Wd luv 2 c xmoor. Cd get down @ wkend.'

'Damn,' he muttered, and put the phone in his pocket. He went out and down the steep narrow stairs. He loved this old house, parts of which were two hundred years old and which was a veritable warren of small, cosy rooms. He passed through the parlour where the ashes of last night's fire still glowed in the wood-burner and where another staircase, broader and less steep, climbed and turned out of sight. The breakfast room was empty but he could hear Milo just beyond the archway in the kitchen.

'I don't believe you for a moment. I think you've had your breakfast already and you're not getting any more. Think I was born yesterday, don't you?'

'Good morning,' Matt said.

There was a brief silence and Milo appeared, Pud at his heels. 'Sorry, old chap. Wasn't talking to you.'

Matt laughed and bent to stroke Pud, gently pulling the long treacle-coloured ears. 'I realize that. OK if I make myself some coffee?'

'Of course it is. Lottie was wondering if you wanted to go into Porlock with her. She's got shopping to do and then she might go on to see Imogen. She's just phoning her.'

'Sounds good to me.'

Matt wondered whether to introduce the subject of Annabel but decided to speak to Lottie first. There was no hurry, he told himself; surely he could enjoy his first day without making any commitment.

CHAPTER FOUR

A few days later Sara phoned just before lunch.

'Hallo, Charlotte. How's life in La-la Land?'

Lottie sighed. She knew that Sara needed to see Milo's gesture in giving her, Lottie, a permanent home as a purely philanthropic and slightly ridiculous act: something to be mocked and made light of, as if both of them were silly children living in a fantasy world. Beneath her disdainful banter, however, was a very real anxiety that Nick might lose out on some material advantage.

'Life is very good, thank you, Sara. How are you?'

'I've got some rather bad news. Has Nick been in touch?'

'Not very recently. What is it?'

'It appears that there's some trouble between him and Alice.'

Lottie took a sharp breath. 'Oh, no! I'm so sorry. I had no idea, they seem so . . .' She hesitated. She'd been about to say 'happy together', which wasn't exactly right; at least not in the sense that Im and Jules were. Nick and Alice tolerated each other in a good-natured manner. 'They seem so well suited,' she finished.

'I thought so too.' Sara sounded irritated. 'Of course, Alice isn't communicating with me and Nick is prevaricating, so I'm not certain what the real truth of it is. I thought I'd better warn you in case either of them gets in touch.'

'Would you like to speak to Milo?'

'Not particularly.'

'I'm so sorry, Sara. What about the children?'

'What about them? Nick has simply said that Alice has taken them to her parents' place in Hampshire for the half-term fortnight and that Nick is not invited. He's coming over for lunch.'

'Well, give him my love. Matt's here for a few days—'

'Oh?' Sara's voice was sharp.

Lottie resisted the need to explain Matt's presence, to apologize for it. Even now Sara clung to all the rights of a wife when it came to life at the High House and fiercely protected Nick's future claims.

'She hasn't any rights,' Milo would say crossly when the pressure became overwhelming. 'I can do what I like with my own property. She must know by now that I shall look after Nick.'

'Yes,' Lottie now said calmly to Sara. 'It's lovely to see him.'

'And how's the new book coming along? A bit of a time, isn't it, since the great success?'

Lottie bit her lips and swallowed her wrath. 'These things *take* time. He's in very good form and it's lovely for him to be able to see Im.'

'Have they found anywhere to live yet?'

'No, not yet.'

'Well, I hope Milo doesn't get another pathetic urge to use the High House as an orphanage. Once is enough.'

Lottie switched off the phone. The result of doing something so positive, so rude, still gave her a sense of shock. It was Milo who had advised her to do it having listened to so many phone calls descending into arguments and protests and irritation.

'It's the only way to deal with Sara,' he'd said. 'She'll always have the last word and leave you feeling thoroughly miserable. Try it!'

He was right; it worked remarkably well, and Sara never commented on it, but it still left Lottie feeling equivocal.

Matt came in. He stood for a moment, eyebrows raised, and she smiled ruefully at him.

'Sara,' she said. 'Bad news, actually. She says that Nick and Alice are having a few marital problems.'

'I'm sorry to hear that. Did she say why?'

'No, not really. It was just to warn us in case Nick phoned. Have you seen anything of them lately?'

'Not very lately. They enjoy the occasional literary party, and they just adored the film premiere, of course, and I get invited to dinner now and then. They're always so busy, both working so hard, and the children have amazing social lives given that they're barely out of nursery school.'

'Perhaps it's just the pressure of work and it will all blow over. A funny five minutes in a marriage, as Milo's mother used to say. What have you got there?'

He was holding a large brown envelope, folded in half, and now he stepped forward and put a photograph on the table between them.

'First of all, I thought you might like to see this one.' He pushed the photograph towards her and she picked it up. Her own face smiled back at her, Tom beside her, laughing. He had his arm casually about her shoulder and their eyes were screwed up against the sun.

'Oh,' she said. 'Oh,' and then pulled herself together. Matt was watching her, half smiling, as if he understood. But how could he? 'I remember this,' she said, making a great effort. 'We'd made an offer for his book and I'd taken him out to lunch to discuss it. It was so exciting. We were such a tiny publishing house, mostly academic stuff; a few poets. Tom was a very successful journalist and I was so thrilled to meet him and to be publishing *Leopoldville*. He persuaded me to go back with him to meet Helen. It was just after you'd all come back from Afghanistan in the seventies and she was rather down. Post-natal depression after Imogen's birth. He hoped that the publication of the book would cheer her up.'

'And did it?'

Lottie hesitated. 'Not really. Not in the long term. Though we had a lovely afternoon together. It was Helen that took the photograph.'

'I wondered if you'd like it. Unless you've got a copy?'

'No.' She still held it, studying it. She could recall the heat of the sun on her head, the scent of lilac in the garden – and the light pressure of Tom's arm across her shoulder. Someone in a nearby house had been playing the piano: Chopin's sonata in B minor, the phrases drifting from the open window. Always, since that afternoon, it had reminded her of Tom.

Remembering, Lottie's heart contracted with pain. 'I'd like it very much. Thanks, Matt.'

'It was in Mum's rosewood box. And then there are these.' He tipped out the contents of the packet and the photographs slid fanwise on to the table. She bent over them. 'Do you see anything odd?'

She shuffled through them; hazarded a guess. 'All of you? None of Im?'

'It's strange, isn't it?' He picked one up. 'It's more than that, though.' He frowned. 'I know it sounds weird but I can't quite relate to them, if you see what I mean.'

She picked another one up. 'How d'you mean?'

He shook his head as if dismissing some bizarre notion. 'Well, for instance, I don't recognize that jersey. How old am I there? Six? Seven? I simply can't remember having a stripy jersey in those bright colours. And look at the background of this one. Whose car is that?'

Lottie peered. 'I don't know. What are you trying to say?'

'I'm not sure. It's just this sense of disorientation I have when I look at them.'

'Have you shown them to Imogen?'

'No. I don't like to tell her that there aren't any of her.'

'But we've got albums full of photos of both of you. She knows how odd Helen was at the end. I think you're being oversensitive.'

'Perhaps.' He shuffled the photographs together and put them away.

She watched him, once more aware of the strange sensation she'd had when he'd first arrived: of a shadow at his shoulder.

'What is it?' he asked sharply.

'Nothing.' She looked away. 'I was thinking of lots of different things. Of where Im and Jules will go at Easter. And of Nick.'

He looked relieved. 'Yes, of course. It's all a bit worrying, isn't it?'

'What's worrying?' Milo came in behind him.

Matt made a little face at Lottie and slipped tactfully away.

'Sara just phoned,' she said. 'She says that Nick and Alice are having a few disagreements. She makes it sound rather serious.'

His broad shoulders sagged and his bleak expression filled her with compassion. She wondered whether it was especially difficult for divorced people to comment on other people's marital problems. What must Sara and Milo be feeling now; what memories must be surfacing?

'Maybe it's just a bad patch,' she suggested diffidently. 'All marriages have them.'

'Are other people involved?'

'Sara didn't say. She doesn't really know. Alice

has gone off to her mother with the children for the half-term break and Nick isn't invited. Sara was expecting him to lunch. I expect he'll tell her more when he sees her.'

'What else did she say?'

Lottie decided to distract him from his anxiety for Nick. 'She said that she hoped you weren't going to exercise your talent for philanthropy again and offer Im and Jules a home.'

He laughed unwillingly. 'Oh, for God's sake! The woman's obsessed. Or perhaps she has second sight.'

'I know. After our conversation about the Summer House I wondered about that too. I hung up on her.'

'Good for you. Shall we have a drink? Lunch is nearly ready. Where did Matt disappear to?'

'I think he thought he was being tactful. I'd just told him about Nick.'

'Give him a shout.' Milo disappeared into the kitchen. 'We'll try not to worry until we know the whole story.'

CHAPTER FIVE

After lunch, Milo settled in the garden room in the little upright wicker chair that these days he found more comfortable than upholstered armchairs or sofas. He loved this sunny room, with the geraniums ranged along the windowsills, and the chair cushions still covered with the pretty faded chintz that his mother had favoured. There was a low, round oak table – whose two shelves were generally piled with books – which could be wheeled close up to his chair and, on the bench along the wall, Lottie's nests of knitting were heaped into big wicker baskets. She often worked two or three garments concurrently so that there was always a variety of textures and colour.

The afternoon sunshine warmed Milo and he closed his eyes, taking a deep sighing breath, relaxing. He was surprised at how tense he was; after all, he wasn't an introspective kind of fellow. He wasn't one for dwelling on the future and depressing himself about what might lie ahead – a complete waste of energy in his opinion – but just at this moment he felt helpless. Since that wretched operation on his lung he'd been less resilient. The trouble was, he told himself, that he was worrying about all of them; all of those dearest to his heart.

Dear old Im and Jules, for instance, not knowing where they'd go at Easter. He'd believed that the Summer House might be the answer to their problem but he could see Lottie's point about Sara's reaction and keeping it all for Nick. Though, to be honest, he couldn't really imagine any of them wanting to live in the High House. Not that it was any of Sara's business how much he sold the Summer House for – and anyway, the money would revert to his estate and Nick would get it all eventually and then, no doubt, he'd sell up. And then what about Lottie?

Milo shifted uneasily: what *would* Lottie do if anything should happen to him? He knew she wouldn't stay here without him but where would she go?

'I've been one of the foolish virgins,' she'd said to him once. 'I've kept no oil in my lamp for the cold dark future.'

She'd said it cheerfully enough, not asking for sympathy, but he knew very well that she'd been supporting Helen and the children in the flat at

Blackheath. Tom had left enough for them to buy the flat but very little else and Lottie had contributed a great deal more than simply her rent.

'I love them, you see,' she'd told him when he'd murmured something about thinking of herself for once. 'Helen simply couldn't work, she's completely unreliable, and I can't abandon her or the children.'

He'd muttered something else about her always having a home with him, and she'd got up suddenly from her chair and put her arms around him and hugged him. Little Lottie: funny little Lottie. Such an odd little girl she'd been with her dark mop of hair and those strange grey eyes fringed with sooty black lashes. Her hair had gone a silvery grey by the time she was thirty but she'd never bothered to dye it and he'd liked that; she'd looked so arresting, so *different*, and it had suited her somehow. Of course, Helen had left her some recompense in her will but all that home care, and finally the nursing home, had cost so much that, at the end, there wasn't much left for any of them.

Secretly, selfishly, he was glad. He'd been surprised at the depth of his relief when Lottie had agreed to make the High House her home when she'd taken early retirement last year. She might so easily have stayed in London amongst all her friends, but she had friends here, too, she'd said, and she'd rather be at the High House than anywhere else, though they both knew that the real reason was because he'd had to have the operation and she'd wanted to be there to look after him. Of course, Sara had kicked up; she'd seen the complications that might so easily arise and had told him exactly what she thought about it all.

'You've never thought about anyone but yourself,' she'd said. 'Where will Lottie go when you die? Remember how much older than her you are. Much better that she sorts herself out now. You've always spoiled and protected her. It's about time she lived in the real world.'

He'd laughed out loud at that. For Sara, supported and provided for all her life, to criticize Lottie, who'd worked full time whilst trying to keep Helen sane and her children happy, was completely out of order, and he'd said so.

'I shall make certain that she can stay here for as long as she wants to,' he'd told her – and she'd positively screamed at him so that he'd simply hung up on her. Yet he'd loved her once.

He was gripped with an unexpected and terrible sadness. She'd been so beautiful, so amusing, such fun – and she'd been so much in love with him. Or so it had seemed. He'd been naïve, of course; too young at twenty-two or -three to know much about love. It wasn't too long before he'd realized that Sara's affectionate behaviour in public was rather different from the sharp, critical way she behaved when they were alone. He'd remarked on it once and she'd slapped him down very firmly. By then they were married and he'd begun to understand that he was a one-way ticket out of a dull lonely life with an elderly, detached father and a tiresome small sister.

Poor old love, he thought now. Poor old Sara.

She'd divorced him for a wealthy stockbroker who'd cheated on her with a string of mistresses and finally left her with a tiny house in Sussex, a reasonably comfortable divorce settlement and a great deal of humiliation to live down amongst their friends. Poor Sara. She'd approached him, then; tried to sweet-talk him back to her.

Milo shook his head: nothing doing. By then he'd fallen in love with Venetia and she with him. They'd fought it to begin with; tried to pretend it wasn't happening. Neither of them wanted to hurt old Bunny, after all: he was a good, if dull, husband and a loyal officer. Then Bunny had been very badly wounded in Northern Ireland, confined to a wheelchair, and Venetia had decided that she must stick with him.

Of course, old Bunny had known the truth about their affair. He'd even hinted – only the slightest of hints – that he was glad of it, that Venetia needed a normal physical life and that he'd rather it was with someone he knew and trusted. And they'd always been very discreet. He'd felt guilty when Lottie had said that about Matt being a bit shocked by his callousness to Venetia; but it didn't do to become sentimental. It was far too late for him and Venetia to make a try at marriage. He'd been alone too long and she was a stiff-necked woman who wouldn't want to change her ways; she was, after all, a good few years older than he was. No, no, by the time Bunny died it was already too late. Much better to leave well alone; to keep the sensation of romance alive by maintaining a little distance whilst, at the same time, watching out for her and making her feel part of the family whenever possible.

But all the same, it was a waste. God, what a mess it all was; what an utter bloody mess. And now it seemed that Nick might be heading down that same road.

Milo sagged a little in his chair: he felt old and tired and dispirited. His loved ones were all in trouble: poor Matt with agonizing writer's block; darling Im and Jules and that sweet baby about to be made homeless; and now dear old Nick on the brink of divorce.

He heard footsteps behind him, felt a hand on his shoulder. He turned and looked up into Lottie's eyes, those amazing eyes, and his spirits lifted slightly. She always seemed to know when his courage ebbed; her touch revitalized him.

'Matt's going off to see Imogen and Jules,' she said. 'He's just phoned her and she's invited him over to tea. I thought I'd take Pud for a walk up on Crawter. We might go on around Pool Bridge and over Wilmersham Common. Like to come?'

She knew it was one of his favourite drives, and the walk would do him good.

'Bless you, darling,' he said gratefully. 'I'd love it.'

Driving out from Bossington, Matt was trying to contain his sense of guilt. He'd told Annabel that it was going to be a busy weekend and therefore not a good one for her first visit to Exmoor. To make himself feel better about it, he'd actually phoned her; made it sound as if it was going to be one long whirl of social engagements and family commitments, but agreed that she must come down one of these days. Meanwhile, he'd phone, he said, as soon as he was back in London. She'd been so understanding that it made him feel even worse, but he hadn't wavered.

There was simply too much on his mind to undertake the role of host and, anyway, it was the wrong time of year. Perhaps at Easter or in the spring: Annabel was a true urbanite and he suspected that only the most obviously pretty aspects of moor and the coastline would really appeal to her.

He drove along Bossington Lane and into Porlock, which on this cold Sunday afternoon was almost deserted, and then out on to the Toll Road. He loved this steep lane winding through Allerpark Combe, with those huge trees clinging to its sides and the clatter of the water far below him. He slowed to watch a swirl of starlings settle like a ragged grey cloud on a gaunt, bare tree, and saw delicate, pretty snowdrops gleaming pale amongst a thick covering of crisp, crunchy beech leaves. He'd forgotten about Annabel now and was thinking about something Lottie had said to him just after lunch when they'd been clearing up together. He'd talked about all the travelling he'd done in the last two years, and how he'd still had no inspiration for the new book, although he'd been able to use the experiences for some travel articles and short stories. Not only that, he'd told her, it was as if the travelling had made his restlessness worse and his sense of incompleteness had grown stronger. She'd been stacking the dishwasher, rinsing dishes at the sink. The kitchen was long and narrow and they moved like dancers, pausing, waiting, as they passed to and fro, in and out of the breakfast room.

'Have you thought about spending some time down here?' she'd asked. 'Oh, not necessarily here at the High House. But a bit closer to us all. You know, Matt, I have a feeling that the answer to your searching is here with us. I don't know how. I just feel that something will guide you towards some kind of answer to your restlessness *and* the subject of your new book, and it will be all part of the same thing.'

He'd paused to look at her, a wineglass in each hand, longing to believe her. He had great faith in Lottie.

'But how d'you mean?' He'd sounded like a child longing to be convinced.

She'd frowned, taking the wineglasses from him and putting them into the dishwasher. Matt knew that later Milo would come in and repack it all. He could always get three times more stuff in than any-one else.

'It's just a feeling I've got,' she'd answered. 'That the two things are tied up together and that you need to step back from everything and wait.'

'And you don't think that I can do that in London?'

'No, I don't. There's too much going on, and even your travelling has an ulterior motive. It's not simply holiday, is it? You're always making notes, testing your reactions for ideas. Step right out of it just for a few months.'

'And the family bit? Being with you all?'

She'd dried her hands and turned to look at him.

'Your mother has just died, Matt. The death of someone close to us reveals all kinds of terrors and pain within ourselves. I think that you've never truly come to terms with Tom's death though you've written out a lot of it over the years. What you don't need to do is to fill your life with more clamour and busyness and travelling so as to silence the fears and deny the mourning. You need to allow thoughts and memories to surface. I don't mean that you have to be introspective, cudgelling your brain to remember things; just a period of quiet emptiness with people who love you close by in case you need company or to talk about the past. We're frightened of silence, aren't we? Switch on the television, pick up a book, make a telephone call. Anything rather than sit in silence. We're always trying to get away from where we are, from the here and now. We think that life is always going to begin tomorrow, or somewhere else. But sometimes waiting patiently in silence reveals things . . .'

She'd rubbed her fingers across her eyes. 'Look, what do I know? It's just what's come to me over these last few days, that's all. And then you being here, and the photographs . . .'

'They're odd, aren't they?' he'd said eagerly, relieved that she'd agreed with him about the photographs. 'As if Mum and I had a secret life somewhere that I can't remember.'

She'd stared at him, clearly shocked by this idea. 'Show them to Imogen,' she'd said. 'Sorry, Matt. I'm honestly not trying to tell you what to do about all this.'

'I know that,' he'd said quickly. 'And I like the idea of some quiet time. I could clear up all the odds and ends and come down at Easter for a couple of months. It sounds a great idea. I think I'd like to find my own pad, though.'

'Of course you would. But your room is here if you want it. You know that.'

Now, as he passed across Birchanger Bridge and drove up towards the toll cottages, he realized that he was growing excited by the idea. Lottie was right: he'd always made sense of life by writing about it; by retelling it to himself in stories so that he could come to grips with it. Even his grief for his mother he'd re-shaped into an odd, rather gripping short story which had been published by the 'Books' section of *The Times*. It was as if he were unable to grieve normally but must take his grief and turn it into something else: yet the familiar haunting lifelong loneliness remained. It was much worse than loneliness: it was the anguish of real loss and separation from someone dear and irreplaceable – but for whom?

There was nobody at the tollgate so he got out to put the money in the slot and then drove on again, up the hill to the cottage.

CHAPTER SIX

The stone cottage was built into a fold in the hill, facing across Porlock Bay towards Hurlstone Point. With Julian's four-track and Imogen's hatchback pulled on to the hard-standing beside the cottage there was no room for his own car. He pulled off the road, parked opposite and climbed out. From this vantage point he could see across to Bossington: there was the High House, with its tall round chimneys, clearly visible perched high above the village and, lower down by the stream amongst the trees, he could make out the red-tiled mansard roof of the Summer House. The sea was a soft pearly grey, smooth as ice; a container ship seemed to skate on its surface, gliding down the Channel from Bristol.

He turned as Imogen opened the door, a finger to her lips.

'Rosie is asleep,' she said. 'We'll be able to have a proper grown-up conversation. Come in here. Jules is asleep too, in front of the television. So tell me about Nick.'

He sat at one of the stools at the pine counter while she switched on the kettle.

'I don't know anything more than I told you when I phoned. They're having problems and Alice has taken the children off to her parents.'

'I wonder if Nick's been playing around.'

He shrugged, uncomfortable with this kind of speculation. She grinned at him.

'OK. I know you hate a good gossip. Listen, we've had details of a cottage in Dulverton. Like to come with me to have a look at it tomorrow?'

He nodded; it would give him a chance to see if there might be anything to rent for a couple of months. It would be unlikely, of course. Most holiday cottages would be already booked for the spring and summer, and any that weren't would be very expensive. He wondered whether to mention this new plan to Im now but, instead, decided to show her the photographs before Jules woke up.

'I've got something to show you. I found them in Mum's rosewood box.' He took the folded brown envelope from his pocket and slid the photographs on to the counter. Im bent eagerly over them.

'Oh, how sweet. Photos of when you were little.

Oh, and older ones, too. I wonder why she kept them separate from all the others.'

He was relieved that she showed no sign of jealousy that there was not even one of her.

'Look at this one,' she was saying, laughing in a kind of disbelief. 'Hey, wasn't your hair short then? And look at this one . . .'

He waited, and she glanced across at him enquiringly.

'What's the matter? Are you worried that she kept them apart from the others or is it that there are none of me?'

He smiled then, and shrugged. 'Well, it's a bit weird, isn't it? But it's not just that. Do you see anything odd about them?'

She peered at them again, frowning. 'What d'you mean, odd?'

'I can't quite decide. First of all, yes, it's odd that you aren't in any of them. But this one, for instance. I just don't remember this jersey – or this baseball cap. And did I really have my hair that short? And I don't recognize this car. Do you?'

She stared at him and then looked again at the photographs. 'So what are you saying?'

'I don't know,' he answered, frustrated. 'I just know there's something wrong.'

Across the passage, Julian stirred, and got up.

They heard the sitting-room door open. Swiftly, Matt swept the photographs together and slid them into the big brown envelope. He shook his head at Im and she turned away and began to make the tea.

'Hi,' she said, as Jules came in. 'Did we wake you? I'm just making some tea.'

'No,' he said. 'Hi, Matt. I wasn't really asleep.'

'Of course not,' said Imogen immediately. 'So what was that you were watching? A snoring competition?'

Before Jules could respond they heard a wailing cry, and Imogen groaned.

'Well, that's our civilized tea party done for. Rosie's awake. Go up and get her, would you, Jules? She'll be so pleased to see Uncle Matt.' When he'd gone she turned to Matt. 'Why don't you want him to see the photos? You're not really worried, are you? Nobody can remember all the things that they wore when they were young. It's always a bit of a shock, isn't it, seeing old family photos?'

'Well, it was,' he said. 'I think it was just coming across them unexpectedly like that in Mum's box. You know?'

'I can understand that,' she said quickly. 'Of course I can. Do you mind if we have tea in here? Rosie's more manageable if I can corral her in the playpen. I'll show you the details of the cottage in a minute. Jules quite likes it but it's still further away from Simonsbath than we're happy with.'

He smiled, nodded; preparing to be a jolly uncle. Jules came in, carrying Rosie, who immediately stretched out a pudgy fist to him. Her beaming smile touched his heart and he took her in his arms while Jules and Im smiled upon them both with a mixture of affection and pride.

Venetia stared at herself in the looking-glass: she approved of what she saw and smiled a little, as if sharing her self-congratulation with her reflection. She turned her head slightly, raising her chin, checking her jaw-line. Pretty good, all things considering.

God, she was lucky to have been born a blonde with fine, fair skin. And these striped pie-crust-collar shirts were still very good value, hiding the less than flattering neck and lending a youthful look, very Princess Di. Lucky, too, to be naturally thin. Clothes hung well on her and her ankles were still excellent. She stuck out a leg to approve the narrow elegance of her calf and ankle. She liked to wear sheer tights and high heels, not like darling Lottie in her long skirts and Ugg boots and hand-knitted garments; mind, Milo was a mean old devil when it came to the heating bills. He still stuck to the military rule: the heating never turned on until the first of October – and not even then if the weather was mild – and off again punctually on the first of April, even if there should be snow on the ground. Lottie never complained, she simply added another layer, and they both lived in the breakfast room all day as close to the Aga as they could get without actually moving right into the kitchen. Venetia shivered. Much as she loved the High House, she couldn't have borne it; she hated to be cold. And anyway, Dunster suited her for the time being; her pretty little house was always cosy, and it didn't take long to hop into the car and nip down the A39 to Bossington.

Venetia dipped her finger into a small, precious pot of light creamy foundation and gently smoothed it on to her face. Poor old Lottie with that brown skin.

'Darling,' she'd said to her once, 'you look as if you're rusting. Now, I know the most perfect moisturizer for you. And are you remembering to put on your sun block?'

Lottie had simply chuckled. 'It's a bit too late in the day for me, I'm afraid. I've always been a gypsy, you know that.'

Well, it was true: Lottie had always been a little brown girl, like a shaggy pony. Nevertheless . . .

Venetia frowned: she hated it when a woman didn't make the best of herself. That's why dear old Milo still adored her, of course. He loved her femininity, though he had no idea of the punishing routines that supported it. Just as well they'd never married: she'd have had no secrets then.

She gave a tiny shudder at the thought of Milo seeing her with no clothes on. Much better as it was, with both of them playing the little game that continued to admit the possibility of resuming intimacy whilst always postponing it. She loved him, of course she did. Oh, what a handsome man he'd been; well, still was, of course. Still thin and elegant, straight-backed and straight-legged. She couldn't have loved a man who'd let himself go. They were both fortunate that they could eat what they liked and never put on an ounce – and those years looking after poor, darling Bunny had kept her on the run and fit as a fiddle, of course. How patient he'd been; how extraordinarily generous. He'd never grudged her a bit of fun; he'd encouraged her to get as much as she could out of her life. My God, she'd made up to him for it, though. She'd done everything she could to make his own days as bearable as possible.

Venetia blotted away a few tears with a tissue. She'd adored him; oh, not in the mad, passionate way she'd fallen in love with Milo, but nevertheless she'd adored Bunny. And Milo had been perfectly sweet to him: sitting with him for hours, pushing him down to the pub in that wretched wheelchair for a pint. Of course they'd all joined the army more or less together. The Somerset Light Infantry it had been in those days, and one big family. Oh, what fun they'd had! She'd thought about it the last time she'd visited poor old Clara, quite gaga and beginning to be difficult with the girls who were looking after her; shouting at them and fighting them when they needed to cut her nails and wash her hair. Tragic, it was, just tragic.

Venetia stared at herself in the looking-glass, willing back the tears: shoulders down, chin up. She'd found a photograph of Clara from those old, happy days. She'd been so dazzlingly pretty, in a low-cut ball gown, laughing into the camera. She'd managed to look imperious and naughty all at once, and Venetia intended to take the photograph into the nursing home and show the girls and say: 'Look at this. This is the real Clara; this is the person you're looking after. Be kind to her.'

She shivered at the prospect of becoming like Clara; the swift descent into dependency and mindlessness. What would she do then? She'd never got on well with her daughters-in-law, and her sons were quite hopeless. What would she do if she were to become ill? At these moments she wished that she and Milo *had* married after Bunny was gone; that she was safe (if cold) at the High House with darling Lottie – so much younger – looking after them.

Actually, had Milo ever suggested that they should marry? Surely he had; just half-jokingly, perhaps, and she'd made some jolly reply – and that had been that. Would it be sensible, perhaps, to think about it more seriously; to encourage Milo towards the prospect of matrimony? Just a formality, of course, and they could be very civilized about it – and she'd have people around her, looking out for her. Was it worth the loss of independence? It had occurred to her before but she'd never quite convinced herself of the absolute need of it. Things worked so well as they were.

Venetia finished applying her make-up, checked her appearance, got up. She mustn't get anxious; worry was so ageing. She bent to peer again into the looking-glass, gave herself a little wink. Perhaps no need to panic quite yet.

CHAPTER SEVEN

Lottie slipped out of the garden door, a plastic container in her hands, Pud attentive at her heels. She made her way round the side of the house to where the bird table stood outside the breakfast-room window. Carefully she put out the breadcrumbs, some raisins for the blackbird, a few shreds of pastry. Pud quartered the grass beneath the table, hoping for some lucky treat, but presently he gave up and ran across the lawn towards the trees on the trail of some night visitor: fox or badger. Lottie waited for a moment, staring out across the coast to where a half-moon hung, ghostly in the pale early morning sky over Culbone Wood.

From his bedroom window, Milo watched her. He was reminded of his mother performing that same task with the small Lottie beside her, carrying the bird food with a rather touching mixture of importance and anxiety. One of Pud's ancestors would have been with them, hoping for a free morsel, just as some ancestor of the blackbird, which now flew down to seize a piece of bread and carry it away into the safety of the shrubbery, would have been waiting all those years ago to do the same.

He liked the sense of continuity, and was grateful to Lottie for the innumerable odd ways she provided it; though his mother would never have gone out dressed as Lottie was now, with her Kaffe Fassett long, knitted coat pulled over her pyjamas and her feet in gumboots. His mother would have been up early, bathed and dressed and every hair in place. She'd been a tough, strong woman – but she'd loved little Lottie.

'She's the daughter I never had,' she'd say to him, half apologetically, hoping he would understand.

At twenty-three he'd been too old to feel any kind of jealousy; anyway it accorded exactly with his own feelings about Lottie, and her visits to the High House made him feel less neglectful about staying away so much when he might have been able to get home, and often forgetting to write or telephone. Some people actually believed that she *was* his sister whilst others, who'd made suggestive remarks and hints, got very short shrift. He'd guessed that Lottie had been in love with Tom. She'd never said a word, and he'd never asked, but once or twice when she'd talked about him there had been an expression on her face that had wrenched his heart. Of course, he'd never known Tom, never met him, but he, Milo, had always had a great respect for war correspondents and had absolutely agreed with Lottie's support of Tom's family. Thinking about it now, he guessed that Lottie would have met Tom sometime in the seventies when she'd been editing his book and, after he'd died, she'd asked if she could bring the children down to the High House to give their mother a break. Matt would have been about five then, and Imogen two. Dear little things; how they'd loved the freedom of the grounds to play in, and the big attics. Milo smiled, remembering. His mother had adored them – just as she'd adored the small Lottie.

Poor little Lottie; how loyal she'd been to the young fatherless family. He remembered an occasion when he'd been playing a CD; Chopin nocturnes and sonatas. It was in the middle of the B minor sonata that he'd noticed that Lottie had begun to weep, a terrible, silent weeping, so that after a moment he'd moved to sit beside her and put his arm round her. She'd leaned into him, still sobbing, and they'd sat together like that until she'd recovered.

'It was the music,' she'd muttered. 'It's crazy, isn't it? I'm OK now. Sorry.'

He'd known then that the sonata had reminded her of Tom and he'd wondered briefly if they'd ever been lovers. He'd guessed not. But even at those moments, when a different kind of intimacy might possibly have blossomed between them, the old brother and sister relationship was too firmly entrenched for it to be possible. Gradually, friends and acquaintances accepted it for what it was and, fortunately, Venetia had made it even easier; their love affair was more or less an open secret. Indeed, a great many men envied him.

'Lucky devil,' they'd say. 'Having that pretty girl looking after you, and a gorgeous woman like Venetia crazy about you. What's the secret, Milo?'

Only Sara was furious with him for having it all.

Milo frowned. Along with the thought of Sara came the remembrance that Nick would be arriving later. Sara had telephoned first.

'Nick wants to come down to see you,' she'd said aggressively, almost as if his father would have denied him. 'And don't nag him, Milo. The poor boy's very upset. Just be nice to him.'

He'd felt a familiar surge of indignation, even anger: why did she always assume that he was going to be difficult or unpleasant? Or did she want to believe that only she understood their son properly? Milo shook his head: it wasn't true. When Nick had been growing up they'd had some wonderful family times here at the High House, but also, sometimes, just the two of them together; some fantastic sailing holidays. And he'd always made great efforts to be around for important events at school, though the army hadn't always made that easy. This unfair remark of hers used so often in the past had almost made him *want* to be difficult with Nick, but his love for his son – and Nick's own laid-back attitude to his mother's partisanship – always disarmed him. Nevertheless, he suspected that this visit was going to be tricky.

Another blackbird had appeared and a battle for territory was now taking place; Lottie had called to Pud and disappeared. Milo turned away from the window and went to take a shower.

Downstairs, in the parlour, Lottie opened the door of the wood-burner and carefully put a small log on top of the still-hot ashes. She, too, was thinking about Nick and wondering what this visit might be about. Sara had been evasive.

'Nick's going to be phoning,' she'd said in the autocratic voice that implied she was still in charge of life at the High House. 'He wants to come down to see his father. I hope Matt's not still with you.'

'Matt's gone,' she'd answered calmly, 'but even

84

if he were here there would be plenty of room for Nick. We love to see him. You know that.'

'That's not the point. Just occasionally, Charlotte, Nick likes to see his father alone. It's his home, after all.'

'Of course it is. And, anyway, as I said, Matt's gone and I promise that I'll be very tactful and keep out of the way.' She'd hesitated. 'I hope there isn't a serious problem.'

'No.' She'd answered too quickly to be convincing. 'And Alice is overreacting, of course. Get Milo for me, would you?'

Now, Lottie closed the wood-burner's doors and stood up, dusting her hands, pulling the woollen coat closely around her. Sara made no secret of the fact that she'd never really liked Alice; not even to Alice. Her dislike of her daughter-in-law wouldn't help this present situation.

Lottie stood for a moment, watching the birds on the seed and nut feeders and on the table: bluetits, a robin, a flutter of sparrows. Suddenly a much larger bird appeared. Beyond the french doors a pheasant paced the terrace, his richly coloured plumage iridescent with copper and greens and reds. He paused, head lowered, neck stretched, staring at the window in which he saw a rival: a beautiful, aggressive male staring back at him. He came closer and his reflection moved with him, strutting, thrusting, pecking at the glass, until Pud came into the room, hesitated in amazement, and then launched himself at the window, barking. The pheasant reared backwards with a startled staccato cry and ran, stiff-legged, into the shrubbery.

Lottie laughed. 'Come away, Pud. He's gone. Let's go and have some breakfast.'

Her mind ranged over the few things still to be done before Nick arrived that afternoon. His room was ready, a fish pie prepared for supper; it was really just a question of waiting for him to turn up. She gave Pud his breakfast, pausing to smooth his silky head, and then made her porridge and cut some bread for toast. She pottered between kitchen and breakfast room, laying the table, waiting for the toaster to pop, and was surprised when Milo appeared, earlier than usual. She was even more surprised when he smiled at her, touched her shoulder, asked if she were ready for some coffee.

Suddenly she realized that his unusual readiness to communicate was due to restlessness; anxiety, probably, about Nick. Lottie sprinkled brown sugar on her porridge and waited.

'Saw you feeding the birds,' he said. 'Looked jolly cold out there.'

'It was,' she agreed. 'The wind's swung round to

the north-east. Nick's bedroom is like a fridge so I've turned the radiator on. He might need a hottie tonight.'

Milo looked contemptuous but refrained from comment. Lottie grinned at him.

'We're not all as tough as you,' she said. 'Or as inhuman.'

'He's a young man,' Milo protested. 'Hotties! Good grief!'

'He's nearly forty,' Lottie said mildly. 'Not very young. And he's not used to our Spartan existence.'

Milo snorted. 'They keep that house like an oven. No wonder the children are so sickly. Always got coughs and colds and snivels.'

He frowned, as if he'd just reminded himself of Nick's unknown problem, and drank some coffee in silence. Lottie spread marmalade on her toast.

'It seems impossible to believe that Alice would leave him,' she said, refusing to be intimidated by the subject and speaking out. 'He'll have had to have done something pretty serious. I think we're jumping the gun.'

Milo stared at her; he looked stricken. 'What, though?'

Lottie looked back at him compassionately. She shrugged, pulling down the corners of her mouth, speculating on what Nick's crime might be.

'I suppose it'll be sex or money,' she said at last.

'You make it sound like a Jane Austen novel,' he said crossly.

'Sorry,' she said, 'but those are the two usual things, aren't they, when it comes to marital problems? Sorry,' she said again quickly, seeing his expression. 'That was tactless, sorry, Milo.'

'It's true, though.' He poured more coffee. 'It's just . . . You know what they say about children of divorced people being more likely to go through it themselves. God, Lottie, I just feel so guilty about things sometimes.'

'I should think it's much more to do with the characters themselves,' she replied calmly. 'Nick is very attractive and he's very kind, and his gambling instincts make him good at his job, but he's insecure, isn't he? He can't resist flirting because it gives his self-esteem a boost, and once or twice it's gone too far and got him into trouble. On the other hand, they both overspend all the time. It might be either. And it's very early days to be talking about divorce, isn't it? We shall know soon.'

'I hate this,' Milo said grumpily. 'I shan't know what to say to him. I just have this feeling that I shall be irritated by him and want to smack him about a bit and tell him to pull himself together.'

Lottie laughed. 'Rubbish,' she said. 'You always say

88

that. And then he'll come in with that Hugh Grant "I know I've been a naughty boy" expression and you'll give him a huge hug and pour him a Scotch.'

Milo looked sheepish. 'I'm very fond of the boy,' he muttered.

'Of course you are. I told Matt that pussycats don't get to be brigadiers but I wonder, in your case, if they made an exception. Mind you, you can be as hard as nails with Venetia.'

He whistled through his teeth, shook his head. 'Venetia's a dangerous woman,' he said. 'You have to watch your step.'

Lottie drank some coffee. 'She's amazing,' she said reflectively. 'You know I have real difficulty in believing that she's seventy.'

Milo gave a crack of unsympathetic laughter. 'So does she! Did you see those heels she was wearing last week? Tottering about like a duck on stilts. She's going to break an ankle one of these days.'

Lottie couldn't help chuckling. 'I take it all back. You are very cruel.'

'Nonsense. I wouldn't dream of saying it to *her*.'

Lottie shook her head but said no more. She reflected that this was one of the good things about not being married. She felt no responsibility for Milo's character; it was not incumbent upon her to reprove him or feel embarrassed by whatever he might say or do. After all, it was no reflection upon her. There was a great freedom within their relationship: none of those sulks or tempers that arose out of the questioning or doubting of love or rights.

She got up from the table. 'I'm going to get dressed,' she said, and went away.

Milo sat on for a minute, finishing his coffee, feeling more relaxed. Perhaps Nick's problems wouldn't be too serious after all. He stood up and began to clear the breakfast things.

CHAPTER EIGHT

When Imogen hurried to open the door, hoping that Rosie hadn't been wakened by the ringing of the doorbell, she was startled to see Nick standing outside.

'Nick!' she cried, and then automatically put her finger to her lips. 'Rosie's asleep. Come on in. What are you doing here? Did you get down last night?'

'Haven't been home yet.' He followed her into the living room, glancing around, smiling his secret smile. 'I wanted to see you first.'

'Oh?' She'd slid behind the breakfast bar and switched on the kettle, and now she turned to look at him, her eyes narrowed suspiciously. 'Why?'

He shrugged, still smiling. 'Because we're old friends. Aren't we?'

'Of course we are.' She busied herself with mugs and teabags, disturbed as she'd always been by that secret smiling gaze. 'But even so . . .'

He hitched himself up on to one of the stools. 'Well, I need all the friends I can get at the moment.'

'Oh, Nick.' She sounded exasperated. 'Whatever is it this time? Has Alice really left you or is it just a sticky patch?'

He leaned with both arms on the counter, not looking at her now. 'It's a bit more serious this time, Im.'

She experienced a tiny thrill of fear. 'Oh God, Nick. Have you been messing around?'

'Not in the way you mean. There's no woman involved.'

He looked at her, and she knew that he'd seen and recorded the tiny inexplicable flash of relief; though why, after all this time, should it matter to her even if there were? She stared back at him; her stomach contracted and her hands were icy.

'Well, that's something,' she said lightly. 'Alice will be glad to know that.'

His smile told her that he knew that she was glad too, and she turned away, confused, relieved to be occupied with the tea-making.

'I've cocked up big time financially,' he said. 'Borrowed some funds from the golf club I'm treasurer for.'

'Oh, my God . . .' She turned back to stare at him, and he caught one of her hands. She made no attempt to resist him. 'So what does that mean exactly?'

His laugh was impatient. 'Does it matter? Do you really want the details? I took some chances with money that wasn't mine. A gross misjudgement. I was expecting to pay it back out of my end-of-year bonus but things are tricky in the City and I got only a quarter of what I was expecting. I don't know how the hell I'm going to explain it to Dad but I really need some money very quickly.'

Imogen drew back her hand, felt guilty and stretched it out to him again and he held it tightly. 'I'm so sorry, Nick. Honestly. But I can't see what I can do to help.'

'At least you haven't recoiled from me in disgust and shown me the door. I suppose I just wanted a bit of . . . oh, I don't know. Affection? Friendship? Before I face Dad.' He lifted her hand to his lips, kissed it lightly, and let it go. 'You were always special, Im, you know that.'

'It was a long time ago,' she muttered, pushing a mug of tea across the counter to him.

'But nothing was quite the same afterwards, was it?' he asked.

'We agreed,' she said, not answering him directly. 'We said that we were too close. Almost like brother

93

and sister. We *agreed*,' she repeated more firmly. 'We were rather like Milo and Lottie.'

'We weren't a bit like Milo and Lottie,' he said. 'There was no family connection at all between us.'

'We were brought up almost like brother and sister,' she protested. 'Or at least like cousins.'

He watched her thoughtfully. 'I'm right though, aren't I? Nothing was quite the same afterwards. I've never been so happy, Im, as I was then with you.'

She flushed. 'It's in the past, Nick. Ten years ago. And what's it got to do with now? What will you tell Milo?'

He took a deep sighing breath. 'It's going to have to be the truth, I'm afraid.' He smiled at her expression. 'Surprised? Oh, make no mistake, I've thought of every possible story that might be believable but even I can't think of anything plausible. I just hope he doesn't throw me out.'

'You know very well that Milo would never do that.'

He looked so desperate that her heart was wrung with anxiety and pity for him. There was no point in telling him what a fool he was; clearly he knew that well enough already.

'Is Alice very cross?' She'd never really much liked Alice.

'She's utterly disgusted with me,' he muttered.

94

'Said she couldn't bear to look at me. I can't blame her.'

'But what made you do it?' she asked more gently. She realized that she was feeling very slightly virtuous, more tolerant of his weakness than the upright, unforgiving Alice. Of course, she'd known him for ever; knew his weaknesses – and strengths.

Nick swallowed some tea. 'You have really no idea, Im, what it's like to live in a very commercial society. Where even at the school gate you're judged by your shoes, and your kids are likely to be losers if they carry the wrong pencil boxes, or if your skiing holiday isn't in this year's socially acceptable resort. The pressure is huge. Children's parties are a competitive nightmare. I'd maxed my credit cards, got behind with the mortgage and I needed extra money; it's as simple as that. The trouble is, you feel that you have to keep up with your friends.'

'Then move. Live somewhere else, where those values don't apply.'

He laughed at her. 'Will you be the one to tell Alice that she needs to change the habits of a life-time? It's what she's used to, and I knew that when I married her. I thought I could hack it. It's not her fault that I couldn't quite cut it. If I can borrow some money quickly I can just about deal with it and she might – *might* – just bring herself to overlook it.'

'How much, Nick?'

He grimaced. 'Twenty-three thousand?'

'Jesus!'

'I know. But I'm strapped whichever way I turn when it comes to borrowing, and the mortgage can't take another penny, so Dad's my last resort.'

'Is Milo likely to have that much spare? He's only got his pension, hasn't he?'

Nick looked away from her. 'He's got the Summer House,' he said reluctantly. 'And Ma says that the tenants are about to move out.'

'You mean sell it?' She felt a pang of real grief. 'Oh, Nick, that would be so sad. It's always been part of the High House, hasn't it?'

He shrugged. 'Have you got any better ideas?' He put down his mug. 'I must get on. They'll be wondering if I'm OK. See you later?'

'Of course. Let me know what happens.'

'Thanks, Im. I mean, really, thanks.'

She came round the end of the counter to give him a hug, feeling rather pleasantly compassionate and horrified, both at the same time. He put his arms around her and held her tightly.

'Good luck,' she said, releasing herself quickly.

She hurried him to the door, shut it behind him, and stood staring at it. To her relief Rosie began to shout, and Im turned and ran quickly up the stairs.

Nick drove slowly: he had no stomach for the meeting to come and, as he drove, he rehearsed the words that he would use to his father. In his heart he blessed Im for her partisanship; he'd never let his mother know just how fond of Im he was: even when they'd been small children she'd been determined to make him see Matt and Im as usurpers and he'd played along with it to please her. But Im had been such a sweetie, and she'd grown up to be a very pretty girl. The fact that none of the family had known about their *tendresse* had made it even more exciting: not even Matt had guessed. Nick almost smiled: it had been fun fooling them all. But he'd always had his suspicions about Lottie; that direct way she'd looked at him sometimes so that he'd been unable to meet her eye. Funny woman, his aunt Lottie; she wasn't at all how one might imagine an aunt. He wondered whether he could count on her to support him; perhaps he ought to tell her first and let her break the news to Dad.

Nick beat his fist lightly on the steering wheel and shook his head in disgust at the thought. But his gut turned to water as he imagined the coming interview. His father was so old school, so straight; though he'd always stood by him, always taken his side. Nick made a face. Of course, there had been a few occasions in the past when he'd been in disgrace: that shoplifting stunt when he'd been at boarding school, for instance, and a bit of a drugs problem at uni; but nothing really bad, nothing serious. Not like this.

He groaned aloud in his despair. He'd give anything, anything at all, to turn the clock back. He slowed down as he approached the tollgate but there was no one in the booth. He wasn't surprised, it was too cold to be standing about today – and too bloody cold to get out of the car to put the money in the slot and, anyway, he hadn't got any change. He'd pay double next time. Meanwhile he drove on with a placatory wave of the hand to anyone who might be watching from the cottage window. Maybe they'd recognize him, and they'd understand.

All the way down the winding road, through Allerpark Combe and into Porlock, he was thinking about Alice and the children.

'Will you tell your parents?' he'd asked diffidently.

She'd given him the cool, contemptuous stare that seemed to be her habitual expression just lately.

'No,' she answered. 'I don't think I could bear them to know just what a stupid immoral prat you are. If you can sort it then nobody except us will know. I certainly couldn't go on if it became common knowledge.'

Humiliated, he'd accepted all of her strictures: he had no choice.

'If you had to do something so despicable at least the timing was good. The half-term fortnight's been booked for ages so my parents won't suspect anything. Except that you were going to get down to see us whenever you could. Well, you can forget that, I'm afraid. I shall invent some crisis for you. When you know what Milo says you can text me.'

'Don't forget,' he'd wanted to cry defensively, 'what the money was spent on. That two-week skiing holiday in Verbier, for instance, when you insisted on taking a chalet and inviting six friends as pay-back for hospitality, not to mention your new must-have Mercedes hatchback.'

Of course, he'd said nothing: there were no excuses. Driving ever more slowly along Bossington Lane and into the village, Nick tried to brace himself: at least Im was on his side. He looked up at the High House standing up on the hill and with a sinking heart turned up the drive.

CHAPTER NINE

Milo came strolling out to meet him. He could see at once that Nick was stiff with apprehension, his face clenched and pale. All the older man's irritation drained away, though his anxiety increased, and he put an arm around his son's shoulders and hugged him.

'Good trip?' Stupid question: he knew quite well that the journey must have been hell. 'Lottie is out with Pud but she'll be back later. Like some tea?'

He sensed Nick's relief. It had been Lottie's decision to be out when Nick arrived.

'He'll probably want to unburden himself at once,' she'd said. 'He's always been like that, hasn't he? It'll be agony for him to sit around making polite conversation over the teacups. I'll take Pud for a long walk and hope that you have enough time together before I get back.'

Leading the way into the house, Milo felt

unbearably nervous; he was too old, he told himself, for this kind of crisis. He felt vulnerable. He made tea while Nick talked rather aimlessly about the journey from London and tried not to get in the way; but as soon as he put the mug into Nick's hand he wasted no more time.

'So what is it?' he asked. He knew that he looked severe and that his voice was brusque but it was the only way that he could manage to control his own nerves. 'Sit down and tell me what's happened.'

Nick put his mug on the table – his hand was shaking too much to hold it – sat down and began to speak. It was clear that he had rehearsed the little recital but he stumbled through it – expenses to be met, afraid of not having enough to pay the mortgage, the school fees; of course, he'd planned to return the money out of his bonus . . . He mumbled on wretchedly and Milo watched him, at first with compassion, followed by disbelief and horror.

'*How* much?' he cried when Nick muttered the sum involved. And, 'You bloody fool,' he said almost dispassionately when Nick repeated it.

'I know,' he answered simply. 'I know that, Dad. But I've nowhere else to go.'

Milo thought about the expensive holidays, the school fees, the quantities of toys and the extensive wardrobes of Alice and her children.

'Have you ever thought,' he asked, 'of saying "No" to Alice and the children occasionally?'

Nick was clearly taken aback by the question. He considered it – and shook his head.

'Part of the deal was keeping up with the lifestyle,' he answered simply. 'I really believed that I could.'

'"Part of the deal"?' Milo repeated disbelievingly. 'Are you by any chance talking about your wedding vows?'

Nick almost smiled. 'I suppose you could put it like that. Alice is high maintenance and I knew that when I married her.'

'But she makes no contribution to this must-have lifestyle? Couldn't she get a job?'

Nick actually laughed. 'Alice? Work? What at?'

'Surely she could train for something? She's young enough. Can you think of any good reason why I, at my age, should use my hard-earned savings to pay for her extravagances while she does nothing? What about her parents? They're a great deal better off than I am.'

'She says that she doesn't want them to know what a "stupid immoral prat" I am. I think those were her words. I have to deal with it or my marriage is on the line.'

'So I have to subsidize your family's high-maintenance lifestyle, Alice's idle extravagance and your criminal weakness? You realize that what you've done is criminal?'

Nick bit his lips, humiliated. 'I promise I'll try to pay it back. The trouble is – I haven't got much time.'

'How much time?'

A short silence. 'Two weeks,' Nick answered reluctantly. 'The books have to go in then.'

Milo closed his eyes. 'My God, Nick.'

'I know,' he said miserably. 'I tried everything I could think of before I came to you . . . Good God, Dad!' He smashed his fist on the table. 'I didn't want to have to do this.'

Milo was unmoved by the outburst – Nick was inclined to become theatrical when the situation demanded it – but he got up and went to the drinks tray and poured him a small Scotch. Standing behind him while he drank it, Milo stared unseeingly down upon his son's thick, fair hair. How could he help him? He dropped a hand on Nick's shoulder, sensing his misery and humiliation.

'What did your mother say?'

Under his hand he felt Nick's shoulder move in a shrug. 'She's furious with me but she blames Alice, which isn't really fair. You're right. I should have more courage and stand up to her now and then.

103

The trouble is, I feel a failure if I can't deliver, you see.'

Milo involuntarily tightened his grip as his own sense of failure assaulted him. He'd made similar mistakes with Sara and because of it the marriage had broken down – with what damage to Nick? Quite suddenly the little scene dislimned and he was back nearly forty years, and this time it was his father sitting at the table staring at him with a shocked, disbelieving expression.

'Divorce?' he was repeating incredulously. 'You and Sara want to divorce? But what about the child? And whatever will your mother say . . .?'

His mother had been distraught, angry, condemnatory. Even now Milo's gut churned with a remembrance of his helplessness and humiliation.

'We'll manage somehow,' he said now – and felt Nick's shoulder sag with relief. 'I'll have to think how,' he warned him, 'and you must promise to use this experience to get your relationship with Alice on to a new footing. If she wants more than you can provide then you must tell her that she must get out and earn it herself.'

Nick nodded earnestly – he looked ill with relief – and Milo knew that his son's readiness to agree to reform was simply a reaction to his thankfulness: nothing would change. He sighed.

'Lottie will be back soon,' he said. 'Do you want this kept as a secret between you and me?'

Nick shook his head. 'I told Im,' he said. 'I don't mind Lottie knowing that I'm a stupid immoral prat. She's my aunt. It won't be news to her, after all.'

The bitterness in his voice, the emphasis on the little phrase he'd used before, wrenched Milo's heart; at the same time he felt impatient with Nick's foolishness and anxious at how he might be able to help him.

'Would it be better,' Nick was asking diffidently, 'if I go back to London?' He smiled, a rather forced hangdog grimace. 'You won't be able to be really rude about me to Lottie with me sitting there, will you?'

Milo smiled too, remembering Lottie's remark about Hugh Grant and the Scotch. 'I don't see why not,' he answered. 'It's never stopped me before. She's your aunt, after all.'

Nick looked at him gratefully. 'Thanks, Dad. I mean, really, thanks. You've saved my life.' He got up. 'I'll go and unpack. Is it OK if I have a shower?'

Milo watched him go and then poured himself a drink. He sat down at the table and began to think how he could help Nick. He was still sitting there when Lottie and Pud came back. She raised her eyebrows and he nodded and pointed towards the ceiling.

'Twenty-three thousand,' he muttered – and her eyes widened in horror. 'I know,' he said. 'But it's pretty desperate this time.'

'You seem quite calm about it.' Lottie kept her voice down. 'How on earth will you manage?'

He gave a little shrug. 'I was thinking about what we were talking about earlier. My idea of selling the Summer House to Im and Jules. After all, neither Sara nor Nick could complain now if I sold it to them at a very competitive rate, could they?'

Lottie looked anxious. 'But is it right for *you*, Milo? The Summer House is a bit of an insurance policy, isn't it? That's what you always said, anyway. A buffer against old age or illness.'

'The Summer House will be difficult to let again without doing a great deal of modernizing. If I sell it I can buy two small letting properties in Minehead or Dulverton – much more sensible – and Im and Jules will have a home. They won't care that it's a bit run-down, and I'll have the rental incomes to boost my pension.'

Lottie frowned. 'It sounds quite sensible,' she admitted cautiously.

They heard Nick's footsteps, exchanged a quick glance. 'It's OK,' Milo said, 'he wants you to know,' and Lottie turned to greet her nephew. She hugged him, aware of the fear and despair beneath his relief, seeing in his shamed glance a question: did she know yet? Would she condemn him?

'It's good to see you, Nick,' she told him.

He smiled at her. 'Thanks, Lottie. It's good to be home. I thought I'd just take a little walk. Get some fresh air and stretch my legs.'

He went out, gently closing the door behind him, and Lottie sat down opposite Milo.

'Very tactful of him,' she said. 'Pour me a drink, please, Milo, and start at the beginning.'

Nick walked down the drive, his head bent against the cold wind, hands in his pockets.

'It'll be OK,' he said to himself once or twice rather drearily, but he felt no real lightening of spirits.

He would have given anything to be back at that point in his life before he'd succumbed to fear: to return to that particular moment and do it all differently. He still felt ill with regret and shame though his gut-churning terror of discovery had receded.

The whole length of the drive he argued with himself; trying to justify his actions. It was easy now, he told himself despairingly, to imagine that he would have had the courage to tell Alice that they were overdrawn in every possible area: that they could no longer go on living at such a rate and that together they must face serious cutbacks. At the mere thought of such a confrontation he felt sick again in the pit of his stomach, fearful at the prospect of her contempt at his failure. And here was the real nub of the thing: not that *she* might be at fault for her extravagances and snobbery; only that *he* was to blame because he couldn't provide for them. Dimly he recognized that he was overanxious to retain the goodwill of his family and friends; that he was diminished by their criticism. Because of his need to please all the people all the time he'd allowed himself to make bad decisions, trying to double guess what would make this friend or that member of the family happy. This invariably led on to secret resentment, yet he continued to be driven by this need.

As he turned out of the drive into the village street, he began to recall numerous occasions in his life when his desire to remain popular, loved, admired, had been stronger than the instinct to be true to himself. He was easily swayed, too unconfident to have the courage of his own convictions. Oh, he could brazen things out if necessary, put on a swagger to cover his uncertainties and give the impression of being confident and cheerful. He was so successful at this Jekyll and Hyde existence that sometimes he'd wondered if he were schizophrenic. He was good at being very jolly; a bit of a clown. Alice had responded to it.

'You make me laugh,' she'd said once, early on in their relationship. 'I like that.'

He'd been flattered; determined to keep up this aspect of his character, thus retaining her approval and love.

Now, as he strode on through the village, past the pretty cottages with their tall, stone chimneys, out towards Allerford, he knew the reason why his brief relationship with Im had been so magical. She'd accepted him for what he was – and there'd been the confidence of consanguinity.

'We were like cousins,' she'd said, and it was true, but that loving closeness had been incomparable and precious during that brief period of their love affair. She'd been eighteen and had her first job working at a racing stable near Newbury; he, an immature thirty-year-old, had been doing well in futures trading after a few disastrous early career moves, and driving down from London at weekends to see her.

Here was another area in which he yearned to reinvent the past; to have another shot at something he'd rejected out of fear.

'Nobody must know,' Im had said to him anxiously. 'What would your mum say if she suspected?'

Her fear had infected him and even now he could remember the terror he'd felt at the prospect of telling his mother that he was in love with Imogen. All too often, right through his life, his mother had expressed herself forcibly on the subject of the 'usurpers'. As a child he'd walked a stressful line between his mother's potential wrath and his easy, natural love for his father and Lottie, and for Matt and Imogen. Yet he'd always needed his mother's love and approval too, fearful that she might cease to love him just as she'd ceased to love his father.

'It's my fault, isn't it?' the small Nick had asked anxiously. 'It's because of me that you and Daddy don't want to be together any more,' and neither of them had been able to give an adequate explanation to the contrary, though his father had remained unwavering in his love and attention to him; more stable and reliable than his mother, who had been given to angry tirades against his father in those early years after the divorce.

Looking back, he guessed that this was because his mother had been the one who'd left, and had felt guilty – and was trying to justify herself to her son – but he knew now that he'd simply been far too young to understand the complexities of adult relationships. He'd worked hard to sustain the fragile connection that remained between his parents.

Nick passed West Lynch Farm and suddenly turned aside, through a little wooden picket gate. He walked up the path that led to the small stone chapel, and let himself in. Sitting in the back pew he gazed upon the scene that was so familiar. Here he'd sat as a child with his father at Christmas-time and at Easter, during holidays from boarding school, and more recently with his own children. The silence and the atmosphere of peaceful prayerfulness brought him unexpected comfort and he began to dread the moment that he must stand up and go back into the depressing reality of his life. He bent his head, trying to think of some appeal, some prayer that he might make, but the only word that came to his confused mind was 'Help'. He prayed it anyway. 'Please help me,' he muttered, then, after a little pause, he stood up and went out into the cold March evening.

CHAPTER TEN

During the night the temperature dropped below freezing and by morning the daffodils along the banks each side of the drive were weighted down by the thick frost, lightly iced like some exotic lemon pudding. Catkins hung like stalactites in the chill air.

Lottie stood at her bedroom window wrapping herself into her thick woollen dressing gown. Overnight a lamb had been born in the field below the house: a tiny grey-white form, like a stone on the ground, with two ewes standing over it. A jug-handle ear suddenly showed and then sank again into the huddle of skin and bone. A magpie landed nearby and the ewes faced up to it. It hopped closer and Lottie leaned from the window, flapping a shawl, so that it hesitated and then flew away. The two ewes gently nudged the inanimate form and now a crow flew in, landing near the little group, swaggering forward. Once again the ewes faced up to it, one of them making a little run forward, but it stood its ground and Lottie opened the window again, clapping her hands to frighten it away. But now, at last, the lamb was on its feet, staggering, pitifully weak, and the ewes shielded its trembling body, bending their heads to nuzzle it. The magpie was down in a monochrome flash, seizing the bloody afterbirth in its beak, dragging it away whilst the disgruntled crow watched from a low bare bough.

Lottie stood at the window for a little longer, until she believed the lamb to be out of danger, and then went out of her room. She paused on the landing to look up the stairs that led to Matt's quarters in the attic; empty again now. It was odd that from his earliest visits Matt had claimed the attic for his own. Even as a small boy he'd loved the isolation and privacy of his eyrie whilst glad to know that the people that mattered to him were not too far away. Lottie and Imogen shared this staircase whilst Milo's bedroom was at the other end of the house with Nick's room and the spare room.

As she went down the stairs, through the parlour and into the breakfast room she wondered how Nick was feeling this morning. Supper had been a sombre affair: Milo in a quiet and rather uncommunicative mood, whilst Nick grasped gratefully at any conversational opening.

The trouble was, thought Lottie as she bent to receive Pud's morning welcome, that at times like these almost any subject was likely to lead eventually into dangerous waters. She'd cast around in her mind to find a topic that might not somehow refer to Nick's family or work and finally decided to sacrifice Matt's pride on the altar of social necessity. They'd talked about the difficulty of following a successful novel and a film with something equally good, if not better, and the pressure he was under. Nick had been sympathetic and thoroughly agreed with Lottie's idea that Matt needed a break away from London and the constant reminders of his failure to come up with the goods.

'He's coming down again at Easter,' she'd said. 'He can't find a place to rent at the moment so he'll be here for a while. He'd like to take a couple of months off.'

She'd smiled at Nick, not actually seeking his approval but hoping that he wouldn't feel in any way dispossessed by the prospect of Matt being around for such a long time.

'I think it's a great idea,' he'd said at once. 'Perhaps he'll find inspiration once he's away from all his usual haunts. I loved *Epiphany*. It's such an amazing book, isn't it? *The Lord of the Rings* meets *Harry Potter*. It's packed with images and plots and ideas. I should think he'd need years to write another one like that. Or perhaps he wants to do something different this time?'

She'd shaken her head. 'I don't think he knows what he wants to do. He's trying too hard to come up with something. He needs time with Im and Rosie. Normal family life.'

'And his mum's death. He needs time to adjust to that, too. Poor old Helen. It's probably worse for Matt and Im that she had such a troubled life.'

She'd been touched by his intuitiveness, smiled at him with warm affection, and he'd smiled back; such a genuinely sad, little self-aware smile that she'd wanted to get up and go round the table to give him a hug. And then Milo had stirred, poured more wine and begun to talk about selling the Summer House. She'd tensed with trepidation but it was clear that this was not a new idea to Nick, and when Milo had suggested that he might let Im and Jules have it for a sum they could afford she could see that Nick was genuinely delighted.

It was also clear to see that Nick's ready generosity on Im's behalf had afforded Milo a grim kind of amusement. She'd been able to read his thoughts without difficulty; after all, the only one who would be down on the deal would be Milo himself – but Nick was so relieved, so anxious to show himself willing for the sale of the Summer House to benefit Im and Jules, that it didn't occur to him to sympathize with his father's financial loss. Across the table she'd watched Milo struggling with himself, reminding himself that this was what he'd wanted to do in the first place before he'd known about Nick's dilemma, and finally resisting making any sarcastic observation that would humiliate his son further. She'd raised her glass to Milo then, silently acknowledging his private battle, and he'd understood and grinned back at her, admitting the temptation with a small, slightly shame-faced wink.

As she and Pud made the morning pilgrimage to the bird table, Lottie felt a lightening of spirits: the difficult moment was over and Nick was out of danger. She wondered how Milo would broach the subject of the Summer House to Imogen and tried to imagine her delight. A chill current of air shivered the stiff leaves of the rhododendron bushes and touched her cheeks; she huddled the collar of her long, knitted dressing gown higher around her neck and hurried back into the house.

To the relief of all three of them, Nick left in the middle of the morning. Milo had made the necessary call to his bank and had written out a cheque, which Nick had accepted with incoherent mutterings of gratitude and promises never to do such a thing again. All three of them were embarrassed, none of them knowing how to say goodbye in a normal manner. It was clear that Nick was longing to be gone, however much he tried to convince them that this was solely because he needed to get the cheque paid in and the accounts finished. Then, once he'd handed over the cheque, Milo had a sudden and violent resurgence of irritation at Nick's 'criminal stupidity' and made him promise that he would resign from the post of golf club treasurer. Nick, looking slightly injured, told him that he'd already decided to do that as soon as the moment was right.

Since this little scene took place in the breakfast room with Lottie present, she tried to smooth over the awkwardness by offering to make Nick a sandwich or some coffee before he went, but he shook his head, smiling at her, and went away to fetch his overnight case.

Milo looked uncomfortable, slightly regretting his outburst but resentful at having to feel remorse. Lottie grinned at him.

'"Rich gifts wax poor when givers prove unkind",' she quoted softly.

'Shut up!' he muttered back, but they were both smiling when Nick came back into the room.

He looked from one to the other, his spirits lifting with relief, and they all went out together to the car.

'Honestly, though,' Milo said, still aggrieved, as they waved Nick off down the drive. 'That my son should behave so . . . well, so *dishonourably*, dammit. I can still hardly believe it.'

'He genuinely meant to pay it back,' Lottie said gently. 'He told me that he was so horrified when he saw the size of his bonus that he was physically sick. Try to see it through Nick's eyes. It was as if he were simply borrowing it for a few weeks. That's how he saw it. I'm not condoning it, Milo, of course I'm not, but it wasn't the action of a criminal. We've all been tempted at some time, haven't we, and done things that other people might consider dishonourable?'

Milo opened his mouth to retort that he had never been in such a position, and shut it again, suddenly wondering how many of his friends saw his relationship with Venetia in the same self-forgiving light that he himself considered it. Perhaps some of them might well have considered that it was dishonourable to have an affair with his crippled friend's wife.

But it wasn't quite *like* that, he told himself

defensively, and saw that Lottie was watching him with those strange eyes narrowed slightly as if willing him to make the connection.

'I might take Pud for a walk,' he said abruptly. 'Up to the post office to get my pension. Anything you need?'

She shook her head. 'I don't think so.'

He hesitated. 'Shall you tell Im about the Summer House? Or shall I?'

'Oh!' She thought about it for a moment. 'I imagined you'd want to. Whichever you like.'

'You do it,' he said. 'Go and see her and tell her that they can have it. You know what they can afford.'

'I'd like that,' she said. 'I'll find Pud while you get your coat, and then I'll phone Im.'

CHAPTER ELEVEN

Imogen was sitting on the sofa in the Cellar Bar of the Dunster Castle Hotel, a cup of coffee on the table before her and Rosie in the buggy beside her.

'Can we meet before I go back?' Nick had asked during his very hurried telephone call the previous evening. 'Yes, everything's going to be OK, thank God, but I'd love to see you if you can make it. Dunster? Great. Eleven-ish in the Castle? See you then.'

Now she watched the entrance to the bar and talked to Rosie, who was drowsy and relaxed, having been pushed up to the Conygar Tower in the brisk cold air and then bumped over the cobbles on a stroll around the town. Imogen smiled at Greyam behind the bar and wondered why her meetings with Nick always gave her a slightly guilty feeling. They'd known each other for nearly all their lives and there was no reason why they shouldn't have coffee or a drink together – yet there was a little edgy sensation going way back to that mad moment that they'd had ten years ago. For instance, she hadn't told Jules that she'd be seeing Nick this morning – and she'd been oddly reluctant to explain to Jules exactly what Nick had been up to, merely saying that he'd got behind with his mortgage payments and that Alice was playing up about money. Not that Jules was all that interested; the new job was very demanding and he'd never had a lot of time for Nick.

Imogen shifted uneasily as three women came into the bar and settled themselves at the table in the corner. She wondered if Venetia ever came into the Castle for coffee with her chums and turned instinctively away from them towards Rosie.

'Hi,' said Nick from behind her. 'Hi, Rosie,' and he held out a little toy, a soft, velvety rabbit.

Rosie reached eagerly for it, making sounds of delight that made Imogen smile.

'Oh, darling,' she said to her child, 'isn't that nice? Say, "Thank you, Nick," or should we call you "Uncle Nick"?' she asked, glancing up at him and feeling embarrassed suddenly, now that he was here, trying to emphasize the family note.

'I'm not sure that I'm uncle material,' he was saying, sitting on the other sofa, which was at right angles, shielding her from the rest of the tables. 'Am

121

I, Rosie? Do you like him?' And he set the rabbit dancing, making Rosie chuckle.

Imogen poured him some coffee. 'So everything's OK?' she asked, keeping her voice low. 'Gosh, what a relief. Honestly, I'm just so thankful for you. And Milo didn't do the heavy father act?'

Nick shrugged. 'A bit. But he was entitled to, wasn't he? Actually, he was brilliant.' He took a deep breath and exhaled slowly. 'He's saved my life.'

'Dear old Milo. So what will you do now?'

'I'm on my way home. I need to get everything sorted and, anyway, it would have been a bit tricky to stay. You know what it's like, everyone a bit embarrassed? I'll come down again soon and try to be a bit more normal.'

'And what did Alice say?'

Nick drew back a little; his face was unexpectedly suffused with colour and she watched him curiously.

'I haven't told her yet,' he admitted reluctantly.

Once again, Imogen was seized with various sensations: that peculiar mix of triumph and shock; of pleasure at knowing more than Alice did; of being firmly on Nick's side.

'But why not?' she asked, pretending indignation on Alice's behalf. 'Honestly, Nick, she must be worried sick.'

122

He looked uncomfortable, even grumpy. 'I'm just not looking forward to the conversation. She won't be pleased like you were. Not for me, anyway. She'll be thankful that we're off the hook, that's all. She won't give a damn about Dad and I'll get another earful, that's why.'

'Oh, Nick.' She touched his knee lightly, then took her hand away quickly as he reached for it, and picked up the coffee pot. Rosie nodded sleepily, head askew, the rabbit still clutched to her chest. Imogen looked at her, her heart melting with love. Guilt twisted her gut. 'But you'll have to tell her, won't you?' she said rather briskly to Nick, refilling his cup.

'She's with her mother for the next two weeks,' he said, as if that were some kind of answer. 'Oh, well, yes, of course I shall tell her. But it won't make much difference. I was wondering, Im, whether to come down again next week for a day or two. I'd planned a few days off, you see, to go down to see the kids but I don't think this will change anything as far as Alice is concerned and, anyway, I can't say I'm that keen on facing her parents just at the moment.'

She didn't look at him but reached to pull Rosie's rug more firmly over her legs. 'I expect Milo would be pleased to see you.'

'I'd hate him to think I only come when I want something. Do you think it would work or is it too close to all this and he'll just be embarrassed?'

'Of course he won't be,' she said firmly. 'Milo's not like that. And Lottie certainly isn't. Bring him a little present and take him out for a pint.'

He nodded. 'I'd like to do that. And what about you? Shall I bring you a present and take you out for a pint, too?'

She laughed, keeping it light. 'Why not?'

They smiled at each other, warmed by their mutual affection. Nick was looking at her, as if he was wondering whether to tell her something, a strange excited look. She stared back at him, frowning.

'What?' she asked. 'What is it?'

'You know what I was saying about Dad having to sell the Summer House?' he asked. She nodded, eyes wide. 'Well, he is going to sell it.'

'Oh, Nick.' She looked sad. 'Oh, I'm sorry.'

'Listen, though. Dad isn't sorry, and neither am I. He wants to sell it to you and Jules. At a price you can afford. He wants to, Im.'

'But he can't do that,' she gasped. 'He mustn't. I mean, he can sell it, obviously – it's his house – but he must sell it at the proper price. Not to us.'

'But he wants to,' Nick repeated. 'He looks upon you and Matt as part of the family, and it's a way of,

124

well, you know, giving you something, just as if you were his daughter.'

'Even so. He shouldn't.' Im was in a state of shock. 'I can't believe it.'

'I shouldn't have told you. I just wanted you to know that I'm absolutely delighted, just in case you thought I might feel . . . well, you know.'

'But your mum will be incandescent. She'll go nuts. After all, it's still your inheritance, isn't it?'

'That's why I want you to know that I'm completely with Dad. I hope you're a good actress, Im. You'll have to pretend you don't know when Dad or Lottie tells you.'

'You're right. You shouldn't have said anything.'

He looked disappointed and she knew that he'd wanted to have this share in Milo's generosity, to ameliorate his own foolishness by being able to attribute some good to it. As usual she responded to his hurt at once, stretching a hand to him and smiling.

'I shan't dare to believe it until Milo says something,' she said. 'It's too good to be true. I utterly love the Summer House.'

'I know.' He was holding her hand tightly, smiling back at her – and then Rosie woke suddenly, scrabbling for her dropped toy; she let out a howl, and the moment passed.

125

As she drove out of Dunster through Alcombe, Imogen was filled with misgiving. Even if Milo did intend to offer her and Jules the Summer House she wished that Nick hadn't told her about it. She knew that she wasn't a good actress and she wondered how on earth she could pretend amazement at such kindness. She comforted herself by thinking that Milo would quickly repent of his first generous idea and nobody would ever mention it again – and was immediately seized with disappointment lest this might be true.

'Don't forget,' Nick had warned her as they'd said goodbye in the car park, 'you don't know anything. We haven't met. Sorry, sweetie, but it seemed the best way.'

They'd hugged and he'd driven away, but she'd felt slightly irritated by the fact that she would have to play-act her way out of it. Now as she drove through Tivington and passed below Selworthy Church, dazzlingly white in the bright sunshine, she came to a decision. She turned right into Allerford and continued along the lane into Bossington until she reached the drive to the High House. Milo's car was missing but Lottie came out to meet her, bending to smile at Rosie who stared back at her solemnly and then raised the little rabbit as if in greeting.

At the sight of the rabbit, Imogen's heart seemed to shift in her breast.

She thought: Thank God, Rosie can't talk. But this made her feel even more guilty and she turned quickly to Lottie, chattering about nothing in particular; how they'd been into Dunster and walked up to the Conygar Tower and then had coffee in the Castle, and decided just on the spur of the moment to come in and see how it was all going . . . Suddenly she fell silent, thinking of all the things she mustn't say, pretending that she mustn't even know if Nick was still with them.

Lottie slipped an arm about her and kissed her.

'Nick's gone,' she said, 'and all is well. Can you stay to lunch? If you get Rosie out I'll bring the bag with all her things in. I expect you've got some milk for her, haven't you? Milo's dashed into Porlock but he won't be long.'

Imogen unclipped the straps and lifted Rosie out of her seat. She had a feeling that Lottie knew perfectly well that she and Nick had been in touch, she probably even knew that they'd met, and she felt uncomfortable. When they got inside, Lottie fetched the folding playpen that was kept for Rosie's visits and set it on the floor near the wood-burning stove. Imogen plonked her down in it and Rosie sat on the padded floor, examining the rabbit – which now to Imogen's guilty eyes looked life-size – and murmuring her own peculiar words to it.

'Bah,' Rosie muttered. 'Bah, boh, da.' She pressed the rabbit to her cheek and then with a swift movement flung it against the netting wall of the playpen. She shifted her weight and half shuffled, half crawled, towards a little rag book that hung from the rail.

'She's had her milk.' Im busied herself with the bag full of nappies and juice and toys, hardly able to look Lottie in the face lest she should burst out with the truth. 'But I've got some lunch for her with us, just in case.'

'I expect you've heard from Nick,' Lottie said tranquilly. 'You're his rock at times like these, aren't you? He knows you're always on his side.'

Imogen was silent, her hands briefly stilled, replies jumbling together in her brain although she couldn't find one that was adequate.

'Anyway,' Lottie was saying, not waiting for any response, 'Milo has found a way out for him. And it includes selling the Summer House.'

'Oh!' cried Imogen, her head still buried in the bag. 'Oh, poor Milo.' She simply couldn't look at Lottie and she cursed Nick for putting her into this situation. 'I'm so sorry.'

'Well, *he* isn't.' Lottie sounded almost amused. 'He's been trying to think of a way he could offer the Summer House to you and Jules at a reasonable price that was fair to Nick and wouldn't send Sara into orbit, and now Nick has provided him with the ideal solution.'

Imogen raised her head, her cheeks scarlet, and stared at Lottie. The older woman began to laugh.

'Poor Im,' she said. 'You were never any good at dissembling, were you? Even as a little girl, with Matt threatening to murder you, you'd blurt everything out. So Nick's told you all this already, and that's fine. Perhaps he should have given his father the opportunity to tell you himself but since Milo asked me to tell you, anyway . . .'

'It was just that Nick wanted me to know how pleased he was.' Im burst at last into speech. 'You know. He said that Sara would probably go ballistic but that he was absolutely thrilled. He just wanted me to know and to say goodbye . . . How did you know?'

'Oh, darling. Your face. You looked so guilty and miserable that I guessed at once. Poor Im. And he swore you to secrecy, of course.'

'Well, he did. He was so embarrassed about what he'd done, you see, and how generous Milo was

129

being, but he thought it ought to come as a surprise to me when Milo told me. Honestly, Lottie, I can't take it in even now. I can't believe Milo could be so kind. Why should he be?'

'Because he loves you. You and Matt are very dear to him. Nick's had lots of help and will inherit all this, and Matt's financially secure after his terrific success. Milo was looking for a way that he could help you and Jules, that's all. He knows how much you love the Summer House and that you need somewhere to live. You'll still have to raise a mortgage, you know. He's not giving it to you.'

'Of course not,' cried Imogen. 'We wouldn't want him to. It's just so . . . amazing. Isn't it, Rosie?' She bent down and took Rosie out of the playpen, swinging her up into the air. 'Gosh, this child smells appalling. I'll take her up and change her.' She hesitated, holding Rosie close to her, their faces almost touching. 'And thanks, Lottie. I might have guessed, mightn't I, that you'd see straight through me?'

'You've always loved Nick,' she answered simply. 'He's very lucky. We all need one person who's always unconditionally on our side. You've always been on Nick's.'

Im looked confused, embarrassed, opened her

mouth to attempt an explanation, but Rosie began to wriggle and to cry, and Im smiled gratefully at the older woman, picked up the big bag and hurried away up the stairs.

CHAPTER TWELVE

All the way back to the cottage Imogen wondered how she might tell Jules the exciting news.

'Of course, Jules doesn't really know the Summer House at all,' she'd said to Lottie. 'He's only seen glimpses of it through the trees. Do you think the Moretons would let us have a look around it? After all, if they're leaving it wouldn't make much difference to them, would it?'

At the bottom of the drive where it forked away to the Summer House she'd slowed the car, peering to get a glimpse of the little whitewashed house with its red-tiled roof and pretty veranda. She knew that it had been built at the whim of Milo's great-great-grandmother, who had wanted a studio where she might go to paint her charming watercolours in peace; the next generation used it as a rather special summer house where the children could picnic and have parties. Just after the war Milo's father had extended it from the studio-summer house into a delightful cottage for the couple who worked for him. Imogen recalled the accommodation: the two big downstairs rooms, now a sitting room and a kitchen-breakfast room, divided by the hall which opened on to the veranda; and, a much later addition, upstairs two good-sized bedrooms, a smaller room (perfect for Rosie) and a bathroom.

Joyful with anticipation she drove into Porlock, waved to Richard – the owner of Antlers, the pet shop – and pulled suddenly into the kerb beside him, stopping on the double yellow line.

'We're getting a puppy,' she called to him. 'Picking him up in a couple of weeks' time. I'll be in to get some things for him.' She glanced in her mirror as a car pulled up behind her, unable to pass. 'Oh dear. Better dash . . .'

She drove on again, still fizzing with exhilaration, chatting to Rosie, speeding away up the toll road to the cottage. Ray came out of the booth, recognized the car and waved her on. She smiled at him, almost tempted to stop and tell him the news, but she resisted the temptation, knowing that Jules must be the first to know. She thought about how she might tell him:

'You'll never guess what's happened!'

'I've got the most amazing news.'

'Milo wants to sell us the Summer House.'

She pulled into the drive and glanced at her watch: nearly half past three. Rosie had fallen asleep, and Imogen decided to leave her there sleeping in the patch of sunlight for another ten minutes. She climbed out, clicking the door quietly closed, standing for a moment breathing in the crisp cold air. Today, the coast of Wales, clear and sharply defined, appeared to be only a step away across the narrow shimmering strip of blue water where a tiny motorboat sped northwards like a shining arrow, its creaming bow wave sparkling in the late afternoon sunshine. A solitary seagull tilted and swooped above her.

Imogen sighed with pleasure. She let herself into the cottage, wondering what she might cook for supper – there were some lamb cutlets in the fridge – and checked to see that there was a bottle of wine with which to celebrate the good news. She'd wait until Rosie was in bed, she decided – bath-time was always such chaos and she wanted to be able to talk to Jules properly without distraction – and then she'd pour him a drink and just tell him. With luck, it might be one of his late nights when he arrived home just in time to read Rosie a story and kiss her goodnight. That would mean less temptation to blurt it all out the minute he walked in through the door before Rosie was tucked up. She let out a little cry of anticipatory joy just as her mobile beeped: a text.

She seized the phone, pressed the buttons: it was from Nick.

'Home. R u ok? Has Dad told u yet? x'

She texted quickly back to him: 'Lottie told me. Cant wait 2 tell Jules.' She hesitated, wondering whether to add some message of affection, then added an x and pressed 'send'.

Another message arrived almost at once.

'Gt. Stay in touch. Luv u lots x'

Im stared at the message, shrugged away her unease. After all, Nick always sent affectionate messages; there was no harm in it. It was strange how, just this last day or two, she had become supersensitive about him. She was just being silly. She texted quickly, giving herself no time to brood on it, and sent it: 'Will txt later. Luv u 2.'

She glanced at her watch: time to wake Rosie or she wouldn't sleep this evening. Imogen went out to fetch her. Rosie was heavily asleep and resented being wakened: she grizzled, struggling, reaching for the velvet rabbit and wailing when she couldn't reach him.

'Stop fussing.' Imogen hoisted her daughter on to her hip. 'Here's the rabbit. Come on. We're going to have some tea.'

She picked up the big Cath Kidston holdall from the back seat, locked the car, and carried Rosie into the cottage.

'But I don't want to buy the Summer House,' Jules said. Half perched on the high stool, he turned to look at her, one elbow resting on the wide pine bar. 'I don't want to live in Bossington.'

Imogen remained quite still, kneeling on the floor, some of Rosie's toys still in her hands. She'd been tossing them into the playpen but now she stared up at him, shocked into stillness. Her expression, and the way she kneeled like a supplicant, irritated Jules. It made him feel guilty, as if he were bullying her, which was unfair.

'Come on, Im. We've talked about this a hundred times. We want to live near Simonsbath. You've always said you wanted to. It wasn't just me.'

'I *know* I have,' she cried in anguish, willing him to understand how crucial this was to her, 'but that was before this happened. I never thought for a *minute* there would ever be a chance of buying the Summer House. And at a price we can afford. It's worth twice that, Jules. Apart from anything else, can't you see what a bargain it is?'

'Something is only a bargain if it's what you want. I don't want the Summer House.'

She flung the last of the toys into the playpen and stood up. Jules subconsciously braced himself. Her cheeks were brightly pink, which made her eyes look even bluer than usual, and in her jeans and the slouchy jersey she looked very young and very pretty. He wanted to put out his arms to her but her expression did not encourage it.

'And what about me?' she asked.

He stared back at her. Suddenly he no longer wanted to put his arms round her; instead he was filled with resentment.

'I'm not thinking about you,' he told her bluntly, 'or only indirectly.' He turned to face her as she marched round the end of the bar into the galley. 'We've talked about the distance we are here from the practice and we've said over and over again that the drive is hell when I'm called out at night. We both hate it, not just me. OK, here I can be on the A39 very quickly, but even then I've got miles of winding lanes. You know very well that we cover farms and stables down as far as Twitchen and Molland, and it's you that makes a fuss when I have to go out in fog or snow at two in the morning. And you hate it if I spend the night in the flat at the surgery. It's a small practice, Im, there's just the two of us, and I'm the assistant who's on call four nights a week and can't afford to get it wrong.'

'But that will change,' she argued, 'as the practice grows.' She bit her lip, trying to contain her bitter disappointment. He made her feel selfish, but her longing for the Summer House was so great that she couldn't think straight.

Jules was watching her. Her answer had hurt him deeply. 'You mean that the Summer House is more important than my safety. That's what we're talking about, Im. Driving around Exmoor is brilliant on a fine day with no pressures but you try it on a foggy night with a sick animal on the end of it, and then coming home exhausted with another day's work ahead. We're adding another three miles if we move to Bossington and we're not talking nice straight roads here.'

She leaned back against the draining board, her arms crossed over her breast: she felt defiant and defensive, both at once. She knew that it was perfectly reasonable of Jules to say these things, yet she could hardly believe that he was not thinking for a single minute of what this opportunity might mean to her: to own the darling little Summer House, and to be close to Milo and Lottie, with Matt and Nick around, and Rosie growing up surrounded by a real family. And – her heart gave a little anxious jolt – if they didn't buy it would Milo still be able to help Nick out? Milo knew that she and Jules had the money for the deposit in the bank and a mortgage lined up, ready to go. If they didn't buy the Summer House it might not sell for ages. How would Milo find the money then? She couldn't say these things to Jules; it might look a bit odd to be worrying about Nick to that extent. She'd already had a bad moment with the rabbit. Rosie had refused to go to sleep without it and Jules had said, 'Is this new?' and Im had answered hurriedly, 'Yes, we got it in Dunster this morning,' which wasn't absolutely a lie but wasn't absolutely all of the truth, either. She simply hadn't wanted to mention her meeting with Nick and now she was in a turmoil of disappointment, shock and anger.

'Look at the map,' Jules was saying. He'd got off the stool and had reached down the map book from the bookshelf. 'Look.' He was jabbing a forefinger along the squiggly lines of lanes, head bent so that she could see his very nearly bald bit, and she'd never liked him less than she did at that moment. 'Look at the terrain across the moor between here and Simonsbath. It takes me the best part of half an hour from here. And that only gets me to the practice. What if I have to go on to the stables at Molland or to Twitchen?'

He looked up at her and she stared at the map, unwilling to meet his eyes. He shut the book with a snap; put it back on the shelf.

'You don't really give a damn, do you?'

'I just want an opportunity to discuss it sensibly, that's all,' she said angrily.

They stared at each other, neither ready to back down, the evening in ruins about them. Jules stood up and went into the hall whilst Im stood motionless, listening intently: surely he wouldn't just walk out. Where would he go? He came back in with his Barbour on, his face shuttered.

'I'm on call tonight,' he said, 'and I'll almost certainly have to go over to Molland at some point. I'll spend the night in the flat at the practice and grab some supper at the pub.' He paused, waiting for her to protest, to make some gesture, and then shrugged, said, ''Night, then,' and went out.

Im could hardly believe that he'd gone: she'd been certain that he was bluffing and would come back. She heard the four-track's engine start up and then the sound of it die away as Jules drove off. Resentment and disappointment blocked any tendency towards regret, though she knew, deep down, that Jules had every right to make his points.

But even so . . . Im came out from behind the bar. She hardly knew what to do with herself: her expectations had been so high, she'd been so happy. And she couldn't talk about it to anyone; not yet.

Her close friends would understand, of course they would, but it might be a bit tricky presenting Jules' point of view without them suspecting that she was being a bit selfish. On the other hand, they'd absolutely understand how she'd be feeling about the Summer House. Just thinking about it made her want to weep. Im filled a glass with wine and put away the food she'd been assembling for their celebratory supper: she simply wasn't hungry any more. In the hall she paused to check for any sounds from upstairs and went on into the sitting room. She made up the fire, switched on the television and sat down, deciding that she daren't even phone Nick. After a few moments of reflection she realized why: she couldn't bear it if his anxiety about the money were to be greater than his concern for her disappointment.

She took a few sips of wine and on an impulse picked up her mobile from the arm of the chair and scrolled to Matt's number. He answered after a few rings.

'Hi, Im.' As usual he sounded rather detached but comfortingly familiar. 'How's it going?'

'Oh, Matt,' she said chokily. 'I'm having a beastly time. You can't imagine.'

'No, I probably can't.' He sounded more alert; concerned. 'What's going on?'

'You've got a minute? You're not dashing off anywhere?'

'No. You have my undivided attention.'

'Well . . .' Im settled herself with relief in the corner of the sofa and began to talk.

CHAPTER THIRTEEN

Matt put his mobile down and sat for a moment, thinking about his conversation with Im. What a mess it all was, and what was the right of it? He could understand Jules' viewpoint: apart from the very real concern about the distance from the practice, he could also see why Jules might not want to live quite so near to Milo and Lottie.

'Think about it,' he'd said to Im. 'Would you want to live so close to Jules' parents? I know they live in Scotland so there are all sorts of reasons why it's not a real possibility, but think about it, Im.'

'Milo and Lottie aren't my parents,' she'd answered stubbornly. 'It's different.'

'No, it's not. Not really,' he'd said. 'Be honest. Lottie was always *in loco parentis* for us in her own particular boho way. And Milo was the father figure in our lives. And that's how Jules sees them. But

I know how you love the Summer House and the thought of having Lottie and Milo around . . .'

He'd tried to be fair, to show her both sides, but he'd felt really sorry for her; it must have come as a terrific shock to find Jules set so firmly against her own desires. And then there had been all the stuff about Nick, about him needing money and not getting his bonus. Well, at least it wasn't another woman, although, knowing Alice as he did, Matt suspected that she might overlook an extra-marital affair much more readily than she'd forgive a real financial problem: she'd never accept a loss of status.

Of course, he could see that Jules buying the Summer House was a perfect all-round solution but why should Jules be sacrificed for Nick?

'How shall I tell them?' Im had cried in anguish. 'Milo will be thinking he's making my dreams come true and it will solve Nick's problem. And Lottie will be really hurt to think that Jules doesn't want to live that close to them.'

'Hey, cool it,' he'd said. 'Try to be rational. Neither Milo nor Lottie will be in the least bit surprised that Jules is worrying about the travelling to and fro. It's a hell of a journey, especially in bad weather and with sick animals on the end of it. They might be disappointed but they'll be OK with it. I'm not sure about Milo raising the money for Nick but that isn't your problem. It's between Milo and Nick. Anyway, I really can't see Milo's bank making a fuss with all the equity he's sitting on. And he can still sell the Summer House.'

'It's so cruel,' she'd said in a small voice. 'It was like my dream come true. I couldn't believe it when Jules just turned it down flat. He didn't think for a single second what it might mean to me. To have all the family around for me and Rosie.'

And that's the real problem, thought Matt. Im is hurt because Jules isn't considering her feelings and Jules is upset because it seems that Im doesn't care about him. God, what a muddle it all is. All these misunderstandings and wounded feelings sloshing about; all the emotional blackmail that goes with relationships. I'm well out of it.

He thought about his mother; the never-quite-drunk, but never-quite-sober behaviour that had made him anxious about taking friends home; the complexities that made him so wary about forming a close relationship of his own. On a few occasions he'd imagined that a close, loving relationship would answer the need inside him and dispel the haunting loneliness. Yet it had never worked out that way. Instead, his sense of incompleteness blocked his ability to love and to give himself totally, and women grew puzzled and then irritated by his apparent self-sufficiency. Each time he told himself that it would be different; that this time he would be able to be open, to be honest about these strange feelings and the nightmares that dogged him – but as yet, no woman had ever come that close. He'd never yet felt emotionally safe enough to risk the look of love disintegrating into a stare of contempt – and, anyway, he wouldn't want to go into such an important relationship pleading such weakness. One day, if he were lucky, he might meet a woman with whom he felt such rapport that the telling would be easy – but it hadn't happened yet . . .

As if on cue the phone rang again and he picked it up and glanced at the screen: Annabel. He groaned briefly, hesitated and then answered.

'Hi,' he said, keeping his voice especially calm in an attempt not to give an impression of eagerness, nor yet of disinterest. 'How was the party?'

'You should have been there,' she told him. Her own voice was part jolly, part reproving. 'You would have loved it. It was such fun.'

'Great.' His tone now implied delight that she had enjoyed herself but refusal to be drawn into any kind of regret. 'That's good then.'

'The trouble with these early evening launch parties is that you feel a bit flat afterwards. You know? You're still on a high but you've got nowhere to go.'

Don't fall for it, Matt told himself. Just don't.

'Has everyone else gone?' He sounded interested but not concerned, and he congratulated himself on his ability to keep it all friendly.

'Well, not everyone.' She was clearly reluctant to admit this; slightly irritated that he hadn't picked up on his cue and invited her round, or suggested that they should meet somewhere. 'A couple of them are going out for some supper, I think.'

'Sounds a great idea,' he said enthusiastically. 'I should go for it.'

'Why don't you come and meet us?' She was trying to sound casual, making an effort not to be too keen. 'It would be fun.'

'Me?' He implied surprise. 'It's a bit short notice. I'm working on an article for *The Times* travel section and I'm running late with it as it is.'

'I'm not surprised,' she retorted. She was aggrieved now, making no attempt to hide it. 'I tried to phone before but you've been engaged for ages.'

'My sister, Imogen,' he answered briefly, resenting it that he should need to explain to Annabel. 'Bit of a problem, that's all. That's what delayed me.'

'Oh, well, I won't hold you up.' Her voice was brittle, hurt. 'See you on Saturday.'

Even in her irritation, she couldn't quite bear to go without reminding him of their next meeting and he felt equal parts of guilt and annoyance.

'Sure, see you then,' he said cheerfully. 'Enjoy the rest of your evening. 'Bye.'

He put the phone down. It was possible that, had Annabel spoken to him before Im had phoned, he might well have gone out to join her but Im's problems had reignited all his deep-seated fears regarding commitment and he'd reacted accordingly. Annabel was very keen, even though she was playing it carefully, and he was wary. The fact that he'd agreed to go down to Exmoor at Easter for a long stay meant that he could keep her at arm's length for a little longer: he liked her very much but he simply didn't want to be rushed into a closer relationship. Although it was a pity that he hadn't found anywhere to rent, he was rather looking forward to a spell at the High House – and now it seemed that he might be able to be of some use; at least he could be there for Im and cheer old Jules up a bit.

Matt sighed, frustrated. What he really needed was inspiration; some exciting ideas for the new book. This sensation of being only half alive, of being mentally crippled, was disabling; it affected all parts of his life. This was why he hadn't wanted to go to the launch party or meet Annabel afterwards. There were too many friends and colleagues who would ask the usual question – or remain tactfully silent – about his work. So many people were waiting to see if he could do it again or if his great success had merely been a flash in the pan.

Lottie had been right to suggest a change of scene; and perhaps she'd also been right when she'd talked about the death of someone close to you revealing hidden terrors. Just recently the nightmares had started up again, and the lifelong, overwhelming sense of loneliness and loss, held at bay throughout the writing of *Epiphany* and its attendant success, had resurfaced with a vengeance.

Remembering his mother, the way *she* had been disabled by grief, a great sorrow welled in him.

'She must have loved Dad so much,' he'd said to Lottie once, almost bitterly.

He'd felt it deeply that neither he nor Im could in any way make up for that crippling loss.

'Yes,' she'd answered. 'Yes, she did, Matt. But she also had post-natal depression after Imogen, and then Tom's death on top of that seemed to make recovery impossible. A double whammy. But we must keep hoping that one day she'll get better.'

She never had – but whilst she'd lived there had been hope. Now, it was too late. The sorrow, kept banked down as a rule, welled within him, swelling his heart with misery. It had all been such a *waste*: such a bloody waste. Even the birth of her granddaughter had been viewed through a haze of alcohol and pain; she'd seemed detached, almost disinterested. He'd been so disappointed – 'Perhaps,' he'd said hopefully to Lottie, 'this will trigger something' – as well as hurt on Im's behalf. Im, as usual, had been philosophical.

'She's never been like a proper mother,' she'd reminded him. 'She can't help it and I'm used to it. Jules' mum and dad are euphoric, and Lottie and Milo are thrilled to bits.' She'd shrugged. 'We're luckier than lots of people, Matt.'

He knew she was right but still there had been that interior struggle. He could remember, very dimly, a different Helen: one who laughed and sang to them, who lifted them in her arms. There seemed to be a whole piece of his life, waiting just beyond his memory, that he continually strained to recall: a life in which their mother was a joyful, happy person who hugged and kissed them, and played silly games with them. These shadowy memories confused him because as soon as Imogen had been born his mother's depression had descended and his father had been killed. Yet they remained to tantalize him: those flashes on his inward eye of a happy woman playing with her children. All through the years of growing up he'd wanted her back.

'Grow up,' he told himself now, savagely. 'Grow up and get a life.'

He stood up with an impatient quickness that dislodged some books and papers from the small table beside the chair. He bent to pick them up and saw a few envelopes: the morning post as yet unopened. All three were addressed to his mother at the Blackheath flat and redirected by the Post Office, and he glanced at them without much interest. One was about double glazing; one was from a charity. The third envelope had been handwritten and he slit it open. Another envelope was inside, addressed to his mother at the news agency where his father had been employed, and marked 'Please forward'. He opened it curiously but there was nothing inside except a photograph.

He held it, staring at his own face laughing back at him; his stomach contracted, as if in fear, and his heart beat quickly. He turned the photograph over but nothing was written on the back. He looked inside the envelope, shaking it, but nothing else was enclosed and the envelope bore a foreign stamp that he did not recognize and a smudged postmark that he could not decipher. He studied the photograph again. The camera had been a little behind him and his head was turned, chin on shoulder, and he was smiling at the photographer.

Matt tried to remember when it might have been taken, and where – on one of his trips abroad? – and by whom, and wondered why it had been sent to his mother with no message. He was gripped by an irrational fear, and great confusion clouded his mind.

When his mobile signalled that it had received a text he seized the phone with relief. The text was from Lottie and it was brief.

'R u OK?'

He stared at it. This was not the first time that Lottie had demonstrated her powers of second sight. He and Im had often teased her about it. Somehow the text steadied him; confirmed his decision to leave London for a while and spend time with his family. He put the photograph back into its envelope, studying the stamp and postmark again but making no sense of it, and then texted to Lottie.

His mind was made up: he would go down to Exmoor next week.

CHAPTER FOURTEEN

During March there was heavy snowfall followed by hail showers. Snow settled on the high, bare hills and along the gaunt, naked branches of the trees; it drifted in the coombes and filled the valleys. Even in Bossington the snow lay for a few hours.

Staring out from his attic window, Matt marvelled at the transformation; at the concealing and magical properties of snow. The landscape was a wonderland. Wolves might roam on the high, gleaming slopes of Dunkery Hill and not seem out of place; trolls might lurk in icy caves deep in Culbone Wood whilst, here in the garden, Kay and Gerda might be having a snowball fight. Even Lottie's little octagonal pagoda, with its pointed roof, looked like a house in a fairy story, overhung with dipping, snow-weighted branches of the surrounding trees. It seemed that at any moment the door would open and a Hans Andersen character, warmly cloaked and wearing heavy wooden clogs, would appear on the threshold. Beyond the huddled roofs of Bossington, across the silver sheet of water that lay flat as a metal shelf, the mountains of Wales glittered in the late afternoon sunshine, dazzling white and shadowed with indigo.

With a cry of alarm, the blackbird swooped out of the shrubbery up into one of the beeches, dislodging the snow, which fell with a small soft explosive plop on to the roof of the pagoda. As Matt watched, Pud appeared from the tangle of rhododendron bushes, his coat a warm golden note of colour against the chill whiteness. It was he, no doubt, who had disturbed the blackbird and now he was making for the warmth of the house and a biscuit. His tracks crisscrossed the snowy ground as he diverged from his path to examine the trodden area around the bird table, but presently he headed off towards the kitchen again and disappeared from sight.

Matt got to his feet, shivering. Lottie had provided him with an electric convector heater in an attempt to warm the two adjoining attic rooms but here, high up beneath the roof, it was still bitterly cold. He went down the steep little staircase to the first floor, and then on down again and through the warren of rooms into the parlour where the wood-burner was blazing and Venetia was sitting with Milo.

'Hallo,' Matt said to Venetia. 'I saw you arrive and thought it was very brave of you to venture out.'

She offered her cheek for a kiss. 'The roads are quite clear,' she said, 'although I admit that I came out through Bossington Lane rather than risk Allerford, but there's hardly any snow left in the village. You're so much higher here. Good heavens, Matt, you're frozen. Come and sit beside me.'

Pushing aside the heap of Lottie's knitting, she edged along the sofa so that he could be next to the fire and he sat down, grinning at Milo's expression.

'Cold!' scoffed the old warrior, right on cue. 'This isn't cold. Now Catterick Camp. *That's* what you'd call cold. Ice on the inside of the windows when you woke up in the morning. Water frozen solid in the pipes. The earth hard as iron. These days, one little fall of snow and you have to have radiators going all day and hot-water bottles at night.' He snorted with contempt.

Venetia touched Matt's knee. 'Of course, Milo isn't human,' she said regretfully, 'but he can't help it, poor darling. Lottie's making us some lovely tea. That'll warm you up. Oh, and here's darling Pud.'

Pud came wagging in with the air of a dog that has been thoroughly rubbed with a towel and given a reward, and he went straight to Venetia with that unerring sense that here was a soft touch; any cake going and she'd give him a share. He sat close against her legs and she stroked him, murmuring words of love to him. His ears flattened appreciatively though he rolled a wary eye at Milo, who was watching sardonically.

'He is not to be fed,' he warned Venetia. 'I don't want any of that nonsense, mind,' and Matt smiled at Venetia's expression of hurt innocence, whilst she continued to smooth Pud's head.

Lottie came in with the tray and he got up to help her. She looked at him with that strange searching glance and he smiled reassuringly at her. Since his arrival they'd discussed the photograph at length and she was just as puzzled as he was.

'It's all of a piece with those other photographs,' he'd insisted. 'Who took them, and why? There's something odd about them.'

She'd sensed his fear but had no answer ready. He'd telephoned the news agency, who'd been unable to help apart from telling him that they had a long-standing arrangement to forward any mail.

'And that's weird in itself,' he'd said to Lottie. 'Dad died over twenty-five years ago. Why should anyone still be writing to him? Anyway this was addressed to Mum.'

'People who'd read his books or articles might try

to contact him or his family that way,' she'd said, 'but I agree that it's unusual after all this time.'

They'd decided that, with all the fuss going on with Im and Jules and the Summer House, they wouldn't mention it to anyone else just yet, and Matt was grateful to be distracted from his preoccupation. He passed Venetia her tea, took his own and sat down again.

'I don't *blame* Jules,' Milo was saying for the umpteenth time, 'but I'm very sad for Im. She would have loved it so much. Well, we all would have. But there it is. Jules has made up his mind, it seems.'

Just for the moment, Matt thought that the older man's curled lip classed Jules amongst the cissies who required heated rooms and warm beds in sub-zero temperatures. No doubt Milo would have been perfectly happy to cross Exmoor in all sorts of weather in the middle of the night and never given it another thought. Matt decided to play devil's advocate.

'It's terribly hard for her,' he said, 'because she's really torn. Of course she quite sees Jules' viewpoint – she hates the travelling he has to do – but then again, she'd love to live at the Summer House. I expect you experience the same sort of difficulties in the services, Milo. You get wives who simply don't want to live in married quarters on the base or get fed up with moving around and want to settle down somewhere and then, I suppose, it can cause problems.'

Milo was silent. He drank his tea, frowning slightly, whilst Venetia glanced sideways at Matt and gave him a complicit wink.

'You're right, of course,' she said with an amused eye on Milo. 'We were expected to be there with the regiment, supporting the chaps, living in the most ghastly accommodation sometimes, and the senior officers and their wives looked very poorly on those wives who couldn't hack it. Poor Sara utterly hated it, didn't she, Milo? Simply couldn't cope at all, especially once she'd had Nick. She wanted her own nice little house in the country. My old pa used to be very tough with me about it if I dared to moan. "Marry the man, marry the job," he used to say. "No good whining afterwards." Not that Im is moaning. She's being very stoical and I expect Jules is feeling rotten at having to put his foot down.'

'I've already said I don't blame Jules,' repeated Milo crossly . . .

Having set the cat amongst the pigeons, Matt sat back and sipped his tea. He felt it was crucial that nobody took sides and that Im and Jules fought it out for themselves. He accepted a slice of cake and steadfastly refused to meet Pud's hopeful eye: he had no desire to tempt Milo's wrath any further.

'We should have thought about the problems earlier,' Lottie was saying. 'I have to admit I thought it was a wonderful idea but now I can really see the drawbacks. It's a very long way across to Simonsbath and it's unfair to expect Jules to do it. I'm just afraid that we've caused trouble between them.'

'Will you sell it anyway, Milo?' asked Venetia. Matt could tell that even she was too wary of Milo's mood to drop the odd crumb to the expectant Pud. 'Now that the Moretons are going?'

Milo shifted in his chair, drawing in his long legs. 'I don't really want to sell on the open market,' he admitted. 'Apart from the fact that it'll cost a fortune to bring it up to date, it's always been in the family and it shares part of the garden. It would be tricky to parcel up the land so as to make it a sellable proposition. Fortunately the Moretons never wanted much in the way of a garden and we were all used to one another after all these years. It'll be very different when it comes to selling. I suppose I'm anxious about getting the neighbours from hell but I'm probably just being an old fogey about that.'

Matt looked at him sympathetically. He could understand that it would be hard for Milo to see the

Summer House in the hands of strangers, and that it would be impossible to have the same easy-going arrangements he'd made with the Moretons twenty years ago – sharing part of the kitchen garden, for instance, and some of the outhouses – with people who wanted to buy it. As he watched the older man's face, Matt had an extraordinary idea. He examined it as the conversation rose and fell, and liked it more with every passing minute.

Why shouldn't *he* buy the Summer House? He'd earned plenty of money out of the film and the book – and was continuing to earn more – and although he'd made some careful investments, he'd been wondering how to utilize some of the remainder sensibly. Why not buy the Summer House? He could use it himself and have friends to stay, Im and Jules could use it as a holiday cottage, and it would mean that Lottie would have somewhere to go if Milo should die first. Catching her eye, smiling at her, Matt felt a true uprush of pleasure at the thought of being able to return some of the love and care that she had poured out on him and Imogen, and he knew that it would remove anxiety from Milo. After all, there really was no question of Alice and Nick ever living at the High House; they'd sell it, no doubt about that – and then where would Lottie go? Of course, Milo had left provision for her to stay on for as long as she wanted to but it was clear that Lottie would do nothing of the kind. Making certain that the Summer House stayed within the family would give her some security.

Matt finished his tea. This was one of the moments when having money to spare brought very real joy. Since his success he'd found it difficult with his friends, walking that fine line between being considered either patronizingly generous or being castigated as a tightwad. Sometimes it seemed that he couldn't win. Of course he liked having the money but he was not by nature extravagant. Even his one real passion – travel – could be indulged without being very rich; huge luxury hotels and the pleasure grounds of places like Dubai had never attracted him. He was like the cat that walked by himself in quiet, secret, undiscovered byways, yet always hoping to discover the one thing that would heal that inner sense of incompleteness.

Lottie was watching him curiously now, and Matt grinned broadly at her. Even the mystery of the photographs couldn't detract from this truly happy moment. He longed to speak out, to surprise them all, but he suspected that Milo wouldn't approve of quite such a public announcement. Matt never knew quite how deeply in Milo's confidence Venetia was – did she know about Nick's misdemeanour, for instance? – and he could see that it would be sensible to wait until he and Milo were alone.

Unable to contain his excitement he stood up.

'I think I'll go out for a walk,' he said. 'A quick one before the snow completely disappears. Come on, Pud. Never mind the cake. Come and get some exercise.'

CHAPTER FIFTEEN

After Matt had gone and Lottie had carried out the tea things, Milo sat for a moment brooding. He felt grumpy, unwilling even to respond to Venetia, who was now chattering about poor old Clara. The whole episode about the Summer House had got him down – and Matt's observations hadn't exactly helped. Of course, the boy was right – and Milo could see that if Imogen were to insist on living in Bossington it might well cause problems between her and Jules – but that didn't make him feel any better about it. He'd been so pleased at the prospect of killing two birds with one stone – and, if he were to be really honest with himself, he'd been looking forward to sharing in Im's happiness and gratitude; to being acknowledged as the good fairy who'd helped to make her dreams come true – whilst sorting Nick out at the same time. He'd wanted Lottie to have the pleasure of giving Im the glad tidings but he'd been confident that she would be coming over to see them, full of joy and ready to celebrate. He'd even put a bottle of champagne in the fridge in readiness.

Instead, there had been an awkward little phone call from Im saying that Jules was very worried about living so far from the practice and it looked as if they'd have to refuse Milo's wonderful offer. Oh, she'd been full of messages from them both of how sweet it was of him to think of it and so on, but the bottom line was that it wasn't going to work. He'd been gutted, and he hadn't quite been able to overcome his immediate reaction: that it was rather feeble of Jules to be so worried about driving to and fro across Exmoor in the comfort of a whacking great four-track. Good grief! The boy was barely in his thirties; at that age he'd been fighting in Northern Ireland . . . Milo gave a mental shrug: there was no point in going down that road.

And, he told himself, it wasn't only because he knew how much Im loved the Summer House that he'd been so pleased but that it was also a kind of safety net for Lottie, much as she might protest that she'd never live there with them. It was the best he could do for her.

He shifted irritably, trying to concentrate on what Venetia was saying to him, and she paused.

'You're not listening to a word I'm saying,' she said plaintively. 'Come and sit beside me, Milo.'

He got up and sat next to her, putting an arm around her thin shoulders, looking down at her with a mix of great affection and slight impatience. Why, for instance, did she put mascara on her eyelashes? Clotted with that black stuff they rayed out like spider's legs, weighting her papery eyelids so cruelly that he longed for some of those wipes that Im used to clean Rosie's face, so as to remove the mascara and allow the fine fair lashes to be free and natural.

'What do you do, Milo, when you wake at three in the morning with the horrors?' she was asking him. She shuddered within his arm and he tightened it protectively about her. 'You know what I mean, don't you? "The fears and terrors of the night". It's a prayer or a hymn or something, isn't it? But it's got it absolutely right. It seems impossible to keep any kind of balance at that time of the night, everything just seems so black, and I plunge into despair. What do you do?'

He sensed the vulnerability behind her question, her need for reassurance, and he answered truthfully.

'I recite a psalm,' he said – and she sat upright in his arm and stared up at him incredulously.

'A *psalm*?' She looked as if she might burst out laughing. 'Doesn't sound quite like you, darling.'

'No, it doesn't, does it?' he agreed placidly. 'But it works. An army padre gave me the tip, oh, years ago when I was out in Northern Ireland and I'd just seen two of my closest friends blown to pieces. "Whenever you're fearful," he said, "pray a few verses of a psalm. You'll be surprised how calming and comforting it is." Well, I was a sceptical young soldier but I decided to humour him. "And which one should it be, Padre?" I asked him, and he answered straight out. "The hundred and twenty-first," he said, and when I stared at him blankly he recited it to me and I have to tell you, Vin, I was very deeply moved. Perhaps it was because they were frightening times and I was mourning my friends, but it struck a chord with me. I went away and looked it up. "The Lord himself watches over you; he is the shade at your right hand so that the sun shall not strike you by day, nor the moon by night. The Lord shall keep you from all evil, it is He who shall keep your soul." I memorized it.' She was still staring up at him and he shrugged away the serious mood. 'Well, you asked me. What do *you* do? Reach for the Mogadon?'

Reluctantly she laughed with him. 'Sometimes,' she admitted.

He turned his wrist behind her shoulder and glanced at his watch. 'Nearly time for a drink,' he said, edging her away from the emotional moment. 'Are you going to stay for supper?'

'Oh, I'd love to. Are you sure? Will there be enough?' She was forgetting her fears and terrors, just as he'd hoped. 'Perhaps we ought to check with Lottie.'

He snorted. 'It's got nothing to do with Lottie. I'm doing the cooking. She'd turn my delicious piece of lamb into something that tasted like roadkill. Stay if you'd like to.'

It was a sop; a gesture of kindness far smaller than the one she was hinting at – or so he suspected. She was testing him, sounding him out as to how the future might work for them both, and his instinct was to play it safe. Lottie came back in and he looked at her with relief; the time for confidences was postponed.

'Did we tell you that Nick's coming down again for a few days?' she asked Venetia. She settled in her chair and picked up her knitting on its thick wooden needles. 'How are all your lot?'

And the conversation turned on children, and children's children, and Milo settled back into the corner of the sofa and reached for the newspaper, wondering how he was going to explain to his bank manager that he wouldn't be selling the Summer House very quickly after all.

'Matt came over today,' Im was telling Jules. 'Lottie looked after Rosie and we went down to Porlock Weir and had lunch at The Ship.'

'Was that good?'

It was clear that Jules was having to make a great effort to be interested and Im was filled with a sudden desire to hit him on the head with something heavy. She was, after all, working very hard to be reasonable about the Summer House, despite her utter misery about it; not nagging, or referring to it, but trying to restore the harmony that had once existed between them. And instead of responding, of being grateful to her for reacting in this positive way, he remained distant; polite but cool.

'It was *very* good,' she answered crossly, getting the ironing board out with a rather unnecessary vigour, plugging in the iron. She surveyed the full washing basket with distaste, half wondering if he might offer to help out. He'd always been good about his own shirts but refused to attempt her things or Rosie's. Instead he glanced at it all and put his hands in his pockets.

'I might watch the television for a bit,' he said, and went out.

She banged the iron to and fro, feeling miserable and resentful. It should be Jules who was feeling guilty for denying her the Summer House instead of behaving as if, in some way, *he* were the injured party.

'He's being totally irrational,' she'd said earlier, to Matt in the pub. 'It's like he's the one who's had the biggest disappointment of his life instead of me. And I'm deliberately not saying a word about it.'

Matt had drunk some beer; he'd looked thoughtful.

'But *how* are you not saying a word about it?' he'd asked at last.

'What do you mean?' she'd said indignantly. 'I'm being jolly noble about it, if you ask me.'

Matt had put his pint down and pretended to sniff the air. 'Do I smell a martyr burning?' he'd asked of nobody in particular, and she'd kicked him on the shin, just as if they were both small again.

Im took another garment from the basket, picked up the iron and ploughed more furrows up and down the board. She'd been delighted to get a text from Nick telling her that he'd be down on Friday. She'd phoned him the morning after she'd phoned Matt and told him the truth about the Summer House, and he'd been full of sympathy and given no hint of any anxiety on his own behalf. A voice in her head had told her that actually he had no reason to be anxious; that, no doubt, the cheque had already been paid in and it was Milo who would need to be anxious, but she was too pleased to hear Nick's words of love and understanding to heed it much. She couldn't wait to see him.

Im folded Jules' shirt, aware of his silent presence across the hall, remembering how she'd planned to tell him about her idea to start an internet company sourcing family holidays on Exmoor and specializing in riding. Then he'd come in quite late with that tight expression on his face so that all her resentment resurfaced and they'd behaved like two strangers. Im shrugged and took one of Rosie's little dresses out of the basket. It was up to him to get over it and start being sensible about it all. She'd done what she could and now it was his turn to try to put things right.

Across the hallway, Jules stared unseeingly at the television. He felt guilty – and more than that: he felt as if he were letting everyone down. After all, Milo wouldn't have suggested that they should buy the Summer House if he hadn't considered it a perfectly reasonable distance from the practice. It was always tricky, living up to Milo: he was such a tough old soldier and it was easy to feel a bit of a weakling when he turned his imperious eye on you. And of *course* it was hard on Im; of *course* he would love to give her the house of her dreams; but, if he weren't careful, he knew he'd weaken and back down, and he had a gut feeling that living at Bossington would put a strain on them that would be simply foolish. Mind you, anything would be better than this cold war that was going on. Im was being very restrained but there was an air of condescension, of suffering nobly borne, that was extraordinarily irritating. She was behaving as if they hadn't come to a joint decision but rather as if she were bearing the brunt of his overbearing selfishness.

He wondered what they were all saying: Milo and Matt and Lottie. Part of him wanted to get up and go and put his arms round her and say: 'Oh, come on. Let's go with it. Let's buy the Summer House.' But he remembered those long night-time drives in thick mist or driving rain, or ice and snow, and always with an anxious farmer and a sick animal at the end of it, and common sense held him in his chair. After all, Im hated it when he was called out; hated the worry and the broken sleep, and they'd both been absolutely adamant that they wanted to be as near to the centre of the practice as possible. Now, it was as if he were insisting on something with which she had no patience or sympathy, which implied that the Summer House meant more to her than he did.

He had no idea how to break the impasse between them and the evening stretched miserably before him.

CHAPTER SIXTEEN

By the time Matt found the opportunity to talk privately with Milo it was late the next morning after Lottie had gone off to lunch with a friend in Dunster.

Milo was in the narrow kitchen assembling the component parts of one of his favourite master-pieces: a terrine. Leaning in the doorway Matt suppressed a smile. The older man looked rather like some great artist preparing a canvas. Tall and lean in his faded butter-yellow cords and soft, checked shirt – he disdained an apron – he hovered above his palette of ingredients. The sage, garlic and lemon zest had been stirred into the softly cooked onion and now waited, cooling on a plate, whilst he chopped the pork fillet, bacon and pheasant and added it to the beaten egg in the mixing bowl. As he worked he recited poetry, anything that inspired him. Today it was *The Hunting of the Snark*:

'Its flavour when cooked is more exquisite far
Than mutton, or oyster, or eggs:
(Some think it keeps best in an ivory jar,
And some, in mahogany kegs:)
You boil it in sawdust: you salt it in glue:
You condense it with locusts and tape:
Still keeping one principal object in view –
To preserve its symmetrical shape.'

'So you're cooking a Jubjub,' observed Matt. 'I thought it was a pheasant.'

Milo added the chopped chestnuts and glanced sideways at him. 'And would any of you be able to taste the difference, I ask myself?' He pressed the mix into the terrine tin and covered it with foil. 'My talents are wasted in this household. Lottie would eat baked beans on toast just as happily as she would eat my terrine, and you're nearly as bad. This will be ready for Nick when he gets down at the weekend. He appreciates good food, I'm glad to say.'

'So do I,' protested Matt. 'I just can't be bothered when I'm on my own. It's easier to get takeaways.'

Milo shook his head and took the deep roasting

tin half full of boiling water from the oven. 'Hope-less. Quite hopeless.'

Matt took a deep breath, suddenly nervous. 'I've had an idea, Milo, and I wanted to run it past you.'

'"Run it past you",' repeated Milo with contempt. 'What does that mean? "Run it past you." Good God! Have you ever read the writings that came back from the trenches? Wonderful letters and poetry from perfectly ordinary soldiers, full of evocation and imagery? Can you imagine what we're getting these days from Iraq or Afghanistan? Assuming that anyone out there can read and write, that is.'

'Emails or text messages,' grinned Matt. 'Nobody writes letters any more, Milo. You know that.'

'No need to brag about it.' Milo stood his terrine in the *bain-marie*, put it in the oven and glanced at the clock. 'An hour and a half,' he muttered. 'So what's this brilliant idea, then? Are you going to take cookery lessons?'

'I'd like to buy the Summer House.' Matt straightened up, instinctively preparing himself for some kind of rejection. 'If Im and Jules don't want it, then I'd like it. If you're OK with it.'

Oven cloth in hand, Milo stared at him, frowning; he shook his head slightly, as if to dispel surprise, and drew down the corners of his mouth.

'If you've decided to sell,' Matt hurried on, 'then

why not to me? Then it will stay in the family. I shall have a place outside London to work and to invite my friends; Jules and Im can use it for weekends, and later on, Lottie . . .'

He halted awkwardly, not wishing to talk about Milo's demise, but Milo had understood him and nodded one short nod, as if to imply that nothing more need be said about that.

'*If* you've decided,' Matt repeated, not wanting to take anything for granted; pretending that he didn't know about Nick's problem. He hadn't been prepared for this sudden onset of nervousness. He wished he hadn't used the words 'then it will stay in the family' as if Milo were somehow failing by not keeping the Summer House; as if he, Matt, were some kind of saviour, keeping everyone together and looking out for Lottie. His love and respect for Milo were enormous and he was beginning to feel deeply uncomfortable. He stared at the older man, willing him to understand, but Milo had turned to pick up his kitchen timer and was pressing buttons.

'You see,' Matt went on anxiously to Milo's back, 'I've been looking for somewhere to buy for quite a while. I've wanted to invest some of the money in property but couldn't decide where. I bought my swish service flat in Chiswick because it's perfect, both to work in and to leave when I go travelling.

But I've been wondering about buy-to-let, and I'm doubtful as to whether I can cope with tenants and all the hassle, and so this would be so perfect. When I'm not here, you and Lottie can keep an eye . . .'

He stopped, feeling sure that he was really putting his foot in it now, casting Milo in the position of caretaker – but Milo was turning, his face showing mixed feelings of delight and relief.

'But it's a simply brilliant idea, Matt. Are you really sure, though, that you want to invest your money in a house so far from London? I would be delighted for you to have it. It solves a thousand problems. If you're really sure?'

Matt could hardly speak, so great was his relief, and not just relief, but pleasure too, that, after all the years of generosity and love that Milo had given him and Im, he was able at last to make some kind of return.

'I'm absolutely sure,' he answered at last. 'It answers lots of my problems too. Honestly. Thanks, Milo.'

He felt odd, as if something momentous had happened; in a state of shock now that an agreement had been reached.

'But you can't have seen the place for ages,' Milo was saying. 'We must ask the Moretons to let you go over it. Well, this is wonderful news and I can't wait to see Lottie's face. Come on. We need to celebrate and I've got some Bollinger in the fridge that will just do the trick.'

'Should we . . . I mean, perhaps we should wait for Lottie,' suggested Matt diffidently. 'You know. She might feel left out. Shall we wait until she gets home?'

'Not bloody likely,' answered the brigadier. 'She could be hours yet. Come on, boy. Get down those glasses and we'll drink to your brilliant idea.'

Much later Matt kneeled at his attic window, staring down at the red roof of the Summer House. He was still in a state of shock. Milo had telephoned the Moretons who had said that of *course* Matt could come down and look around; but they had a friend staying, would tomorrow morning be convenient? If Matt were in a hurry, however . . . ?

Milo had telegraphed this to Matt, who had said that, yes, tomorrow would be perfectly fine and, no, there was no great hurry. He'd been almost relieved for the respite. Milo was so happy that he couldn't wait to get Matt down there and show him around properly.

'I've never been upstairs,' he'd told Milo. 'But Mrs Moreton used to invite me and Im into the kitchen for lemonade and biscuits sometimes. It always felt warm and friendly, and I love the veranda and the little lawn that edges the stream.'

'It means that we can go on sharing the barns,' Milo had said with great relief. 'And you won't want the gardens carved up. In fact, the less ground you have the better. We can look after it for you.'

He'd been so enthusiastic, so full of ideas, that the champagne was finished by the time Lottie returned. She'd glanced at the empty bottle and raised her eyebrows.

'Celebrating?' she'd asked without rancour. 'You might have waited. So what's happened?'

Matt had remained silent whilst Milo told the glad tidings. He'd seen at once that she'd had a reservation; her eyes had drifted beyond Milo, as if she were seeing something else besides his delight.

'What is it?' Matt had asked quickly. 'You're not happy about it, Lottie.'

'Oh, yes,' she'd said at once. 'I am. I feel it's right except . . . well, I was just wondering how Imogen will feel about it.'

Now, leaning forward, his arms folded on the narrow window ledge, Matt thought about Im and how she might react. It hadn't occurred to him that she might feel jealous or angry, but he could see now that it was a possibility. He'd been too taken up with his exciting idea, his own solution to the problem, to think that it might be very hard for Im to see him owning the little house that she loved so much.

'So what shall I do?' he'd asked Lottie anxiously, as if he were a child again. He'd looked at Milo, who had an expression of irritation on his face.

'If Jules and she have decided not to live there I should think that the next best thing for her would be to have her own brother owning it,' he'd said. 'Matt's said that she and Jules can use it. I think it's the obvious solution. I think you're being oversensitive.'

'It just might take a bit of getting used to, that's all.' Lottie had defended herself. 'She's very disappointed, remember. It all depends how Matt tells her. I'm sure she'll be delighted once she gets used to the idea.'

Matt could see that Milo was impatient of this pandering to Im's delicate sensibilities but he'd agreed that they should postpone telling Im until Matt had been down to see the Summer House.

Turning back into the room, with its low-raftered ceiling and boarded, cream-washed walls, Matt was aware of excitement building inside him again. He looked around: at the double mattress that he and Milo had dragged up the steep staircase and squashed through the narrow doorway, at the bookshelves that they'd built along one whole wall, at the small painted chest of drawers and at the toys sitting in a wicker basket in the corner. He picked out the teddy bear, worn and bedraggled with hugs and kisses, and inhaled the musty smell of the past; of childhood. Briefly but powerfully, a strong mental jolting of the senses momentarily transported him to another world: he felt great heat, heard the cries of harsh foreign voices, smelled rich scents; he saw himself, a small child, as in a mirror image, and then knife-sharp came the familiar feeling of loss, of being lifted and whirled away . . .

Matt stood quite still, holding the bear, struggling with the overwhelming loneliness and the sense of agonizing separation from something precious. It was not new; it would pass. Gently he placed the bear back in the basket and went downstairs.

CHAPTER SEVENTEEN

Rosie sat in her playpen, a pop-up book in her hands. Several pieces of the pop-up cards had been torn from the book, sucked, and flung aside; sometimes the whole book would be thrown with all the small strength she could muster. Now, however, she was studying very closely a picture of a rabbit, homogenized and charming, that was driving a small car. Head bent, totally absorbed, she made gentle encouraging noises: 'Mmmm,' she murmured approvingly. 'Bab, bab, bab.'

'Is there a rabbit, darling?' asked Im. She knew now that this was Rosie's word for rabbit. Ever since Nick's present, Rosie had been obsessed by rabbits: every story must have a rabbit in it; each picture must portray one. If the book had no rabbits then Rosie would become at first tearful and then vengeful.

Imogen gazed down at the small figure: the wisps of blonde hair curling on the tender white neck, the fat, curving cheeks, the starfish hands clutching the book. Im's heart seemed to move within her breast, squeezed by love, fear, and inexpressible tenderness. She imagined all the terrible things that might happen to this tiny, vulnerable, defenceless and most beloved person and she bent quickly and caught Rosie, lifting her out of the playpen and holding her close.

'Bab!' shouted Rosie, twisting in her mother's arms, outraged by the interruption. She pointed back, down into the playpen, where Nick's gift lay abandoned, long legs and arms entwined. Im leaned to pick it up.

'Here,' she said. 'Here's Bab. Isn't he nice?'

They studied him together: the rather pleading expression in the large eyes, the deprecating half-smile, the debonair bow tie that was woven into his white-bibbed chest. Suddenly Imogen realized that Bab reminded her – very slightly – of Nick himself; the thought unsettled her and she hurried away from it.

'Shall we have a walk?' she asked Rosie. 'Just up the lane to the road? Shall we?'

She joggled her and swung her round, and Rosie chuckled. She dropped the book but hugged Bab to her chest and made sounds that indicated she approved of the idea.

183

'Come on, then. Coat on. And your nice warm boots. Good girl, then.'

Presently they were out in the road: Rosie in the buggy still clutching Bab, Imogen pulling on her gloves, checking that she had the door key, glancing up to see if there was any imminent sign of rain. The sky was a pure china blue, patched with inky-purple clouds; dense fingers of golden light probed the turbulent green water of the Channel, and the Welsh hills floated behind a translucent glittering veil, distant and unreal. The lane wound uphill, curving out of sight, and Imogen stood for a moment, staring across the farmland that sloped towards the coast. The hawthorn, sculpted and shaped by the wind, was misting greenly with new leaf, and black buds swelled on the ash. The first cold white stars of the blackthorn blossomed in distant hedges and, everywhere she looked, the gorse flower burned brightly gold.

She began to walk quickly, talking to Rosie, breathing in the sharp, cold air. The sun slanted above the hill's shoulder and now the lane levelled a little, and beech trees, their lower branches still thickly clotted with dark bronze, crisp leaves, blocked her view to the sea. She passed the gate to Eastcott Farm and paused to watch a small bird hopping, beak stabbing for insects, on the moss-covered roof of the little wooden building down on the farm track. She could see now that it was a wren and, as she watched, it darted and danced and plunged from sight beneath the hedge.

On she went, the wind cold in her face; the lane opening out again seawards now, with new fence posts and barbed wire strung along the top of the bank. Soon violets and primroses would grow in the mossy bank and, later in the year, purple honey-scented heather would cover the heathland to the south; now only its black brittle bones were to be seen, frail, curving cages growing amongst the whin and furze. Rosie sang a tuneless little song and beat Bab on the side of the stroller and Im bent forward to call to her.

Suddenly, with no warning, hail clattered from the bright blue air; it bounced and cracked in the lane and stung Im's cheeks. Gasping with the shock, she ran to pull the hood over Rosie's head, then crouched to shield the small body with her own whilst the hail pattered on her back and Rosie cried out with fright. Im was trying to turn the pushchair, still crouching to shield Rosie, when the car slid alongside with a swish of tyres on the icy road. She stared upward, hair damp across her face, as the car door slammed and feet crunched around the shining chrome bumper.

'Nick,' she said, unbelieving. '*Nick?* What are *you* doing here?'

'Visiting my two favourite people,' he answered lightly. 'Come on, I'll give you a lift back down to the cottage. Let her out, Im, and get into the car. I'll deal with the buggy.'

Holding Rosie in her arms, Im straightened up, half laughing, half disbelieving.

'Why didn't you say you were coming?' she cried breathlessly as the wind whirled the icy pellets all around them.

'Surprise,' he said briefly, kissing her. 'Hello, Rosie. Hello, rabbit. Get in the warm and we'll go home.'

'Dad knew I was coming,' he said later, as they warmed their hands on mugs of hot coffee whilst Rosie drooped and snoozed amongst the cushions Im had put into the playpen. 'But I decided to take a detour and see if you were around.'

She sipped her coffee, watching him across the rim of the mug. Her cheeks burned but she assured herself that this was due to coming in out of the wind and hail and feeling suddenly glowing with warmth. She tried to ignore the tightening of her gut and the little churning sense of excitement.

'How's Alice?' she asked.

His face changed at the abruptness of her question

and she bit her lip with vexation: poor Nick, how crass of her when he'd been so sweet.

'Anyhow,' she went on quickly, before he could answer, 'it's great to see you.'

'I was so sorry to hear about the Summer House,' he said. It was offered as an excuse; a reason for coming to see her before he went to the High House. 'What rotten luck. Not that I can't see old Jules' point of view, of course, but I know how you love it.' He made a sympathetic face. 'Poor darling.'

'Oh,' she said quickly. 'I'll live with it, though I admit I *am* gutted. But what will Milo do with it? Do you know?'

He shrugged. 'I know he doesn't want to go on renting it out. He'd have to modernize it so much for anyone these days it would cost a fortune. It's just sad that it's going out of the family, and I can't help feeling that it's all my fault.'

'But he'd have had to do something now that the Moretons are going.' She hastened to comfort him, to cheer him up. 'Like you said, he didn't want to go on renting, so selling it must have been on the cards.'

'Anyway, what are you going to do now? Where will you go?'

'Oh.' She sighed, made a little face. 'Jules has a client over near Simonsbath who's got a converted barn for rent. His son has been living in it whilst he builds his own little eco bungalow but he'll be out next week and it's been offered to us on a long let. They absolutely love Jules and they don't want to go back to holiday letting. I haven't seen it yet. To be honest, I really believed a miracle would happen and we'd be buying by now.' She shrugged. 'So there we are.'

There was a short silence. 'Alice is fine,' Nick said, as if Im had only now asked the question, 'in a glacial, critical, contemptuous sort of way. How's Jules?'

Another silence. 'Jules is fine,' Im answered, parodying Nick's answer, 'in a sulky, self-defensive, unfriendly kind of way.'

They looked at one another, half questioning, half fearful, and Im put down her mug and went to make Rosie more comfortable on her cushions where she now drowsed peacefully.

It was odd, Im thought, how the child seemed to protect her from what Nick was offering. She remained, kneeling by the playpen with her back to Nick.

'You shouldn't have come,' she said.

'I know,' he said, not attempting to misunderstand her. 'But I miss you, Im. God, life is so miserable at the moment. I can't stop thinking about you.'

'You mustn't,' she said. It was an effort to say it. She wanted to stand up and put her arms round him.

And why not, she asked herself silently, angrily. Jules wouldn't care. Not the way he is at the moment.

Rosie stirred, put in her thumb, and Im remained, hanging over the playpen, one hand stroking Rosie's shoulder and arm.

'I think you'd better go,' she said miserably. 'Honestly, Nick. We mustn't.'

'But you want to.' He was beside her, his mouth beside her ear, and she shivered, nodded reluctantly, just a tiny movement of her head. He kissed her, pressed his cheek against hers. 'You know I love you,' he said. 'God, what fools we were, Im.'

She heard the door close gently but still she stayed where she was, one hand on the sleeping child as if she were a talisman that might ward off evil.

CHAPTER EIGHTEEN

Matt passed Nick at the end of Allerpark Wood, recognized the car and slowed down. He backed the few yards to where Nick had stopped, and they both wound down windows, leaned out.

'Just popped in to see Im,' said Nick, getting in first. 'Just as well. She and Rosie were walking in that hailstorm and I gave them a lift home. Are you going to see them?'

'Yes.' Matt was slightly nonplussed. 'I thought it might be nice for Milo and Lottie to have you to themselves for lunch and I'm hoping Im will give me a sandwich. See you later, then?'

'Sure. I'm on my way to the High House now.'

He waved cheerfully and pulled away, and Matt drove on, wondering why he felt uneasy.

Imogen opened the door quickly and her expression of surprise was almost comical.

'I heard a car,' she said. 'I didn't know . . .'

'You didn't get my text, then?' He went past her into the hall, and she pointed to the sitting room as she shut the front door.

'Let's go in there,' she said. 'Rosie's fallen asleep in the playpen and I don't want to disturb her. No, I didn't get it. I must have been out with Rosie. We got caught in the hailstorm.'

'So Nick said.' He saw the colour rise in her cheeks. 'I've got something to tell you, so I came on over anyway.'

Im shivered, wrapped her arms around herself. 'It's so *cold*,' she complained. 'Colder than it was in January. I think I'll light the fire.' She kneeled down and then glanced over her shoulder at him. 'Nothing's wrong, is it? Milo and Lottie are OK?'

'They're fine.' Matt perched on the arm of the sofa, watching her. 'It's about the Summer House, Im.'

She half turned. 'What?' she asked quickly. 'What's happened? Oh God, Milo's found another buyer, hasn't he?'

'Yes,' said Matt slowly. 'Hang on, don't get upset. Yes, he has, but only if you're OK with it. It's me. I've offered to buy it so as to keep it in the family. We can all use it, you see. It will be all of ours, not just mine.' He talked quickly, noting the expressions – shock, dismay, anger – flit across her face, knowing

191

that Lottie had been right to warn him. 'He's going to sell it to someone, Im,' he said gently. 'Don't you think that it might as well be to me rather than to a stranger? I know it's a shock, and I suppose you might actually prefer a stranger in an odd sort of way . . .'

He waited for her to contradict him – and, in the silence that followed, realized that she was even more upset than he'd imagined.

'No, I wouldn't,' she said at last, turning back to the fire, arranging sticks over a firelighter, piling logs around them, reaching for the matches. 'Of course I wouldn't. Sorry, Matt. It's just . . . Well, it's just such a shock. I'd never thought about you buying it, and I can see that it's the obvious thing to do since Jules and I . . . since Jules . . .'

She began to weep, leaning forward with her head nearly on her knees, covering her face with her sooty hands.

'Im.' He kneeled beside her, feeling traitorous. 'I'm sorry, love, I didn't realize you'd feel quite so strongly about it. I should have done. Lottie was right.'

'Lottie?' She stared up at him, smearing her cheeks with her wrist. 'What did Lottie say?'

Matt sat back on his heels and dug his handkerchief out of his jeans pocket. 'Lottie thought you'd be upset. She said it was only natural that you'd feel a bit, well, miffed, to see me there when you couldn't have it. Perhaps a stranger *would* be better.'

'No.' She shook her head vigorously, wiped her eyes on his handkerchief, and smiled at him. 'No, it wouldn't. I'm being a spoiled brat. A tiresome little sister. I'm sorry, Matt. It's a brilliant idea. It just kind of underlined it. You know? That it's not going to happen. You always keep hoping for a miracle, don't you? But Jules won't change his mind, and in my saner moments I know that he's right. I just wish he'd be a bit nicer about it, that's all. Still, never mind that.' She got to her feet. 'I bet Milo's dead chuffed?'

'Well, he is.' Matt got up too. 'He's hated the idea of strangers there, and it's somewhere Lottie could go when . . . you know. When . . . if something happens to Milo.'

Im stared at him, her face was serious, shocked. 'I hadn't thought of that,' she admitted. 'I can't bear to imagine either of them not at the High House but I suppose she wouldn't stay on without him. You mean, Lottie could live at the Summer House. Oh, Matt. What a terrific idea.'

'It's just how I saw it,' he said quickly, to avert another emotional response. 'We can share it. I can bring my friends down and you and Jules could use it at weekends or for holidays if you didn't want to go away. You could even rent it now if you can't find somewhere to go.'

'No,' she said shortly, then smiled reassuringly. 'It's OK. It's just I'd rather not do things by halves. I'm coming to terms with not having it and I think that renting it for a while would undermine that. But I'm glad, Matt. Truly I am. And we'll see a bit more of you. It'll be fun.'

'Will you come and see it with me?' he asked diffidently. 'Just to give me advice about furnishing? Stuff like that? Would that be . . . rubbing it in?'

She touched his arm. 'What a nice brother you are,' she said lightly. 'Just try to keep me away, that's all. You know I'd love it.'

'Well, then.' He was surprised at how relieved he was. 'That's great. Milo celebrated with champagne. What have you got?'

'I can't follow Milo,' she said. 'But I've got a nice rough Rioja. If you keep quiet so we don't wake Rosie we'll go and find some glasses and the cork-screw. Can you stay and have a sandwich or have you got to get back?'

He shook his head. 'I thought I'd let them have Nick all to themselves.' He hesitated. 'What was he doing here, Im?'

Her cheeks flamed again at the casual question.

194

'Does he need a reason? He often drops in on his way to the High House.'

'Hardly on his way, is it?'

She stared at him. 'What's all this third-degree stuff?'

'Sorry. I was just surprised to see him, that's all. Shall we have that drink?'

He drove home feeling faintly uneasy: it had been a surprise to see Nick, and, when he'd commented on it, Im's reaction had been odd, almost guilty. Suddenly he remembered, oh, years ago now, Lottie asking him if he'd noticed that Im and Nick were seeing rather a lot of each other. It was just after Im had started working in the stables near Newbury, but there had been no evidence of any relationship and he'd dismissed the idea. Now, he wondered if Lottie could have been right: Im had been unusually defensive.

Matt pulled in to the side of the lane and sat looking out over the marshes. The tide was just turning so that the bleached fields were still flooded with pools of glittering water, sliced with brimming ditches, all reflecting the chill blue of the sky. He could easily imagine the dangers: Nick in the doghouse with Alice; Im angry with Jules and feeling hurt. It was a perfect recipe for trouble, he could see that. But even so, surely it was impossible. Nick and Im had known each other for ever; they were like brother and sister. They might console each other, sympathize about the intractability of spouses, but nothing more . . . And yet there had been that sharp answer: *Does he need a reason?* And the way that she'd blushed, twice, at the mention of Nick's name.

Nick, of course, had been his usual insouciant self, but he'd always had that vulnerable side: the need to be loved and approved of. Was he looking for that from Im – and was she in the mood to respond? Matt swore under his breath. How complicated and tiresome relationships were! This thought reminded him that, having decided to spend at least a month in Bossington, he'd given in at last and invited Annabel down to the High House. Milo and Lottie, thank God, had been perfectly easy about it all: no sly looks or knowing smiles. She wasn't the first to be invited, after all, and he'd played it very low-key, but he felt surprisingly nervous about it. Annabel was keen: very keen. She'd been delighted with the invitation and, though she knew that it wasn't quite the same as being invited home to meet the parents, it was clear that she was viewing her visit rather in that light. Im would help him to keep it very casual; she'd done it before. She had a very clever, sisterly

196

knack in making his girlfriends very welcome whilst managing to imply that they were one of many, and that her brother was a rather hopeless case. Sometimes, afterwards, she'd be quite cross with him – especially if she'd really liked the girl – but she understood his reluctance to commit, though she longed for him to fall in love.

He knew he need not worry about Milo. Milo was the perfect host, enjoying the opportunity to create some amazing culinary feast whilst remaining faintly detached from any emotional overtones. As for Lottie . . . Matt gave an involuntary snort of laughter. Fortunately for him, any matchmaking skills had been completely left out of Lottie's genetic makeup. She loved all his girlfriends – she had an enormous empathy with the young – whilst harbouring no desires to see him permanently attached to any one of them. She was neither practical nor particularly maternal, yet he'd never questioned her love for him or for Im. She and Milo were indeed 'the odd couple' but he was deeply grateful for their love.

It occurred to him that once he'd become the owner of the Summer House, inviting his women friends to stay might take on a whole new connotation. He suddenly realized that he didn't particularly want Annabel to see the Summer House: not this time, not yet. Going to see it with

197

Milo had been so strange; surprisingly exciting. The house was in the throes of being packed up and Mrs Moreton had apologized for the mess, but he hadn't noticed the mess. He'd been completely absorbed by the delightful proportions of the little house: the elegant staircase, and the way that the rooms were wood-panelled and painted creamy-white, just like the cabin of a ship. Tall rhododendron bushes sheltered the little lawn that sloped to the Aller Brook and he'd stood on the veranda with its twisted, barley-sugar pillars and felt an overwhelming thrill of ownership that his very smart flat had never afforded him. He couldn't wait for the Moretons to move out.

Watching a great flock of gulls, swooping and circling at the tide's edge, he decided that he'd get Im over as soon as he could, show her around the Summer House; take her mind off Nick. He remembered that he hadn't shown Im the photograph or told her about the odd manner of its arrival. Somehow it hadn't been appropriate. In fact, her response to his news had put it right out of his mind. He had, however, consulted Lottie and then shown all the photographs to Milo.

'I can't quite see how he could throw any light on them,' Matt had said to her, 'but it's worth it, isn't it? He'll have a new take on them, coming to them fresh,' and she'd agreed at once: the time was right.

And so, after supper, he explained his dilemma, brought out the packet and gently slid the photographs in a sheaf across the table. Milo took in the circumstances without needing to ask endless questions – it was such a relief to have his quick, intelligent response – and picked up first one photo and then another.

'It's not just that there is none of Im amongst them,' Matt said, trying to gauge Milo's silence: he had a horror that the older man might think that he was simply crackers. 'It's just this weird sense of disorientation I have when I look at them. This one, for instance. Did you ever have a car like that, Milo? Or your father, perhaps.'

Milo peered more closely at the picture. 'It's difficult to say, isn't it? You can't see much of it. Of course, you didn't have a car in London, did you, Lottie? Did Tom ever have one?'

'I don't remember Tom having a car.' Lottie leaned over the table to peer at it. 'How old would you say you are in this one, Matt? Four? Five?'

Matt shook his head. 'I wouldn't know but I should guess so. I'd definitely think that it was taken after Dad had died. That's why I wonder whether it might have been Milo's car. It was about then that you first brought us down to the High House to meet Milo, wasn't it, Lottie?'

Milo studied the car again. 'So it wasn't taken when you were all out in Afghanistan?'

'No.' Matt was firm about that. 'The only photo I've got that was taken out there is one of Dad when he went out the second time on his own. He sent me a little letter and the photo was in it. There was none taken of us as a family. Or if there was, I haven't seen it.'

'Which is odd, isn't it?' said Milo thoughtfully, picking up another. 'You'd have thought Tom would have wanted a record of your time there, being a photographer.'

Lottie smiled a little. 'That's the whole point,' she said. 'The last thing a professional photographer does is to take happy family snaps. It was his job, not a hobby. Helen must have taken these. Remember that Matt was only eighteen months when they came home so all these must be post-Afghanistan.'

'You can't remember taking any of them?' Matt asked hopefully, but she shook her head.

'I was never much good with a camera,' she said. 'I probably took a few, of course, but I couldn't swear to it. And not those very early ones. You were four, Matt, when I first met you all, and Im was a baby.'

'So it's the clothes you don't recognize,' murmured Milo. 'But why do you think you'd remember them after all these years?' He turned to the most recent photographs, but these were head-and-shoulder shots, with barely a shirt collar showing, and gave no further clues. He picked up the most recent one, and Matt explained how it had arrived from the news agency with no message.

'I wondered if it had been taken when I was on tour, but why should anyone send it to the news agency; and why no message? Why not through my publishers?'

'I must admit that it is very odd. And you couldn't recognize the stamp at all? Did you try to check it out on the net, for instance?'

Matt flushed. 'It had been really heavily stamped and the ink was so badly smudged that I couldn't decipher it at all.'

Milo glanced up at him. 'So you ditched it?'

Matt's expression gave him his answer. 'You chump,' the older man said, but without heat. 'It was our only clue, wasn't it? Never mind. Now if you wrote thrillers you'd have known to have kept it.' He shook his head. 'It's baffling, isn't it? I wish I could be more helpful.'

Matt began to gather up the photographs; he suspected that secretly Milo was still wondering what all the fuss was about and almost wished he'd never exposed his formless anxieties to this pragmatic old soldier.

Yet now, as he watched the gulls wheeling above the rising tide, he knew that he was glad that Milo shared his secret.

CHAPTER NINETEEN

Nick and Lottie sat together in silence in the garden room. Lottie was knitting. He watched as the knitting slowly grew, the soft wool bundling over her knees, the big multicoloured ball rolling away and being retrieved, the rhythmic action of the needles. He felt soothed, infinitely relaxed, wondering why it was possible to sit in such contented silence with some people and not with others. His aunt finished a purl row, reversed the knitting, and began on a plain row. It might have been a shawl, or a blanket. She made beautiful clothes for little children – in fact most of the knitting she did was for charity, very occasionally for herself; never for Milo or Matt or Im.

'Would you knit me a jersey, Lottie?' he asked suddenly, hardly knowing why, except that he believed that there might be some special magical quality about a garment worked with love by someone close to you.

'Oh, my darling,' she said, amused at the suggestion. 'Are you certain? Are you the type of man who would wear a jersey knitted by his aunt?'

He laughed too. 'Why not? My friends would believe that it was from Brora or Toast or something. I'd like something rugged and tough. It would be good for my image.'

She glanced at him, and it was as if those clear grey eyes looked right into him, past all his posturing and pretence. He braced himself lest she should make some light, hurtful remark about it needing more than a jersey to make him tough – as Alice would have – but instead she nodded.

'I'd like to,' she said. 'A fisherman's jersey, I think. You can wear it when you go out sailing with Milo. Navy blue. I'll measure you before you go back.'

'I don't want to go back,' he said. He rocked gently on the big revolving cane chair. 'Do you ever wish, Lottie, that you could just step out of life?'

She knitted a full row before she answered him. 'I think my problem is exactly the reverse,' she said at last. 'I've never felt part of life at all. I feel as if there's always been something missing in my brain that has prevented me from connecting properly with the rest of the human race. It's very uncomfortable and very lonely. It's as if everyone else speaks a language I can't quite understand and behaves according to a set of rules that nobody has ever explained to me. I fumble about, trying to pick it up as I go along, but I've never been very successful. That's why I'm so grateful to Milo. He's been a refuge for me, you see.'

Nick was silent for a moment, taken aback, searching for words that might reassure her.

'But you managed all those years in London, looking after Im and Matt. They always say that their lives would have been so miserable without you.'

'They probably would have been,' she answered candidly, 'given that poor Helen suffered so terribly from depression. But the point is that I found it very hard. Looking after them didn't come naturally to me at all. I never knew my mother so I had no experience to fall back on. Poor things; I still wonder how we survived. We were like the babes in the wood, all of us looking after one another, and it was only because I loved them so much that we survived it at all. I watch other people with awe, especially young people. They seem to know things without being told, they have their hands on all the ropes, and their wisdom is amazing. I have to struggle all the time to keep up.'

'Well, if it's true, all I can say is that you have many other qualities to make up for it,' he told her loyally. 'I don't know what Dad would do without you.'

She smiled to herself, but didn't answer him, and he cast around for something else to encourage her. Of course, his mother had always been sarcastic about her younger sister but he'd assumed that it was simply the usual sibling rivalry – especially as Lottie got on so well with Milo.

'You worked in a publishing house,' Nick reminded her. 'That's pretty impressive.'

'A very small, esoteric one,' she said, 'but I *did* connect with the oddball writers we published. I could see at once that most of them inhabited a parallel universe, just as I do, and I got on with them very well. Dreamers, most of them; people who lived within the worlds of the books that they wrote and found reality dull or even frightening. I understood that, though my parallel universe seemed to have been thrust upon me, and they invented their own. I was a very lonely child and my refuge was books. This was how I saw the world; through the pages of children's fiction. That's great if you have a full, balanced, normal life running alongside a passion for reading, but it's not so good if it's the only world you know. Your grandparents were particularly kind to me when I was a little girl. Well, you know all that. They allowed me to come to stay here and, when you think about it, that's like a fairy tale in itself. I'd never known what it was like to have a mother, or a proper family life. And then later on, when Tom died, I was presented with another ready-made family of my own. Very odd, in a way, but it all fitted with my particular take on life. After all, in books miracles happen; Cinderella gets to go to the ball.'

'I suppose that's why you connect so well with Matt, him being a writer, I mean?'

'Yes.' Lottie rested her hands on her lap and stared out of the window. 'Matt has always inhabited a parallel universe, and I recognized that, but in his case it's one of his own making rather than one created by other people.'

'You mean because he's a writer?'

'Yes.' She hesitated, frowning. 'But I think it's not just that. There's something else from way back that informs his writing. Tom's death, of course. Helen's withdrawal . . .' She shook her head. 'Anyway. His particular alternative world has certainly been a terrific success.'

'What will he write next, I wonder?'

Lottie picked up her knitting again, smoothed it out. 'I think it will be very different from *Epiphany*.'

Nick raised his eyebrows. 'Not a sequel? It's been such a massive success that he must be under a lot of pressure to do it again.'

'I'm sure he is. But Matt's not a formulaic writer

and he won't do it simply for the money. No, I think something's waiting for Matt. Something special – and different.'

She was still staring out of the window, past the geraniums, into the gathering dusk. Nick felt the ghost of a shiver on his skin and he, too, looked out into the garden. Through the trees he could see the roof of the Summer House.

'Dad's thrilled that he's going to buy the Summer House, isn't he?' He was glad to turn the subject a little. 'Good old Matt. It's a great idea.'

'What will Sara say?' She turned to look at him anxiously. 'She won't be pleased.'

He shrugged, guilt edging into his contentedness. 'At least it stays in the family,' he muttered.

Lottie chuckled. 'I don't think Sara considers Matt and Im as members of her family.'

'Well, I do,' he said crossly. 'Matt and Im are . . .' He paused. He'd been about to say that they were like brother and sister to him, except that his feelings for Im were not in the least brotherly and now he couldn't think quite what to say.

'And how *was* Im?' Lottie was asking, head bent over her work.

'She was fine,' he answered distractedly, then remembered suddenly that he hadn't mentioned dropping in on Im, and cast a quick glance at Lottie.

'She's in a state,' Lottie said placidly, counting stitches. 'I expect Matt's found it hard to tell her that he'll be buying the Summer House now, but she'll soon see that it's the right thing to do for everyone. She's very emotional just now.' She began to knit again, not looking at him. 'You'll be careful, my darling, won't you?'

He was confused and embarrassed, wondering exactly how much Lottie suspected. 'Yes, of course,' he muttered – and changed the subject. 'I expect you're looking forward to meeting Annabel. Is she special?'

'Well, we all hope that one day Matt will find someone special but I haven't got the impression that Annabel is more special than the other girls he's brought to meet us. He's been quite firm in insisting that she's a publishing friend. Nothing more. We shall have a better insight when we meet her and see them together.'

'He's a funny chap, old Matt. I get the sense that he's waiting for something cataclysmic to happen to him.' Nick laughed. 'Outside his phenomenal success, that is. Something personal.'

'I think you're absolutely right,' she answered seriously.

She looked so serious, so thoughtful, that he was slightly taken aback and cast about for a lighter topic.

'Do you think that Dad will bring Venetia home with him this evening?'

'After a bridge session? Good Lord, no.' Lottie laughed out loud at such a suggestion. 'Poor Milo will be in a state of advanced irritation, so I warn you. Venetia has never been the world's sharpest bridge player but now she gets even more confused, and Milo's too loyal to chuck her over for a new partner. He'll be breathing fire and we'll have the whole rubber, blow by blow.' She finished the row, rolled the knitting together and put it into the big wicker basket. 'Shall we take Pud for a walk?' she suggested. 'Before it gets dark? Would you like to?'

'I'd love it.' He got up out of his chair. 'Now this is when that jersey would come in very useful,' he joked. 'It's freezing out there. You'll have to get started on it quickly.'

'You shall have it soon,' she promised cheerfully. 'Come on, Pud. We're going out.'

Venetia knew at once that when Milo turned left out of the Briscoes' drive that she was not going to be invited back to the High House for supper. She slumped slightly in her seat, disappointed and slightly miffed. And when he said irritably: 'Why on earth did you lead with that club, Vin?' she knew that he'd be in no mood for persuasion.

'Nonsense, darling,' she answered airily. 'I couldn't possibly have done anything else.'

Never give in, she told herself grimly, peering out into the twilight, rather dreading the coming evening. Really she couldn't see why the Briscoes couldn't finish off with a little bite of supper. When it was her turn she always managed something tasty after the game: some smoked salmon sandwiches and a glass or two of wine and then coffee. Anything rather than be left with an empty evening stretching ahead. She shivered as they fled through the dark, narrow lanes, between box-shaped beech hedges, solid as walls. Mist drifted in the fields and hung in the hedges, and suddenly, as the car swung round a sharp bend, they saw a fox, caught for a few brief seconds in the bright glare of the headlights. They waited, engine idling, while he paused, eyes shining green and watchful, one paw lifted, before he vanished into the shadows of the ditch.

'Ooooh.' Venetia let out a long breath of satisfaction as Milo accelerated away again. 'Wasn't he nice, sweetie?' She relaxed a little. The sight of the fox had very slightly changed the atmosphere inside the car: Milo's irritation at losing the rubber was passing. 'Shall you come in for a drink or must you hurry home?'

'I shall have to crack on.' He was on the defensive

now. 'I told you we've got Nick and Matt staying at the moment, and lots to talk about. You know how it is.'

There was a very slight indication that she was being unreasonable and she made a little face in the darkness of the car.

Definitely not your evening, she told herself. Never mind.

'OK, sweetie,' she said in a bright little sing-song voice. 'I can *quite* understand that. Give the boys my love,' – and waited.

'Come to lunch on Sunday,' he said as they turned left into St George's Street and drove round behind the Priory to the Ball. 'We'll all be there.'

She smiled triumphantly to herself: brave cheer-fulness always paid off with Milo, pressed his guilt button, and generally resulted in some small offer-ing.

'Lovely,' she exclaimed as he stopped outside her little house. 'Now that's something to look forward to. I *do* love seeing the boys.' She leaned forward to kiss him lightly on the cheek. 'Thanks so much, sweetie. Off you go now. Hurry away.'

And she nipped smartly out and slammed the door before he could speak. She experienced a tiny glow of pleasure as she acknowledged the very slight look of chagrin on his face at this abrupt cutting off to his farewell, and she was still smiling as she unlocked the front door and went inside. The satisfaction lasted until she was standing alone in her smart little hall, turning on the light, listening to the silence. Her smile faded; she shrugged off her coat and threw it over the banisters before going into the kitchen to pour herself a drink.

CHAPTER TWENTY

Imogen wakened early. She lay quite still, listening for any sounds from Rosie, sharply aware of Jules lying curled in a ball and turned away from her. She had a longing to touch him on the shoulder; to feel his arms go round her and to inhale his sleepy night-time scent and feel the scrape of his early morning chin against her cheek. She hadn't realized how indescribably lonely it would be to have that warm current of affection and companionship cut off from her; yet she knew that she was just as much to blame as he was. Neither of them was prepared to back down; to admit to pride and hurt.

Cautiously she turned her head to look at him; watching the rise and fall of his regular breathing. If he were to turn now, rolling sleepily on to his back, stretching an arm to gather her to his side, how would she react? Would she lie stiffly, as she had on the one or two occasions when he'd attempted a reconciliation, or would she relax against him? Im stared miserably at the ceiling again; she wanted things to be right but some tiny stubborn demon muscled within her, whispering that it wasn't quite fair, that Jules was being selfish and inconsiderate, and that some notable gesture on his part – some acknowledgement of her unselfishness – was needed before she could agree to restore the equilibrium. So far, Jules had merely taken it for granted that they weren't going to buy the Summer House and was showing no real remorse or understanding for her or how she might be feeling. Even last night when she'd told him about Matt buying it Jules hadn't shown any emotion, or any indication that she might be finding it a bit hard to think of her brother owning the house she loved so much. No. He'd merely implied that everything was OK then, problem solved, and that she ought to be feeling delighted.

And then he'd said rather abruptly: 'So are we going to look at Billy Webster's barn, now, or what? Time's beginning to run out, isn't it? Or do you have any other ideas?'

There had been a coolness, almost an indifference, in his voice, as if it really didn't matter much to him and although deep down she knew that it wasn't true, yet she'd been incapable of steering the discussion into a course that might have led to initiating some warmth between them.

'I suppose there's no alternative,' she'd said icily. 'I'll go and look at it tomorrow morning, then. I suppose you've already seen it. You'd better leave his telephone number.'

She'd seen his look of disappointment, known that he'd hoped that they'd go together to look at the barn, but he'd said nothing more and she'd got up from the table and banged about in the kitchen, clearing up the supper and feeling angry and frustrated. She'd known she was being unreasonable and expecting too much. After all, Jules had never been a particularly oversensitive man; he was down-to-earth, practical and quite tough. Not like Nick, for instance, who was much gentler, much more aware of people's sensibilities.

Now, thinking about Nick, remembering how much she'd longed for him when he'd been with her yesterday, Im felt a scalding twinge of guilt. She looked again at Jules' recumbent form, hesitated, half lifted a hand towards him. At the same moment there was a high imperious cry; then another one: Rosie was awake. Im pushed back the quilt and slid quietly and quickly out of bed.

*   *   *

216

Jules waited until the door had closed behind her, then he turned on to his back, took a deep breath, and stretched. He'd grown adept at feigning sleep, hating those moments when they'd lie side by side, stiff as a pair of skittles, each locked into silence with the stretch of icy sheet between them. The fact was that he simply didn't know what to do. He absolutely refused to put himself totally in the wrong, though, and beg forgiveness for something that wasn't his fault. After all, they both knew that Bossington was too far away from the practice to make it a sensible place to live, and he wasn't going to grovel about it: she knew all about the pressures of the job. He expected Im to behave like an adult and accept her disappointment. Anyway, now that Matt was going to buy it – oh, the triumphant way she'd announced that Matt was going to keep the dear old Summer House in the family, as if Matt were the only person to understand how important *that* was – she'd be able to go over as often as she wanted to. And when he'd said as much, imagining that she'd be pleased, she'd stared at him as if he were a monster. 'Thanks,' she'd said. Sarcastic and contemptuous. Just that: 'Thanks.'

He resented this suggestion that he was some kind of unfeeling moron. In fact, on the few occasions when he'd attempted to break the impasse she'd absolutely rejected him: refused to meet him halfway. And now there was this nonsense about the barn, and the way she was insisting on going alone to see it. Well, he'd look a fool, that was all. Billy Webster would wonder what the hell was going on, and it meant a phone call to try to make out that Im could manage to come over this morning but that he'd be too busy to come with her; something like that. He didn't want Billy suspecting that there was anything wrong and he hoped to God that Im was nice to Billy and his wife. It was damned embarrassing, and too bad of Im to put him into this position.

Jules lay for a moment, seething with impotence and unhappiness. He glanced at the bedside clock, threw back the covers and headed for the bathroom.

Nick phoned about half an hour after Jules had left the cottage, hardly speaking and much earlier than usual.

'Where are you?' asked Im, guessing that Nick was alone. She wiped Rosie's face clumsily with the cloth in her left hand. 'Keep still, Rosie. I should have said that this was a tad early for you to be out.'

'I'm walking Pud,' he told her. He sounded amused. 'I'd no idea how useful it is to have a dog. He's a wonderful excuse for an early walk and a bit

218

of privacy. I was wondering whether we could meet up for coffee. Or lunch?'

'It's a bit tricky. Hang on, I'm just getting something to keep Rosie amused. Here you are, darling, here's Bab and your rabbit book. Sorry, Nick. Listen. I'm going over to Simonsbath to see a barn that we might rent. Jules is pretty sure that the farmer or his wife will be around but he's going to double-check and then phone me. I want to go this morning if I can. We've simply got to make a decision.'

'I'll come with you,' he said at once. 'It'll be fun. Why not?'

She hesitated, terribly tempted. 'I don't think we should,' she said reluctantly at last. 'It's very near the practice, and it's possible that Jules might turn up unannounced. It would be . . . well, it would be embarrassing.'

'OK.' He sounded disappointed. 'But we could meet somewhere afterwards, couldn't we?'

'I don't know.' She was flustered; trying to collect the breakfast plates one-handed. 'What's Matt doing this morning? I mean, won't they all be a bit surprised that you're going off on your own?'

'He and Lottie are going to see some old chum. A writer who lives over near Dulverton. I was invited but I don't really know whoever it is so I cried off, and Dad's got things to do in the garden. I think

Matt's getting nervous about this girl Annabel who's coming down on Sunday. Dad and Lottie are wondering whether he's really serious about her, hoping that this time she might be the one. That kind of thing. They aren't pressuring him but I think they want to know how to behave towards her; whether she's extra-special. Of course, Matt is insisting that she's just a friend, like he always does.'

'Well, we'd all like to meet the girl that Matt could really fall for,' Imogen agreed. 'But he seems completely incapable of finding one that he can commit to. You and Matt and I never really had any good role models when it came to happy marriages, did we?'

'Well, you seemed to have managed it,' he answered lightly. 'How *is* Jules?'

The question pulled her up short and reignited all her grievances. 'Grumpy,' she answered. 'He's in Eeyore mode.'

Nick laughed. 'Poor darling. I couldn't sympathize more. Perhaps he and Alice should get together. We'll find them a nice damp corner in Hundred Acre Wood and build them a little wooden house and they can grump about together at Pooh Corner. Come on, Im. What about lunch in Lynmouth?'

'I have to think about Rosie,' she said uncertainly, watching her daughter crooning over the battered pages of the little book, Bab clutched lovingly against her chest. 'It's not always easy in pubs. Some don't allow children, except in dreary family rooms, and she's a nightmare in a restaurant. I have to fit around her lunchtime too, you see.'

'I'll bring a picnic,' he said instantly. 'Fantastic. You bring something for Rosie and I'll manage our lunch and we'll eat it in your car. Is it a deal? Pick a place.'

She began to laugh; her spirits rose at the prospect and the black cloud of her misery drew back a little: 'It's a deal,' she agreed. 'What about up on Brendon Common? There's that car park in a kind of quarry under Shilstone Hill. You know where I mean?'

'Yes, I know. About one-ish?'

'No, earlier than that. Rosie will be wanting her lunch soon after twelve. I'm hoping to get over to this barn fairly early but I expect it will mean having coffee and a chat with Mr Webster or his wife. I just hope it's as good as Jules says it is, that's all. We've left it so late but that's my fault really. I suppose that, knowing that we could go to the High House if we were really stuck, kind of took the pressure off. And now Matt's saying we could camp at the Summer House if we want to.'

'But you'd hate that, wouldn't you?' He sounded

concerned. 'I mean, it would be like really rubbing it in, I should think.'

She warmed to him afresh for his intuition: 'It would,' she agreed. 'Keep your fingers crossed that the barn is good. And luckily it would be furnished. We've never had our own place yet and I wouldn't want to buy furniture until I buy the house it's going into. We've got a few bits and pieces that Milo's stored for us but nothing serious. Anyway, I'll let you know later what it's like. And if I'm a bit late, or something goes wrong—'

'I'll wait,' he told her, 'for as long as it takes. See you later, Im.'

She switched her mobile off, flustered and confused. How could there be anything wrong with having a picnic with Nick; after all, he was practically Rosie's uncle? Yet she knew that she wouldn't tell Jules about it. She wondered if Nick would tell Matt and Lottie where he was going – and knew deep down that he wouldn't.

CHAPTER TWENTY-ONE

Venetia arrived early for lunch on Sunday: too early. She knew it but simply couldn't resist. There was nothing worse, she told herself, than getting ready and then sitting about, glancing at the clock, waiting to go; and, anyway, this new girl of Matt's was arriving and she wanted to be there so as to see it all. So much happened just at those first moments of introductions and she didn't want to miss a minute of it. How she loved the bustle and excitement of new people: of watching their reactions, of sizing them up.

'She's not a girlfriend,' Lottie had said when she'd phoned to say that Annabel would be there. 'We've asked him and he's been very firm about it. Just one of his publishing friends. You know what I mean, Venetia.'

Of course she knew what she meant. Darling Lottie was warning her not to put her foot in it. In fact she suspected that Lottie was hoping that she might cry off; insist that she mustn't intrude on their family party.

'Of *course* I know, sweetie,' she'd answered instead. 'What fun. I can't wait to meet her.'

So now she sat close to the wood-burner, gin and tonic at hand, chatting easily to Nick whilst Lottie laid the table in the breakfast room and Milo appeared from time to time fresh from his preparations in the kitchen.

'And *don't* eat all the nibblies,' he told them. 'Leave some for Matt and Annabel.'

Behind his back Venetia pulled down the corners of her mouth and made big eyes at Nick, inviting complicity.

He grinned back at her. 'We're all dying to meet Annabel,' he said. 'She and Matt should be here any minute.'

'An odd time to arrive from London,' observed Venetia. 'Lunchtime on Sunday.'

'Yesterday was her parents' wedding anniversary. One of those important ones that she couldn't miss. So she's come dashing down this morning on the train and has to go back tomorrow afternoon.'

'Quite long enough to discover whether we like her or not,' she said, pinching another small handful of crisps; they were simply so delicious she couldn't resist. She never bought them for herself: too tempting. 'I always know straight away, don't you?'

Nick looked thoughtful. 'No, not really,' he said at last. 'I often think I do but then I'm usually wrong. I'm not a very good judge of character, I'm afraid.'

'That's because you always expect people to be nice,' she told him. 'You want to like them. It's a great mistake to look for the good in people. So disappointing. Much better to believe the worst and then if something good does appear it's such a pleasant surprise, d'you see?'

He burst out laughing and she laughed with him. 'You are such a cynic,' he said. 'You're nearly as bad as my mother.'

She bit back the answer that sprang to her lips – 'Your mother isn't a cynic, she's just a bad-tempered cow' – and scooped up a few olives, keeping an eye open lest Milo should suddenly reappear.

'It's a pity that Im and Jules couldn't be here too,' she said. 'A real family party.'

Nick didn't reply and she glanced at him; he was biting his lip, frowning a little, and she sat up straighter, wondering if there had been some kind of row that she hadn't heard about yet.

'Rather overwhelming for Annabel, wouldn't you say?' Lottie had come out of the breakfast room and now she sat down beside Nick. 'I should think we'll be quite daunting enough as it is for the poor girl. I think I'll have that drink now, Nick. Yes, gin and tonic would be good, thanks. Are any of your lot down for Easter, Venetia?'

Milo reappeared before she had a chance to answer, which was a relief, because it was a bit embarrassing to admit to the fact that neither of her sons and their families had been down for a very long time. Of course, her house was tiny and it was a problem trying to fit them all in – but still . . .

The sound of an engine, car doors slamming, saved her from having to answer, and Matt was coming in, leading the way, followed by a very small dark girl who smiled sweetly as Nick and Lottie got up to greet them.

Venetia watched, not moving yet. The girl was quite pretty, she decided, though she'd never admired that tiny, dark-haired, simpering type. She disliked undersized women: too much like small dogs that were always treated as if they were sweet little puppies instead of the snappy, full-grown adults that they really were. She noted that Annabel was already playing the girlish part with Milo, bridling slightly and looking shy, whilst trying to keep Pud at bay by edging him away with her foot. And now Nick was exerting his charm, bending slightly from his great height, and Venetia wanted to laugh out loud at Annabel's expression that subtly acknowledged his attractiveness whilst hinting that she was already committed elsewhere otherwise she might be interested. Nick was looking flattered – a wonderful example of his lack of judgement of character – and asking about her journey. Annabel was answering, giving Pud another unobserved shove with her foot, taking a glass of wine from Matt and sending him a quick little glance that implied she was just the tiniest bit overwhelmed and needed his protection. He, however, didn't pick up the subtle signal.

Venetia took a deep, satisfying breath. One thing was certain: Annabel wouldn't do for Matt. She knew though, now, exactly how she would deal with her.

She saw that Lottie was watching her. Her lips were curved in a half-smile but her eyes were slightly narrowed as if she were warning Venetia to behave herself. Venetia beamed back at her – of course, darling Lottie never missed a trick – and got to her feet as Matt brought Annabel forward, saying, 'And this is Venetia.'

It was typical of Matt that he saw no need to

put Venetia into any kind of context for Annabel; as far as he was concerned no qualification was necessary. Venetia approved of that. She toyed with the pleasure to be had from the reaction of saying, 'I'm Milo's mistress,' but resisted out of her love for them all, although only Nick would have been really embarrassed. Instead she took Annabel's hand and murmured greetings. She could see that the girl wasn't the least bit interested in her but was prettily polite, briefly deferential, whilst her eyes darted back at once to Nick and Matt.

Venetia disliked being treated like an invisible old woman rather than a person in her own right.

'And this is Pud,' she said brightly. 'The most important member of the family. I hope you like dogs?'

For one blissful second Venetia saw an unguarded expression of irritation on Annabel's face, swiftly veiled as she bent down to the hopeful spaniel with insincere cries of delight. Venetia smiled triumphantly as she watched Annabel reluctantly stroking Pud and trying to look as if she were enjoying it.

'I can see he's taken to you,' she observed. 'Next thing he'll be sleeping on your bed.'

And then Milo came back to say that lunch was ready and Venetia swallowed the last of her gin and tonic and followed them into the breakfast room.

It was Lottie who showed Annabel to her room. She made all the right noises, grateful appreciation and amazed delight at the view, but after Lottie had gone she sat on the bed and allowed herself to relax for the first time since she'd got off the train. She felt quite exhausted by the effort she'd been making. Of course she'd known that it might not be that easy; after all, it was she who'd made all the running and edged Matt into a corner so that he'd finally invited her to meet his family. Even so, she'd believed that, once she was here, he would have been much more . . . much more what?

Annabel stood up and wandered over to the window. The view was pretty amazing, if you liked high bare hills and little square fields and stuff like that, but it wasn't really her scene. Still, she was prepared to learn to love it if Matt gave her the chance. And that was the trouble. He was still behaving as if they were friends, nothing more, and she'd hoped that once she was here, on his patch, the friendship would segue into a closer intimacy. She'd got off the train – and she'd known she was looking really good – and he'd been standing there, very sexy in dark grey jeans and a half-zip jumper over a rugby shirt, and he'd simply given her a kiss on the cheek; very cool, very contained. And even in the car she hadn't been able to force that sense of intimacy. She'd tried everything she knew to charm him and now she was feeling a bit foolish as well as cross because Matt simply wasn't playing up to her and she knew that back in London all her mates were waiting, holding their respective breaths, to hear how she'd got on.

She couldn't prevent a little grin of satisfaction when she remembered the reaction when she'd told them he'd invited her down to Exmoor.

'You have got to be kidding,' they'd said. 'Matt Lle*well*yn? How did you manage that?'

Well, of course everyone knew his reputation for privacy, the cat that walked by himself and so on; just as everyone knew that his well-known journalist father had been killed covering the wars in Afghanistan. But despite all the media coverage and the huge success of Matt's book and the film, he still managed to keep his personal life just beyond the reach of critics and journalists. So it had been a real triumph when she'd managed to arrange a few dates with him, generally after some book launch or at a literary festival.

Annabel frowned discontentedly: not that there had been much to write home about, to be honest.

Matt had very good manners and he was amusing but he'd stayed well on the side of friendship even after she'd made it clear that she'd like it to go much further. She was convinced, though, that by gentle pressure she'd get there in the end. She sensed that he wasn't particularly comfortable with women and she was sure that she could win him over simply by being around. He'd get used to her, begin to depend on her.

Actually, she preferred men like Nick: charming, flirtatious, easily impressed – but Nick wasn't an internationally bestselling author who'd made a stash of money with his first book. And, anyway, he was already married. During lunch she'd discovered that he had two children and a wife in London. It was a bit tricky trying to work out the scenario here. The old brigadier, Milo, was Nick's father, and Lottie was Nick's aunt, fair enough, but their relationship to Matt was all a bit woolly and she hadn't liked to be too inquisitive, and Matt had given her only the briefest of sketches. And then there was the old bat who'd shown her up about the damned dog. God, how she hated those tall, thin old women who looked like retired greyhounds. Who the hell was she, anyway? Not his mother, that was for sure.

She knew that Matt's mother had died recently

but, though she'd made one or two very tactful and sympathetic noises, he'd refused any kind of bait to draw him into talking about her. It was common knowledge that his mother had been an invalid for a long time and by the time his book had begun to top the bestseller charts she'd already been in a nursing home for ages. Annabel shrugged. At least she didn't have a doting mother to contend with, although she knew there was a sister that might be a bit of a challenge. From what she'd gathered so far, Matt and Imogen were quite close. It was a possibility that she and her husband might be coming over later on, someone had said. And there was a baby: Ruby? Rosie? Whatever, the baby might give her an opportunity to impress by doing the maternal bit, though she wasn't all that keen on screaming brats. Still, she had to find some key; some way of making Matt really *see* her.

Maybe a very slight flirtation with Nick might be one way; or even with Milo. He was still a good-looking old boy with a twinkle in his eye – but there was something else beside the twinkle: a hint of steeliness that made her suspect that he might not be quite a pushover. Lottie was easy, thank God; she could just talk publishing with Lottie. But even with Lottie there was that slight detachment that indicated she wouldn't be easily charmed.

Feeling frustrated, Annabel turned away from the window and began to unpack her overnight case, her brain turning and twisting; plotting and scheming.

CHAPTER TWENTY-TWO

By the time Annabel got back downstairs Nick had already set off for London and Matt was suggesting a walk with the dog. Lottie found Annabel's coat and she and Matt and Pud prepared to set off. Venetia watched the proceedings sardonically.

'Have a lovely time,' she called after them.

'Not very kind, darling,' Milo said, as the door closed behind them. He sat down by the fire and picked up the newspaper, pleased by the success of his lunch. Annabel had been very appreciative. 'You could see that the last thing she wanted was to go out.'

'I know,' said Venetia contentedly. 'I don't like her much, do you?'

'Pretty girl,' he said cautiously. She *was* pretty but some essential quality was missing though he couldn't quite define it. 'Not really my type, though. What do you say, Lottie?'

Lottie was staring into the fire. 'Odd,' she remarked. 'It's rather odd and very disappointing. I hoped that she might be a bit special but Matt certainly isn't all that keen and I really can't quite see why he's invited her down.'

'She's pushed him into it,' Venetia said promptly. 'You'll have to keep an eye on her.'

'Honestly, Vin,' said Milo uncomfortably. 'She seems a thoroughly nice girl.'

'"Seems",' repeated Venetia contemptuously. 'I tell you, she's after him and she means to get him.'

'I agree that she's keener than he is,' Lottie said, 'but Matt's old enough to look after himself.'

'No man is ever old enough to look after himself,' said Venetia. 'Not with a woman like that around. Trust me.'

Imogen and Julian arrived. Lottie saw that Jules looked faintly truculent; Im, carrying Rosie in her arms, glanced round quickly, half hopefully, half anxiously.

Lottie had already erected Rosie's playpen in the corner and now she held out her arms to her.

'What a pity you've just missed Nick,' she said, and saw Im's expression change to a mixture of disappointment and relief. 'Matt and Annabel have taken Pud for a walk but they'll be back soon. How are you, Jules?'

He smiled at her rather warily. He looked very strained and so tired that her heart gave a little tick of anxiety.

'I'm OK,' he said. 'Busy time of year. Lambing. You know?'

'I know,' she agreed sympathetically.

She put Rosie down in the playpen and they both watched as she began to examine the toys that were kept for her at the High House. Im was talking to Milo and Venetia now, and Jules, having glanced round at them, spoke in a lower voice.

'I wanted to say that I'm sorry about the Summer House,' he said. 'I hope to have a word with Milo later on. He must think I'm a bit of a wuss as well as very ungrateful.'

'He doesn't think anything of the sort,' Lottie said swiftly. 'He's the first person to understand that the job must come first and when we all thought about it properly we could totally see your point.'

Jules looked at her gratefully. 'Thanks, Lottie. It's very disappointing for Im, of course.'

He hesitated, looking so thoroughly miserable that she put her hand over his where it gripped the playpen's rail.

'Im will come to terms with it,' she said softly. 'Of

course it's a disappointment but she'll get over it. Has she seen the barn?'

He nodded. 'She liked it, actually. I knew she would. But even so . . .'

Rosie looked up at them, holding out a toy and making unintelligible Rosie-noises. Jules bent over to take the toy and Lottie gave his hand a squeeze and turned away to the others.

'I hope you're not being rude about Annabel, Venetia,' she said, 'and giving Im a totally false impression?'

Im turned, laughing. 'She says that the poor girl has designs on Matt.'

'And I told her that Matt can look after himself,' said Lottie. 'Ssh. I think they're back.'

'So what do you think?' Lottie murmured to Im, who had come into the kitchen to help make the tea.

'Predatory,' muttered Im. 'Putting on an act. Pity, isn't it? I hoped she might be special. She's very keen, though. Matt doesn't seem to be seriously involved.'

Lottie smiled to herself. 'You sound like Venetia. I don't think Matt's at all involved but I suppose there's always a danger.'

'I shall speak to him in a sisterly manner,' Im said. 'It won't be the first time.' She glanced around the narrow kitchen – at the gleaming work surfaces, the shelves with Milo's well-used cookery books, the wooden block with its dangerous cargo of shining knives. 'Milo keeps this place so clean,' she said. 'It's amazing.'

Lottie warmed the teapot and took the tea caddy from its place on the shelf. 'You know the old saying? "The navy protects the world and the army cleans it." Only, don't repeat it to Milo. Luckily I'm hardly allowed in his sanctuary except to make tea and coffee.'

Im chuckled. 'It's a good thing that you don't mind.'

'Mind? You're joking? Far from minding I encourage him to believe that I'm useless at everything culinary. It suits me splendidly. He won't even allow me to cut bread because he says I can't slice the loaf straight.'

'But you get on so well together.'

'That's because we don't interfere with one another in the areas that really matter to each of us. If he wants to choose the menus and organize the kitchen his way it's just fine with me. On the other hand I don't have to check with him as to when I see my friends or what I do, and he plays bridge and goes off shooting when he wants to, and we meet very happily on the common ground.

None of the third-degree stuff or criticisms that married couples have to put up with. I suppose that it's because we've never had the problem of sex to contend with, or all the emotional muddles that come with a sexual relationship.' Im stared at her, and Lottie smiled at her expression. 'Why is it that you and Jules are having such a problem about the Summer House? You both know it isn't the right thing but you're tearing each other to pieces over it. Why?'

Im looked away. 'It's just not that easy,' she mumbled defensively.

'Why not?' asked Lottie. The kettle boiled and she began to make the tea. 'Is it because you're muddling a perfectly straightforward, sensible decision not to buy the Summer House with your emotional responses? Perhaps you think Jules ought to be able to sympathize more with your disappointment and therefore he doesn't care about you enough. Perhaps he thinks you shouldn't need sympathy because you can see the decision is the right one, given his job, and so he thinks you're undervaluing him.' She paused, and when Im didn't speak, she added, 'And how does Nick come into it?'

'Nick,' began Im quickly. 'Well, Nick is—'

'Hi,' said Annabel from the doorway. She leaned against the archway, dainty and demure, whilst the two other women turned quickly to look at her. 'I wondered if I could help?'

'That's very sweet of you,' said Lottie. 'But as you can see there isn't really room. Even Im is in the way. Here.' She put the loaded tray into Im's hands. 'You take that and I'll bring the teapot.'

'Of course, my mother was an amazing woman,' Venetia was saying to Matt.

Milo and Jules had disappeared and Matt was sitting beside Venetia with Rosie on his lap. With Matt's help she held a large cardboard book adorned with bright, plastic buttons. When she pressed a button, a nursery rhyme jingle would play and, each time she pressed a button, she beamed at Matt with delight and expectation and he would obediently sing along to the nursery rhyme. Venetia was watching them both with amusement whilst undeterred from her own train of thought.

'I was telling Matt about my mother,' she told them, as the tea tray was unloaded. 'She had this quite unintentional gift of making people feel very special. It was simply a kind of social politeness, of course, but each person would imagine that she was really interested in him, or her, and everyone simply adored her. She found it quite amusing but occasionally rather wearing. She said that she ought to carry a placard which read: "I think you have mistaken me for someone who cares."'

Everyone laughed, except Annabel, who looked faintly shocked.

'Where's Jules?' asked Lottie. 'And Milo? Could someone tell them tea's ready?'

Im went out; she needed a moment to recover from Lottie's question about Nick. She guessed they'd be in the garden room but she didn't hurry. On the way to the High House earlier, Jules had told her that he was hoping for a private moment with Milo.

'I've never thanked him for offering us the Summer House,' he'd said. 'I'd like to do that. I expect he's pleased that Matt's going to buy it.'

'Yes, he is,' she'd answered. Glancing at him sideways, feeling a queer, almost painful stab of affection for him, she'd suddenly wanted to say something more; something that implied that she was coming to terms with it now.

And then he'd added: 'Well, thank God you like the barn. I knew you would once you'd made the effort to go and see it. If only you'd gone when I asked you to we might not have had all this fuss.'

And in that moment her love had switched to indignation so she'd only reminded him that Venetia knew nothing about the sale of the Summer House

241

yet; nothing more. Anyway, she'd been anxious about seeing Nick again and wondering how on earth they'd be able to behave quite naturally with everyone around. It had been almost a relief when Lottie told her that he'd already gone: almost, but not quite. A part of her was disappointed. The picnic had been such fun – and she'd been feeling good because she really had liked the barn . . .

She could hear voices, and here were Milo and Jules coming out of the garden room, so she called out quite naturally: 'Come on, you two. Tea's ready.'

Annabel watched the tea ritual with disbelief. She hadn't imagined that there were still people around who actually drank tea poured from a teapot using a tea-strainer and ate cake at half past four in the afternoon. And it was clear that this hadn't been done for her benefit: they all looked too used to it. She took a piece of cake with well-simulated delight – mentally adding up the calories with an inward shudder – and smiled at Lottie, ready with a compliment.

'Did you make this? It looks delicious,' and was disconcerted when Lottie burst out laughing.

'Good grief, no,' she said cheerfully. 'You need have no fear.'

242

'Lottie's cakes make excellent ballast,' Milo said. 'Do you like cooking, Annabel?'

'Oh, yes. Yes, I do.' She was flustered, because she wanted to impress him, to get him on her side, but was fearful in case he questioned her too closely. 'I just wish I had more time.'

She glanced about, seeking desperately for some distraction, smiled up at Im's husband – James, Jeremy? – and was relieved when he smiled back at her. He seemed rather a sweetie and she was pleased when he came to sit beside her. She remembered that he was a vet and, miraculously, she had a friend whose brother was a vet so she could probably manage to hold her own. Anyway, it was rather fun to sit next to this attractive man and pretend to be utterly absorbed in him, whilst Matt looked on. To be honest, she was rather bored by his 'Aren't I a good uncle?' act and the child was far too noisy and demanding.

Annabel smiled dazzlingly to cover the fact that she'd forgotten his name and asked, 'Are you mainly a small-animal practice or do you deal with large ones too?'

He looked rather surprised that she had any clue about his work, and quite pleased, and she leaned forward, just a little bit, so as to look really keen and interested. He began to explain but she didn't concentrate too hard, just enough to wing it, watching Matt from the corner of her eye, and waiting to make her next comment.

'It's just terrible, isn't it,' she asked, wide-eyed with distress, 'that the suicide rate is so high amongst vets? The pressure from manic pet owners and the travelling, and being called out at night and all that. A brother of a friend of mine, he's a vet, worked with a man who killed himself just before Christmas. Of course, he had the means to hand with all those drugs available but he left a wife with a young family. It was tragic.'

She glanced round, slightly surprised at the silence, gratified to see that everyone seemed to be watching and listening. She turned back to – what *was* his name? Julian. That was it.

'Do you have those problems down here, Julian? The practice I'm talking about was a very busy one in Berkshire. I expect it's a bit more laid-back down here.'

He hesitated for a minute, looking oddly embarrassed: she waited, watching him, keeping her face alert and interested.

'We're pretty busy too,' he said at last, almost reluctantly. 'Though we're not that big yet. There's just me and my boss and a nurse, but it's growing quite quickly.'

'Oh,' she cried sympathetically, 'but that can almost be the worst situation to be in, can't it? Too much work for the two of you but not quite enough to pay for a third person.' She touched his knee lightly, playfully. 'You'll have to be careful that you don't overdo it.'

She sat back to sip some tea, delighted with the reaction: the whole party seemed riveted, except for the wretched child, who had dropped her book and was now scrambling around over the sofa, though Matt wasn't paying the child any attention. It really did seem that, at long last, he was seeing her properly – obviously a bit peeved by her interest in Julian. Only the old bat, Venetia, didn't seem to be taking much notice. She'd obviously been following her own line of thought because, when she spoke, it was clear that she was still thinking about cakes and cooking.

'I must admit,' she was saying, 'that I agree with dear old Hugh Fearnley Eat-it-all that occasionally you can have too much of a good thing. My intentions are always good, and I get just so far with all the clever stuff, and then I think exactly like he does: "Sod it! Where's the corkscrew?"'

PART TWO

CHAPTER TWENTY-THREE

Matt stood on the veranda of the Summer House watching the rain pouring down. He was quite dry beneath the veranda roof and down here in the village, at sea level, even the rain felt surprisingly warm.

'You'll notice the difference,' Mrs Moreton had promised him. 'We always put our coats on if we're walking up to the High House to see the brigadier.'

Well, she was right. The Summer House was snug – and something more than that. Matt tried to analyse the odd sensation he had each time he came into the house. It was as if a welcoming presence embraced him and eased that long-familiar, deep-down loneliness. Living as he did for most of the time in the parallel universe that inhabited the world of his imagination, Matt had no problem in accepting this concept. He liked it. He knew instinctively that the presence went back beyond the

Moretons – though he could see that those gentle, kindly souls had added something of their own to the extraordinary atmosphere – beyond the happy picnic parties and family gatherings, to something in the more distant past.

Watching the rain slanting across the small emerald-green lawn, listening to the bubble and chuckle of the brook's voice, Matt stood well back beneath the veranda's roof. He took a deep breath, emptying his mind; waiting. All at once he felt wrapped about with peace, a sensation that until now had been almost unknown to him, and the joy of it was so great that tears pricked his eyes. The rain clattered on the leaves of the tree-tall rhododendrons but he was no longer aware of it: he was simply caught up in this healing sense of wellbeing. He stood in silence, accepting it.

Presently he straightened, looking around as if emerging from a waking dream, and turned back into the house. As yet there was very little furniture; after all, he was in no hurry and, anyway, he was waiting, giving himself the time to understand what he might need and to discover where he would work. Of this one thing he was now certain: that he would work on the new book here. This knowledge was exhilarating even if, as yet, he still had no clue as to what the book might be about. Just for now, he liked the empty spaces, the uncurtained windows, the lack of clutter. The glass doors on to the veranda let in airy volumes of green, watery light that reflected back from the pale painted wood-lined walls; at night, from the landing window above, he could see the wheeling stars: scattered icy fragments glittering in the soft black darkness. He walked from room to room, dwelling pleasurably on the elegant proportions, the way the sunbeams slanted across the polished oak floors, the scullery at the back of the house with its huge ancient stoneware sink, and the old-fashioned bathroom above it. He liked the pretty glass-fronted bookcases that were built into the alcoves on either side of the red sandstone fireplace in the sitting room, and wondered if this room was where he might work.

This overwhelming sense of ownership was new to him: and yet ownership was the wrong word here. It was as if he had always belonged; as if it were his rightful home, as natural and comfortable as his skin. He knew that everything that he put into the Summer House must be in tune with this feeling and he simply wouldn't be hurried. Milo had offered odd pieces from the High House which Matt had politely but firmly resisted: he was waiting, he'd said, to get the feel of it. He could see that Lottie understood – and Milo was too happy to know that the Summer

House was staying in the family to press it. And Im had been so busy moving into the barn and getting Rosie settled that she'd had no opportunity to hurry him either.

'It's lovely,' she'd said, walking round with him, making suggestions as to what he'd need. 'It really is. I'm still jealous – but actually I love the barn and, to be honest, it's a better layout for us. Anyway, I'd never have a minute's peace with the brook at the end of the lawn and Rosie just learning to walk. We'd have had to fence it right off, which would be a shame.'

She'd been in a rather odd mood for the last few weeks, ever since Annabel's visit, rather quiet and preoccupied, but she'd given him lots of sensible advice about curtains and furniture, and, though he'd listened to her suggestions, he'd taken no steps to implement them. The kitchen already had a built-in dresser along the wall opposite the old Rayburn, which had been converted to oil, and there was a fairly modern stainless-steel sink. The Moretons had left a sturdy oak gate-legged table and a handsome wooden carver which, they'd said, had been in the house when they'd moved in. He'd put these into the bay window at the other end of the kitchen, pleased to have some of the original furniture.

'You were right,' he'd said to Lottie, 'about me

being here. Though I never thought it would be like this. That I'd be buying the Summer House.'

'Neither did I,' she'd admitted. 'But I'm so glad that you're . . . peaceful here.'

It had been an odd word to choose: peaceful. But it was the right word. 'Happy' would have implied an ephemeral state. 'Peaceful' described this unfamiliar sense of wellbeing, as if something important and necessary were soon to be revealed to him and, meanwhile, everything was as it should be. Only Annabel continued to be a slight source of anxiety but she was tethered, luckily, by her job in London so that he couldn't be rushed into a relationship he might regret.

The further away she was, the more he liked her, and the fact that there was no mobile signal at the Summer House protected him even more. She knew now that he was buying a house in Bossington and was very keen to see it. He'd prevaricated and gently held her at bay, but soon she'd be down again. The trouble was that he couldn't make up his mind about her – and part of him was afraid of missing a wonderful opportunity. His friends told him that he'd never really know how he felt about a girl until he let himself go; took a few chances emotionally. But still he held back.

'There's something I don't know about myself,' he'd

said to Lottie, confusedly. 'Something important. And I simply can't make such a huge commitment until I know what it is.'

Being Lottie, she hadn't scoffed, or even questioned him; she'd merely looked thoughtful.

'I think you will know soon,' she'd said at last. 'Do you remember when we talked about it before, when I told you I believed that you needed to be here? Well, I think that the other thing will follow.'

He'd nodded. 'I'm beginning to believe it too, but I don't really know why – or how.'

'Wait,' she'd said, with that odd, far-seeing look of hers. 'Wait and be patient. I don't mean resignation, as in waiting for the rain to stop, or for the end of something over which we have no control because we imagine that, once it does, then, magically, life will be different. I mean the true patience that allows us to live fully in the moment and to be content to be where we are while we wait. And be prepared to confront a few demons.'

So that's what he was doing. He'd decided to go to London to bring a few things down from his flat to the Summer House, and he'd see Annabel while he was there to prevent her from making another visit to Bossington just yet, and so as to give himself a bit of breathing space.

'So what did you think of her?' he'd asked Im,

though he'd known that Annabel hadn't been a great hit with any of them. Even so, he intended to make his own mind up without letting that knowledge put pressure on him.

'She was putting on a bit of an act,' she'd answered candidly: he and Im had always been honest with one another in these matters. 'I didn't absolutely take to her.'

The trouble was, of course, that Annabel's observation about vets had rather hit home and poor Im had clearly been a bit knocked sideways by it. At the same time, it seemed to have made her think carefully about this rift between her and Jules. As far as Matt could see, she was making much more of an effort to come to terms with them not buying the Summer House and Jules was looking more like his old cheerful self.

'How will you use it?' Im had asked, turning the subject back to the house. 'Are you really going to live in it?'

'I think so,' he'd answered cautiously. 'I shall still spend time in London, of course, but I'm going to be here a lot.'

'Then you'd better buy some furniture,' she'd said in her practical way. 'And then you can give a house-warming party.'

Now, he stood in the hall, at the bottom of the

255

staircase, listening; staring at himself in the oval, gilt-framed looking-glass that hung there: another relic from the past. He imagined he could hear noises: footsteps in the kitchen; the swirl of a paintbrush in a jar of water; voices in the garden. He closed his eyes so as to hear them better and, suddenly, time seemed to arc backwards to his childhood. In his mind's eye he saw his own small face as in a mirror image, and he was being lifted, swung up high, and he was crying out in fear and loneliness.

His heart raced and stampeded and he opened his eyes, staring at himself again in the glass. He thought he glimpsed a movement behind him on the veranda and he turned sharply, but there was nobody there. He stood at the door, looking out into the rain-drenched garden, waiting, willing down the panic, and gradually the sense of peace gently took hold of him again. Matt took his jacket from where it hung over the banisters and, shrugging it on, he let himself out into the rain.

CHAPTER TWENTY-FOUR

The path led from the veranda round the side of the house to the walled area at the back. Here he could choose to walk past the open-fronted barns, used for cars and garden implements, along the drive, which wound through the avenue of walnut trees, or he could pass through the wicket gate that led through the kitchen garden into the grounds.

Matt chose the wicket gate. He closed it behind him and, with his head bent against the rain, he made his way around the path under the high walls. A blackbird perched briefly on the corner of the high cage that protected the soft fruit from his predations, his beak full of food for his babies; his sharp, gold-rimmed eye charted Matt's progress before he plunged into the curtain of ivy that grew over the red stone walls and camouflaged his nest hidden amongst the woody branches and sheltering leaves. Just here, by the greenhouses, purple violets grew in a glass frame and there were primroses under the wall. Matt breathed in the scents of newly dug earth and sappy, vegetative growth. He knew how hard Milo worked in the kitchen garden. It looked cherished, well-nourished; the vegetables stood in regimental lines. The grassy paths that cross-sectioned the well-filled beds were edged and mown with precision. At the further point, in the archway in the wall, Matt paused for a moment to give due homage to such effort.

'The weeds are too scared to grow,' Lottie told him. 'Poor Milo. He's going to miss Phil Moreton so much. Phil and Angela were very grateful to be able to have use of the garden and Phil always put in his fair share of hard work, especially since Milo's operation.'

'Perhaps I could help,' Matt had suggested tentatively. 'I'd like to.'

'Be very careful,' she'd warned. 'Milo is a slave driver and you've got a book to write.'

The path through the shrubbery was dank but Matt didn't mind the gloominess of the overarching branches of laurel; today he still carried with him the sense of that presence, never so vivid as when he was in the Summer House, but still here in the gardens. Perhaps it was merely the glint of sunshine on the dark green leaves or a shimmer of light through the rain; but it seemed to him that someone moved along these paths, sometimes glimpsed ahead through the sturdy network of branches, or, should he turn his head suddenly, on the turn of the path behind him just out of sight.

'Do you believe in ghosts?' he'd asked Lottie once, long ago.

'I think that wherever there have been truly strong emotions there will be echoes that remain,' she'd answered, rather obliquely. 'Your great-grandmother had the Sight so you've probably inherited the ability to connect to that. It can be an uncomfortable gift.'

Her matter-of-fact answer had reassured him; oddly it made certain things clear to him and he'd ceased to be anxious. How vital she and Milo had been to him: the odd couple. Dear old Milo, with his soldier's toughness informed by his love of poetry: the Great War poets, of course, but also the absurd: Lear, Carroll, Belloc.

Matt paused at the edge of the shrubbery, looking across the lawn to the bench beneath the lilac tree. He had a clear vision of himself when small, sitting on that wooden seat, his hand clasped in Milo's big one, listening to Milo reciting poetry: 'The Jumblies', perhaps, or 'Jabberwocky'. Milo had been best at reading the night-time story. He entered readily into the world that children inhabit and he could invest the poem or the story with such reality that Matt would cling to his arm, listening in terror as the terrifying Mr Brock was confronted by the cunning Mr Tod, or transfixed with delight by Peter Pan's entry into the Darling children's nursery. By the time he was six he could chant most of A. A. Milne's poems, bouncing on his bed with delight and shouting, "Butter, eh?" at the appropriate moment during 'The King's Breakfast', or repeating 'Disobedience', half in dread because he knew that James James Morrison Morrison Weatherby George Dupree's mummy was going to disappear for ever, and, of course, in a different way, this had happened to him.

As he stood beneath the dripping laurels, hot tears gathered in his eyes. His mother had disappeared just as surely as James's had: that happy, laughing woman who had played with him had vanished, leaving behind an unfamiliar person whose face was clenched with sorrow and whose despair disabled her. He grieved silently for her whilst the rain washed the tears from his cheeks, then he crossed the lawn and went into the house.

Lottie came out from the parlour as Matt came through the hall, almost as if she'd been waiting for him. She looked at him interrogatively, as if reading his recent experiences in his face, but he greeted her cheerfully.

'Milo has something for you.' She spoke quite low, almost warningly, and instinctively he lowered his own voice.

'What sort of thing?'

'I hope you're not giving the secret away!' Milo's voice boomed suddenly from the parlour, and Lottie quickly shook her head and squeezed Matt's arm. He followed her into the room where Milo stood, looking pleased with himself.

'I've been looking everywhere for these,' he said to Matt. 'Couldn't think where they'd gone. What d'you think of them?'

He gestured to the oval mahogany table and Matt moved further into the room to see what Milo had found. The shock was surprisingly intense. Standing together, some self-supporting, some resting on small lecterns, was a group of watercolours. At once he recognized the Summer House, though this was the original building: a single-storey pavilion with pretty pillars and long graceful windows. And here was an interior: the sitting room with its windows opened to the garden, the curtains moving in the breeze, a small marmalade cat curled in a low velvet-covered chair with curving wooden arms. In another, with a thrill of delight, he saw his drop-leaf table and the old carver chair exactly where he had placed them in the kitchen, with a jar of sweet peas standing on the table beside a trug full of fresh-picked runner beans. Another showed the veranda from the hall; a rocking chair looked as if it had just been vacated mid-rock, and a straw hat with pretty ribbons fluttering hung from the rail at its back. The sense of immediacy, the vividness that was inherent in the paintings, gripped Matt. He stared and stared in silent joy, and only when Milo moved suddenly just behind him did he startle back into awareness.

'They are utterly beautiful,' Matt said. 'They are exquisite. Where did you find them? I mean . . .' He shook his head, unable to articulate sensibly. 'Sorry, but they are just so perfect.'

'I knew I had them somewhere.' Milo was looking intensely pleased at Matt's reaction. 'I've been searching everywhere. And then I found them in the little dressing room off the spare bedroom. My mother must have hung them there. I think she thought that they were a bit old-fashioned and insipid. She liked oils.'

'But who painted them?' Even as he asked the question he knew the answer, and he saw that Lottie was watching him, and knew that she knew too.

'My great-grandmother had the Summer House

built so that she could paint in peace,' Milo was saying. 'She spent a great deal of time in it and there were all kinds of rumours that filtered down through the years. Some say that she had a secret lover – she was a great deal younger than her husband – and some say that she had a great tragedy in her life, and others say that she was just a recluse who liked to paint. Anyway, my great-grandfather designed it for her. He died at Bloemfontein. Poor fellow, he died of enteric fever before he ever got to fire a shot. And after that she practically lived down at the Summer House, so the stories go, and her son took over the estate. That was George, my grandfather. He was wounded in the Great War and died soon afterwards. Anyway, I wondered if you might like them.'

Matt stared at the paintings. 'I should love to have them,' he said at last. 'Thank you.'

'They are so fresh,' Lottie said softly. 'How she must have loved her little house.'

'Yes.' He couldn't take his eyes from them. 'And they shall go back there where they belong.'

'And,' said Milo, delighted by the success of his find, 'there's something else.'

Matt turned, almost warily. Anything else must surely be the most awful anticlimax – but no. There, half hidden by the sofa, was a low velvet-covered chair with curling wooden arms: the chair in the painting.

'It was in the same room with the paintings,' Milo told him, 'and I know you don't want anyone interfering with your plans but we thought you'd like this, seeing that it's in the painting there. It's obviously come from the Summer House.'

The rosewood glowed in the firelight though the dusty pink velvet was rubbed and worn. Matt stroked the scrolled wood with his finger. Milo and Lottie were watching him, sharing in his pleasure, and he smiled at the two of them: the odd couple. He couldn't think of anything to say in this emotional mood that might not reduce him to tears, and he saw Milo give Lottie a wink, a little nod, and murmuring about things he had to do, he went out. Lottie followed him and Matt was left alone.

CHAPTER TWENTY-FIVE

The puppy had found a wooden clothes peg. He sniffed at it cautiously at first, then, with growing confidence, he caught it in his mouth and pretended to worry it. He growled and shook it and dropped it again. A flurry of wind whirled around him, distracting him, and he pounced on a dead leaf, which disintegrated at the touch of his paw. He sat down in surprise and stared at the remains of the leaf.

Imogen laughed at him as she hung out the washing; the puppy was another good reason for being at the barn. There was plenty of room for him here, and he slept at night in a slate-floored utility room which was easily washed down when accidents occurred. When he was older there would be wonderful walks over Goat Hill and up to the Chains, and along the Tarka trail. He was a good little fellow; coming on well – and Rosie adored him.

Bab had almost been abandoned in favour of him: almost but not quite. When she was miserable or tired Rosie always reached for Bab to comfort her.

Remembering how she'd once imagined that Bab rather resembled Nick, Im made a little shamefaced grimace. Things were very much better between her and Jules but there were still odd moments when a text from Nick, or the sound of his voice, cheered her. He'd been her comfort blanket and she couldn't quite give him up. She reached for another garment, glancing over her shoulder to check that Rosie wasn't doing something she shouldn't. Another good thing about living at the barn was that the small garden was a very simple area of paving and grass. The holiday-makers had required only an area where they could have a barbecue and sit and look at the stark splendour of the surrounding moorland whilst they ate their charred sausages; and this suited Im very well. The dense beech hedge and sturdy gate kept both Rosie and the puppy in perfect safety and there were no flowerbeds to be dug up or to get muddy in: it was ideal.

On reflection, the Summer House would have presented a great many problems and she was surprised how glad she was, now, that she hadn't insisted on living there. And, of course, this was simply great for Jules, with the practice hardly ten minutes away.

He was delighted that she loved the barn so much and it had been rather sweet how he'd appeared with the puppy one evening, when she'd believed that she'd forfeited her chance to have him because of dithering about where they might live.

'They kept him for us,' Jules had said, holding out the squirming bundle. 'He's a house-warming present.'

Well, she'd been overwhelmed, of course, and swamped with love and guilt and remorse, and that night they'd made love for the first time for ages, whilst the puppy howled mournfully in his new bed, missing his mother.

It was rather nice having the Websters just down the track in the farmhouse. They were so sweet and kind, so delighted to have their favourite vet and his family in the barn, and they adored Rosie and spoiled her to bits, and Mrs Webster – Jane – was always ready to look after her for an hour or so, which was wonderful.

Im hung up the last garment and looked with delight across Goat Bridge to the moor, listening to the clear, bubbling song of a skylark. Below her, two pretty Exmoor Hornies balanced on a rocky outcrop, and she could see a herd of red deer browsing their languid way across the grassy slopes of Roosthitchen. The strong warm west wind was filling the washing; socks and shirts and jeans dancing on the line, yearning towards the Chains: toes pointing, arms outstretched, legs kicking. Behind her, Rosie squealed loudly: she'd crawled out on to the patio and the puppy was licking her face enthusiastically.

'What shall you call him?' Jules had asked – and Im had held the soft, warm bundle and put her cheek against his coat.

'I don't know,' she'd answered. 'Not yet. It's too early.'

So he was still 'Puppy' or Rosie's 'Gog-gog' because no proper name had yet suggested itself. She went to rescue Rosie, swinging her up high – and heard her mobile ringing inside the house. Guilt clutched at her heart: it was probably Nick. He was still looking to her for consolation, having found no comfort or resolution with Alice yet, and it was impossible to ignore him. After all, he'd been so sweet and understanding when Jules had been so unapproachable.

Carrying Rosie, the puppy dancing at her heels, she went in, through the utility room to the amazing interior of the barn: she still caught her breath at the sheer space, the high raftered ceiling, the great doors – now glazed – that had once admitted the wagons, and the big stone inglenook. She set Rosie down on the wooden floor and picked up her mobile: there was a voicemail.

'Hello, sweetie. Just wondering how you are. I'm missing you so much. No change here. Shall I make a quick dash down? It seems ages since I saw you and I expect you're more or less settled in by now, aren't you? Give me a buzz, darling. Make my day. Love you.'

Im put the phone down: she felt anxious. How could she say to Nick that her moment of madness was over: that he'd just been a handy emotional scapegoat? It was so heartless, so cruel. And, after all, the occasional affectionate message could do no harm, could it; just until he and Alice were settled again? Some tiny instinct warned her that it might; that it could be dangerous. She wavered, thinking about Nick and how lonely he was, shrugging away the warning.

Quickly she picked her mobile up again, and began to text.

'So has he got a name yet?' asked Jules, coming in and putting his laptop well out of Rosie's reach. He bent to stroke the puppy, who chewed at his fingers. 'Ouch! His teeth are like pins.'

Im laughed. 'He's a terrible chewer. We could call him "Jaws".'

269

'He ought to have a name. Don't they say that a baby should have a name straight away? Perhaps it's the same thing with puppies.'

'You think he might be psychologically damaged if we keep calling him "puppy"? Well, you could be right. Names are so important, though, aren't they? And you have to live with them for such a long time . . . if you're lucky,' she added. 'And it has to be something you can shout without sounding an idiot. Are you on call tonight?'

'No,' he answered thankfully. 'I can have a drink.'

He looked round happily at their new home; it was all working out just as he'd hoped and the puppy was a great success. He crossed the space of the big living room – Milo called it 'the atrium' – and put his arm around Im's shoulders and kissed her.

'I've been down at Brayford,' he told her. 'A difficult birthing with a mare but they're both OK now.'

Im's mobile rang, and she glanced at it quickly and then pushed it away from them across the table, turning her back on it and smiling at him.

'Answer it if you want to,' he said. 'Who is it?'

She made a little face, wrinkling her nose. 'It's not important,' she said. 'It can wait.'

He was surprised – it was unusual for Im not to answer her phone; a trickle of unease edged down his spine. 'But who is it?' he repeated. 'Is everything OK?'

'It's only Julie,' she said. 'She'll just be confirming a date I texted her earlier for lunch next week. I just don't want to get tied up with her now. Anyway, you haven't said hello to Rosie yet.'

'Where is she? Is she in bed already?' For some reason he still felt slightly uneasy, though he was glad that Im wasn't going to be tied up for ages talking to one of her mates. 'I thought it was a bit early for her bedtime.'

'She's not in bed, but she's in her bedroom. She's had her bath and her milk and now she's taken every single one of her toys out of the toy box and thrown them all over the floor and it looks like a tip. Come and see.'

She slipped her arm through his and hugged it slightly and he pressed it close against his side, too relieved to know that all was well between them to worry any more about the phone call.

'It's wonderful,' she was saying, 'to be all on one level. I thought it would be a bit odd at first but it's great not to have to worry about Rosie on the stairs. And I love the bedrooms with the rafters and the odd-shaped windows. It's like being in Matt's attic.'

She let go of his arm and led the way down the

short passage into the tiny hallway outside the two bedrooms and the bathroom. She pushed the door to Rosie's bedroom further open and stood back to let him see. The scene was one of chaos. Every soft toy and all her books were piled in one heap and Rosie lay amongst them all, with Bab clutched to her chest and sucking her thumb.

'She'll be falling asleep if we're not careful,' Im said. 'Come on, Rosie. Come and say hello to Daddy. He'll read you a story.'

'Hi, Rosie.' Jules bent to pick her up. 'What a mess you've made. Shall we tidy up a bit?'

Rosie screwed her face up, as if she might protest, then she reached out and seized a piece of his hair to twiddle. She put her thumb back in and her eyelids drooped sleepily.

'She's nearly asleep,' Im said. 'Look, put her into her cot and read to her until I've tidied her room up. Here, give her Bab or she'll fuss.'

He put the unresisting Rosie into her cot, covered her with her quilt and gave her the rabbit.

'He was one of your better buys, this rabbit,' he said to Im. 'Funny how she's taken to him and takes no notice of some of the others, isn't it?'

'Mmm,' said Im, kneeling on the floor, sorting toys and books, hair falling forward over her face.

'Here you are, Jules. Read this one until she drops off.'

And so he perched on the chair beside the cot and began to read *The Very Hungry Caterpillar*.

CHAPTER TWENTY-SIX

Venetia towelled her hair dry, peering at herself in the steamy glass over the wash basin, pausing to pull her warm bathrobe more closely around her. She wound the towel into a turban over her hair and stopped to admire the effect. It was rather flattering; the lilac-blue towel against her skin. The severity of it made her look rather beautiful, even without any make-up. She smiled at herself, gave her mirror-image the tiny, private wink that somehow excited her: 'Go, girl,' she murmured, and drained the last of the wine in her glass. She'd been feeling a bit odd today, a bit dizzy and rather shaky, but a long scented soak in the bath had reinvigorated her, and the wine had steadied her and lifted her spirits.

In her adjoining bedroom she pushed her narrow feet into warm sheepskin slipper-boots – rather like Lottie's Uggs but not nearly so clumpy – and went out on to the landing still carrying the glass. She would pour herself another little drink and think about some supper before she dried her hair. Standing for a moment at the landing window, looking down into her pretty little garden in the last of the early evening light, she thought with pleasure of the summer ahead and jolly lunches out there in the sheltered courtyard.

At the top of the stairs she felt dizzy again; she stumbled a little, her hands flew out and the glass smashed against the banister; she gave a cry of fright and fear, and overbalanced, toppling and bumping down the steep narrow staircase.

Some time later she opened her eyes on to darkness and was at once aware of an agonizing pain in her ankle and in the arm that was doubled under her. How cold it was. She tried to remember what had happened and was filled with anguish and a terrible fear. She moved gingerly and the pain stabbed so viciously that she cried out. She lay still. Her head was wrapped in something sodden and heavy and cold – her face and her neck felt wet. Why should they be wet? Dimly the hall swung into focus around her and, slowly, all the previous events clicked into place. She'd washed her hair and had a bath and then she'd fallen – but how long ago? Willing down panic, she tried to edge herself along the hall floor. Every movement was agony and she was obliged to stop every few seconds to rest.

In the sitting room the telephone began to ring; she listened to it, biting her lips, weeping with frustration.

'Please,' she cried, 'help me,' and wept again at her stupidity: nobody could hear her. She lay still, feeling the deathly cold creeping around her, trying to cover her icy limbs with the bathrobe, wincing with pain. Presently she lay still, trying to think what she could do. Even if she could get to the front door, how would she manage to kneel up to unlock it and then open it to cry for help? She must try: she mustn't spend all night on the hall floor, and who knows when anyone might come to find her?

'Milo,' she muttered, her cheeks wet with tears. 'Milo. Help me.'

Crying with pain, she began to force herself along again, inching towards the front door and the oblong edge of light that was cast across the floor from the half-open kitchen door, and then the pain overwhelmed her and she fainted.

When she came to, the telephone was ringing again. Perhaps it would be more sensible to try to get to the phone: it was further away but at this time of the evening – what *was* the time? – it might get better results than lying on the doorstep and calling for help. That was assuming that she could manage to lift the phone and dial for an ambulance. One leg dragging painfully, her left arm useless, she continued the slow progress, praying for help.

Lottie put down the telephone and looked at Milo. His irritation was apparent, the remote held at an expectant angle that indicated that he was waiting to continue with his DVD.

'There's still no answer,' she said, puzzled.

'She might be out to supper with one of her chums,' he said. 'She does go out, you know. Why are you being so twitchy?'

Since early evening Lottie had been restless; rather silent over supper, unable to concentrate on the film that Milo had chosen for their later entertainment, picking up her knitting and putting it down again. Matt was watching her.

'Shall I dash into Dunster?' he suggested. 'Just see if she's OK?'

'Oh, really,' said Milo crossly, drawing in his long legs, preparing to get up. 'If anyone does any dashing it had better be me. But what if she *is* out? What then? Are you going to track down all her friends to see where she is?'

'I'm sorry, Milo.' Lottie came to sit down again. 'It's just a feeling I've got. And it's quite late. Nearly

277

eleven o'clock. I don't think that Venetia and her friends have such late nights these days.'

'Oh, very well.' He allowed them to see his resignation. 'You'd better come with me, so that *you* can be the one to explain exactly why we're waiting for her when she gets home. Or waking her up if she's decided to have a nice early night.'

'I *shall* come,' said Lottie, ignoring his sarcasm. 'She said this morning when she phoned that she was feeling a bit light-headed. Perhaps she isn't well and has gone to bed. But she's got a phone beside her bed . . .'

'Oh, come on,' he said impatiently. 'If we're going let's get on with it. Where's her spare key?'

'In the usual place. On the hook in the hall.' Lottie bundled her knitting away and grimaced at Matt. 'I shall feel such a fool if she's having an early night,' she said.

'It's better to make sure,' he said reassuringly.

She nodded. 'See you later. I'm coming,' she shouted to Milo, who was roaring some instruction from the hall. 'See you later, Matt.'

He'd fallen asleep, and wakened with a shock when the telephone rang.

'Oh, Matt.' Lottie's voice was tremulous. 'She'd fallen down the stairs. A broken arm and ankle and

278

some cuts to her hand. We're in Minehead Hospital and she's OK now but very shaken. She looks so frail, it's heartbreaking. She wept all over Milo and practically had hysterics when we arrived but she's been so brave. She was lying in the hall, absolutely freezing with her hair all wet. Poor Venetia.'

'Thank God you went,' he said. 'She might have been there all night. I bet Milo was horrified to think he nearly didn't go.'

'Well, he was.' Lottie's voice sounded as if she were smiling. 'You know that thing people do when someone they love is hurt. When he saw her there all crumpled up in the hall he practically shouted at her but she didn't seem to mind. I went with her in the ambulance and she told me that the worst thing was Milo and the ambulance men seeing her without her make-up on and her hair in rat's-tails.'

Matt was smiling now. 'I believe you,' he said. 'That sounds so like Venetia. How she'd hate to be caught at a disadvantage, poor old love.'

'Well, they've bandaged her up and sedated her, and they'll be doing some other tests tomorrow. We're on our way home, darling, but don't wait up.'

He put the telephone down and stood up, stretching. The fire was practically out and he was cold. He crouched down before the wood-burner, building up the fire with small twigs and then bigger logs so that it would be warm when they got back. He was remembering an incident from his schooldays in Blackheath, when he'd fallen off one of the climbing bars and concussed himself, and Lottie had suddenly appeared before there'd been time for anyone at home to be notified.

'I was just passing,' she'd said, 'on my way to a meeting just round the corner.'

Matt sat back on his heels, watching the flames and lost in memories, and then he heard the car's engine as it came up the drive and he got up and went out to meet them.

CHAPTER TWENTY-SEVEN

He still couldn't decide where to hang the paintings. He'd brought them all down to the Summer House and now he stood in the kitchen, by the table in the window where he'd arranged them, and studied them. They were even more magical now that they were here in the house, but he knew that until he was living here he wouldn't know where each one should be hung. Meanwhile he gloated over them, marvelling at the delicacy and beauty of the colours and at the evocation of a spring and summer long ago.

'There are others,' Milo had told him casually, 'but I've no idea where they'd be. These were probably the only ones worth framing.'

His words had sent Matt into a frenzy of desire for the other paintings and he'd begun a systematic search of the High House in between moving some furniture into the Summer House. His sense of belonging was very strong today: as if he were moving closer to the unlocking of the mystery that was at the core of his inner loneliness. He stepped back from the table and wandered out into the hall and on to the veranda, wondering how it would have looked all those years ago. The rhododendrons and azaleas would have been small shrubs in those days, planted so as to edge the small square of lawn that had once been a rough, grassy corner of the meadow. Here and there, growing in sheltered corners of the lawn, the delicate pinky-mauve lady's-smocks were a reminder of that meadow.

He crossed the grass and stood looking down into the brook: not much change here. The marsh marigolds would have been casting their richly gold reflection in the water then, and the stiff, brittle rushes would have been rustling in the little shivering breeze; and the long green tresses of weed that floated beneath the surface might have reminded her, as they did him, of Ophelia, clasping her 'fantastic garlands', drifting and drowning in the weeping brook. There was even the willow on the bank – several willows – growing aslant the brook. A low wall separated the lane from the brook and, by crouching on his heels and making a frame with his hands, he believed he could recognize a section of the wall and a stretch of the water from one of the paintings.

'What was her name?' he'd asked Milo, and he'd answered: 'Helena.'

And that in itself had been another shock. Standing now, with his hands in his pockets, Matt stared down into the fast-flowing brook: the connections were being made and he felt excited and scared in equal parts. This young woman, Helena, had had a son and a daughter; then her husband had been killed in a war. So she'd closed herself away in her Summer House, grieving and painting, but not, as far as he knew, succumbing slowly to drink as his own mother, Helen, had. No, Helena had worked out her grief in the paintings to such a successful extent that she'd left a strong impression of tranquillity in her little house. Yet that was not quite all. He had a very strong instinct that there was something more: something to be finished.

He raised his head, listening. A vehicle was coming slowly along the avenue towards the house. This would be the delivery van with some furniture on board: a double bed and a big comfortable sofa and one or two other things. He crossed the lawn at a run and went round the side of the house to meet them. They were pulling in beside the barns, waving cheerfully back; climbing out.

'Hi,' he said. 'This is great. Come and have a look round. I think you may have to bring it all in through the veranda. The back porch is a bit small.'

Several hours later the bed had been erected in the biggest room, over the kitchen, and the long, deep sofa set opposite the fire in the sitting room. On the veranda stood a curving, high-backed wicker chair, shaped like half an egg; its twin had been put in the hall. He'd made the men coffee and given them biscuits, and he'd enjoyed this first occasion of playing host in the Summer House, even in this very simple way, and basked in their compliments.

Once they'd gone he stood by the window, looking at the paintings, allowing the silence to settle again. A thrush was singing in the lilac tree and Matt turned his head to listen to the magic of its song. He could just see the pale speckled breast amongst the heavy purple blossoms and, quite suddenly and unexpectedly, he had a strong mental vision of Selworthy Church, shining white against the hill, set all about with trees. The vision drew him and held him, and then the thrush fell silent. As if released from a spell, Matt turned back into the kitchen and began to wash up the mugs and clear away the remains of the little picnic.

*   *   *

284

Back in the attics at the High House he resumed his search for the rest of the paintings.

'There ought to be hundreds of them,' Milo said. 'She spent years down there, painting away, so the stories go. Of course, a lot of them might well have been ditched.'

There was certainly none hanging on any of the walls and so Matt began systematically to check out all the rooms; all the chests; every drawer, every cupboard – but there was nothing. Across from his own rooms there was another big attic, and now at last he stood amongst the rejects of generations and looked rather helplessly around him. Yet he felt driven, confident that there was more evidence, and he wasn't particularly surprised when he finally found the two big portfolios lying together beneath papers and photograph albums at the bottom of a battered chest of drawers. He drew them out with a kind of exultation and laid them gently on the scored and dusty top of the chest. They were bound with tape, which he undid carefully. He saw at once that he was right, that these were more of the paintings, and though he longed to examine them at once he felt that it was only proper to show his find to Milo first.

*   *   *

As he came downstairs he could hear their voices: Milo and Lottie talking about Venetia. Matt held the portfolios firmly but gently to his chest, rather as though they were beloved children who needed his protection, and went into the parlour.

'We must invite her, at least,' Lottie was saying. She was sitting on the sofa all amongst her knitting as if she were perching in a big soft nest. 'She won't be able to drive so I can't imagine how she'll manage her shopping. Of course, she might not want to come but surely she can't go back to that little house all on her own. How could she look after herself properly?'

Milo sat in the high-backed wing chair; his long legs in old moleskins were crossed, showing a glimpse of red sock. Pud was curled at his feet.

'I'm not quite heartless,' he said rather crossly, glancing briefly at Matt as he came into the room. His eyes rested for a moment on the packages clasped in Matt's arms and his eyes creased a little in a smile before he looked again at Lottie. 'Of course she can come here if she wants to, *but* – and this is important – *but* only if you think you can cope, Lottie. It won't be easy.'

'I realize that.' Lottie, too, looked round at Matt. 'We're talking about Venetia,' she said. 'I think she ought to come here when she's let out of hospital but Milo's a bit worried about it.'

'*Not*,' said Milo defensively, 'because I don't want her here but simply that I'm worried that we can manage. She's going to need a lot of looking after. She's had a very bad shock, apart from her injuries, and she's very weak. It's a lot to take on.'

'I know it is.' Lottie looked anxious. 'But we'll have help, you know. I think they call it a package of care, or something. But there are those two little rooms with the shower that Milo's mother had when she couldn't manage the stairs any more. I think we should offer them to Venetia.'

Milo shrugged. 'That's fine with me. As long as you've thought about it carefully. It'll fall much more on you than on me.'

'I know. What do you think, Matt?' She smiled at him, and then saw the packages. 'Oh! Have you found them?'

He nodded, still holding the portfolios. For some reason he didn't want to look at them now; not publicly. He wanted to wait and savour them. It seemed that Milo understood this because he made no attempt to take the packages but simply looked at him with affection and a faint bafflement. It was clear that he regarded Matt's passion for these watercolours as an odd but charming whim.

'That's good,' was all he said. 'Let us know if there's anything worth seeing.'

But Lottie was watching him with a warm sympathy, and he nodded to her as if answering a question, laid the portfolios down on a little table and prepared to join in the discussion about Venetia.

CHAPTER TWENTY-EIGHT

It was late evening before Matt had a chance to examine his find. He didn't mind: some part of him was glad to postpone the moment of discovery – and to prolong the sense of anticipation. Instead of hurrying away, he set himself to concentrate on the immediate proposition: whether or not Venetia should be offered a temporary home at the High House. He sat down between Lottie on the sofa and Milo in his wing chair, rather like a spectator at a tennis match, alternately shocked by Milo's outspokenness and touched by Lottie's concern for the brigadier's mistress.

'It'll probably be the thin end of the wedge,' Milo was prophesying gloomily. 'Once she's got her feet under the table we'll never be rid of her. You realize that?'

'I think you're being too dramatic.' Lottie refused

to be daunted. 'She loves her little house and she won't be nearly so comfortable here.'

Milo brightened a little. 'That's true. A few days of your ministrations and she'll probably be begging to be allowed home.'

Lottie burst out laughing but Matt was rather shocked, and defensive on Lottie's behalf.

'What do you mean?' he asked rather indignantly.

'My dear fellow,' Milo glanced at him indulgently, 'remembering my experience at her hands after I'd had my operation I can tell you that I'd rather be nibbled to death by ducks than be nursed by Lottie again.'

Matt looked at Lottie to see if she had been hurt by Milo's comments but she'd gone off into another fit of laughter.

'You had a lovely nurse for most of the time,' she reminded him, 'and I did all the bits round the outside, but I agree that nursing is not my thing. I'm rather clumsy and I get distracted and forget the most basic things. Poor Milo. You were very long-suffering. Don't look so indignant, Matt. It's very sweet of you to leap to my defence but I know my shortcomings. It's just lucky for you and Im that you were such healthy children. However, I'm sure that Venetia will have plenty of the right sort of nursing care. It'll be company that she'll need, and lots of

TLC. I'm quite good at that. And so are you, Milo, in short bursts.'

He groaned, but Matt could see that despite his protests he was quite prepared to agree to Lottie's plan. Matt was relieved; he didn't want to think of Milo as a callous man, even though he'd seen plenty of evidence of the older man's toughness. He preferred to continue to believe that, deep down, Milo was a bit of a pussycat. After all, his love and kindness to all of them had been boundless, and it was clear that Venetia adored him.

'Well,' Lottie was saying now, picking up her knitting, 'I've told you what I think and now it's up to you, Milo. After all, it's your house and your mistress.'

This time it was Matt who laughed: they truly were the odd couple. Milo stuck out his long legs and crossed his arms over his chest whilst Lottie placidly knitted a row or two of Nick's jersey.

'Poor old darling,' he said meditatively. 'She's a terrible sight. Black and blue all over, and no slap or "lippy" to cheer her up. Well, let her come here if she wants to, but we must make certain that there's a proper care package, Lottie. I'm not going to give her bed-baths or cut her toenails. Those ghastly stories she's told me about Clara make my blood run cold and I'm not being responsible for anything of that nature.'

'Oh, stop fussing and go and make some supper,' Lottie told him. 'I'm starving. We'll talk to the hospital staff tomorrow and make certain that everything will be in place.'

Milo got to his feet with a sigh and winked at Matt. 'Any problems and I'll be down with you at the Summer House, just so you know.'

He went through the breakfast room into the kitchen and Lottie looked at Matt.

'Annabel phoned,' she said. 'She's having a problem contacting you on your mobile, she said. She was wondering if you were OK. I told her that you were down at the Summer House. I'm glad you've told her about it and that we don't have to keep it a secret any more.'

Matt hunched a shoulder, pulled a face. 'I just didn't want to be crowded,' he said almost irritably. 'It would have been difficult to refuse to take her down and show it to her, wouldn't it? And I wasn't ready for it.'

Lottie nodded, finished a row, and turned the knitting. 'I know exactly what you mean. It was such a special moment, wasn't it, and you wanted to hug it to yourself for a bit before you could share it. Rather like those paintings.'

292

He looked at her quickly. 'I hope Milo didn't mind. I know it's weird but I just want to have a moment to look at them without anybody else around.'

'Milo doesn't mind a bit. Why should he? I think he's rather pleased that you're so taken with them. Shall you phone Annabel before supper? Do you want to invite her down again?'

He shook his head. 'Not yet. I'm going to London next week to pick up a few things from the flat and I'll meet up with her then. I want the Summer House to be pretty much up and running when she sees it so that she doesn't get any false ideas, if you see what I mean?' He got up. 'But I'll go and speak to her now and tell her that I'll see her in London. Give me a shout if I'm not back when supper's ready.'

Later, in his attic, Matt undid the tape and slid the paintings out on to his bed. They were all quite small, some no bigger than three inches square, but as he examined the larger ones he saw at once that the mood had changed. There was a difference in the light and shade; a subtle poignancy, even melancholy, that was missing in the paintings that were now at the Summer House. He bent over them, studying them closely, and wishing he knew more about painting. How had she managed, for instance, to give the impression that some sorrow had touched her? Here was his kitchen table again, but now the flowers in the jar drooped a little and a few petals lay on the polished surface; the trug was missing but a toy engine stood in its place, turned on its side and neglected by its owner. Here was the velvet-covered chair but this time there was no marmalade cat curled comfortably on its seat; instead, a teddy bear lolled against the cushion, once again giving the impression of abandonment.

Yet here was a painting of the child: a small boy. Matt seized it eagerly, turning it towards the light. The child crouched in a puddle of sun on the veranda, concentration visible in every line, a blond thatch of hair falling over his eyes. He wore a sailor suit and the little wooden engine was in his hands. Matt picked up another one: this time the child was sitting in the chair on the veranda, the teddy bear clasped in his arms. Beyond him in the shadows of the hall there seemed to be another figure, so lightly sketched that Matt wondered if he were mistaken. He peered at it closely: surely it was another child there in the shadows? He picked up the other painting and looked at it again. Yes, there in the trees was another small figure. Was he hiding from the little boy who played with his engine in the sunshine? Matt was strongly reminded of his own child hero whose *alter ego* remained in the shadows, yet protected him.

Disturbed, excited, he examined the paintings. Some were simply beautiful little sketches of minutiae: a branch of flowering blackthorn, a clump of purple honesty; pussy-willow buds bursting, fuzzy and diaphanous against a bright blue sky. Helena's touch was sure and confident, and he began to plan where he would hang these perfect evocations of a cold, sweet spring more than a hundred years old. He would keep these smaller ones in groups – but these with the children, where would he put them?

Here was a study of Selworthy Church, and a sketch of part of the churchyard by the west wall, and another of the chapel at Lynch; here was a portrait of the child, his eyes wistful, and here were some studies of the garden still in its early stages: small bushes of rhododendrons and azaleas, now as tall as trees, which had been planted to form the hedge, and a little shrub of a lilac tree, in whose branches earlier today he'd seen the thrush. Matt riffled through his treasures with delight but with a growing awareness that something was being asked of him. It was as if he were being posed some question whose answer would be crucial to him. Carefully he packed them all back into the portfolios, pausing to look again at the paintings of the little boy.

He kneeled at the low window, gazing out into the clear night. Away in the west a waning moon lay on its back, swinging low over the sea, its cold, silvery light spilling into the choppy black water. He could just make out the roof of the Summer House amongst the trees below him and he felt a thrill of excitement at the prospect of his first night in the house. He wanted it to be a special occasion, yet couldn't quite think of how to make it so: but he knew that it was important, and that once he'd made the Summer House his home nothing would ever be quite the same again.

CHAPTER TWENTY-NINE

'I was remembering way back when Lily was born,'
Nick said, 'when we were having another really bad
night with her. We hadn't slept for weeks and we
were both exhausted. Well, Alice had fed her and
put her back in her cot but we hadn't got to the
door before she was screaming again. And I lost it
and said something really rude and Alice just stared
at me in shock and horror and she took Lily out of
her cot and said, "Don't swear in front of her," or
something like that, and stood holding her as if Lily
needed protecting from me. And I felt awful, as if
I'd done something really bad, and I said "Sorry"
a few times. And then she looked at Lily and said,
"It's all right. We forgive you." And, you know, that
was the very first time that "We" didn't mean me
and Alice any more. It meant her and Lily, and I'd
been excluded, and suddenly I felt terribly alone,
as if the balance had changed for ever and I was on

a different side from my wife and my child. I felt like an outsider. And that's what's happening again now.'

Imogen quickly switched her mobile phone from her right hand to the left, shoulder hunched, trying to prepare Rosie's lunch with the other hand. Rosie sat in her high chair, watching her.

'Of course, the girls don't know exactly what's happened,' Nick was saying. 'But they know that Daddy's been silly again and the three of them look at me with that slightly disapproving, slightly resigned expression, as if they're all simply tolerating my presence until someone better turns up. Actually, I think the girls are simply rather enjoying the fact that Daddy is getting some of the treatment Alice reserves for them when they've been naughty, but it's really getting me down.'

Im made a sympathetic noise and began to mash the vegetables and potatoes together.

'I wish I could see you, Im, I really do. I think that you're the only person who's ever really been on my side and never made me feel like a loser. Listen, Alice wants us to go down to Rock for the Bank Holiday; one of her friends has a cottage there. I could make a dash over to see you. Damn, the phone's ringing. I'll call you back.'

She switched off her mobile with relief, feeling

anxious and guilty. How could she tell Nick that, for her part, the brief resurrection of passion had been simply an immature desire to get her own back on Jules because of his cavalier behaviour over the Summer House? It would be so cruel to hurt Nick now, when he was still suffering humiliation at Alice's hands. Im groaned. The fact was that she and Jules had survived their dangerous moment; they'd reconnected, and now they were settling happily into the barn.

She spooned the mashed vegetables on to Rosie's plate. It must be possible to hold it all together for a little bit longer; just until Alice had decided that poor Nick had suffered enough and could be forgiven. When her mobile rang again she picked it up with misgivings and saw with relief that it was Lottie.

'Just to ask a favour,' she said. 'Venetia's settled in and all's well, but if you felt you could come and provide a bit of light relief sometime we'd be very grateful. The poor duck is frustrated by her inability to be able to do much, so a different face is a wonderful distraction. Matt's gone to London for a few days but you probably know that. How about lunch tomorrow? Yes? Fantastic. See you whenever you can make it in the morning, then. Love to Rosie.'

Im sat down beside Rosie, put the plate on her tray and gave her a spoon.

'Now,' she said, 'let's try to get as much food in your mouth as we do over your face and the tray, shall we?'

Rosie turned the spoon over carefully, examining the ducks on the plastic handle. 'Guk,' she enunciated with conviction.

'Duck,' agreed Im. 'Now, try some of this lovely lunch. Look, the puppy wants some. Better eat it all before he gets it.'

Rosie leaned out of her highchair to see the puppy, who was sitting, gazing up hopefully.

'Gog-gog,' she cried.

'Yes, dog-dog. Puppy. We simply must give him a name. What will it be? I'll know it soon, I'm sure of it. Come on, Rosie. Eat up your lunch. Tomorrow we shall be having lunch with Lottie and Milo and Venetia, and I want them to see how clever you are.'

After lunch Lottie took a broom and some cloths in a bucket of hot soapy water and strolled through the garden to the little octagonal wooden chalet to give it its annual spring-clean. The windows were streaked and dirty and, inside, spiders' webs were strung across the panes and in the dark, high

300

corners of the pointed roof. The two wrought-iron chairs and small round table were lightly filmed with dust, and a faint odour of damp rose from the faded, threadbare rug.

Lottie opened the door wide and dragged the rug out on to the grass. Here in the shelter of the beech trees it was hot, and she shook the rug and left it to air in the sunshine. The chairs and table were too heavy, too unwieldy to move, so she wrung out a cloth in the clean soapy water and wiped them over carefully. She struggled with the windows, which were swollen with damp and difficult to open, but she managed them at last, fixing their catches, watching the spiders hastening, long-legged, to safety. She liked to make certain they were all out of the way before she took the broom and began to destroy their webs with the usual pangs of guilt.

'It's someone's home,' she'd protest when Milo scoffed at her reluctance. 'And spiders catch flies, don't forget.'

Now, she wiped all around the panes, shaking the duster out of the windows before changing it for a wet one. Soon the windows were gleaming, the floor swept, and she paused in the doorway, listening to the clamour of birdsong and watching the swallows that returned each spring to nest in the barns down by the Summer House. Matt had asked her to open the veranda doors for a few hours each day, to check the house over whilst he was away, and she was both touched and amused by his care for it. They'd gone together to Pulhams Mill at Brompton Regis to talk to Ian about making some furniture, some special pieces, and Matt was very excited at the result. It was clear that he knew exactly what he wanted and was prepared to wait for it.

It was hot, the thick, heady scent of the lilac drifting in the air; she grew aware of the presence of bygone occupants of the garden, and she wondered what Matt had discovered in those portfolios: as yet she hadn't seen them. She knew that he was waiting, and she had no intention of pressing him.

'I'm starving,' Venetia said, sitting in the sun in the garden room, her left foot in plaster resting on a stool, her right arm in its sling. 'It's funny, isn't it, that I should be so hungry all the time? After all, I'm taking very little exercise.'

'It's boredom,' Milo told her. 'Mealtimes give an important structure to the day when you're convalescing. It's only half past three, so you'll have to wait a bit until teatime. Can't have you getting fat.'

She stretched her thin hand to him and he took

it, noticing the transparent skin, the blue veins and the brown, blotchy freckling. Quite suddenly he realized how dull the world would be without Venetia; without her courage and gaiety and her eye-wateringly barbed comments. His hand tightened over hers, and he touched her fingers very briefly to his lips. They sat in silence for a moment, both pretending nothing particular had happened, each silently acknowledging the need and love they shared.

'Think of all the Brownie points you're clocking up on your afterlife insurance for taking me in,' she said, not looking at him. 'Jesus will definitely want you for a sunbeam. But I say my prayers too, you know. To begin with, I thank God that you're such a good cook, darling. Lottie's an absolute sweetie but she does rather live in a world of her own, doesn't she?'

'She's not practical,' he admitted. He couldn't quite think of how to describe his feelings for Lottie. She'd saved him from loneliness and occasionally from despair, and he couldn't quite imagine life without her, either. Yet how different these two women were; and how lucky he'd been to have their loyalty and affection.

'She's got something else, though,' Venetia was saying. 'Something special. We need Lottie.'

'Yes,' he said gratefully. 'We need Lottie. Look, here she comes. We could have an early cup of tea, I suppose. She'll need it after pushing all that dust about. Isn't it nearly time for your painkillers? I'll get you some water.' He got up and went away.

Venetia leaned forward to wave to Lottie, who raised the broom in a kind of salute, and then sat back in her chair trying to ignore the dull ache in her wrist and the sharper pain in her ankle. It was rather sweet of Milo to have remembered her tablets; perhaps she'd been fidgeting. God, she was lucky to be here and not to be sitting alone at home, hoping that somebody would drop in to entertain her for an hour. Milo was perfectly happy to allow her friends to come visiting: in fact he was rather enjoying it. They'd arrive, bringing flowers or chocolates, and, depending on what time of day it was, Milo and Lottie would make coffee or tea or produce the drinks tray. Then there would be a bit of a party, which she'd thoroughly enjoy.

Milo had found the wheelchair his mother had used and persuaded her to try it, though at first she'd protested against being wheeled about like a baby – or worse, like an invalid.

'Oh, Milo,' she'd said sadly when they'd had a trial run in the garden, 'it reminds me of darling Bunny.

He was so brave and cheerful but I'd never quite understood before how ghastly the helplessness must have been for him of all people. He was so vital, wasn't he? So physical. It must have been terrible for him. And yet he was so . . . peaceful.'

Milo had parked the wheelchair next to the garden seat and he'd sat down beside her. He'd remained silent for a while.

'Bunny realized that one word was crucial to his mental survival,' he'd said at last. '"Acceptance". He gradually trained himself to be able to live in the present moment and to take something positive from it. I don't mean in a shallow, manic kind of "live now, pay later" sense but in that he accepted what was now, however dire it was, and lived it fully to the best of his ability.' He'd frowned then. 'We saw it, didn't we? Not just a stoic, determined, brave front that he presented to the world but something much deeper that went to the essence of what was happening to him. True acceptance. And out of that battle with frustration and self-pity grew an amazing spiritual serenity. Being with him was a joy.'

After that, she'd allowed him to push her down the drive, through the village and up the lane – Pud running alongside – and, though she still hated the sense of helplessness and dependency, he turned these outings into such fun that she'd begun to look forward to them. They'd stop to look at the fearsome, beautiful birds of prey chained to their perches outside West Lynch Farm, or pause to watch the pretty bantams scurrying and running around the farm gate beside the chapel. Then, after the long march through the narrow, winding lane, they'd get to the post office at Allerford and Milo would push the wheelchair into the tea-garden, and June or Steve would bring out coffee and stop for a little chat. It was fun and, after all, she'd never have made it all that way on her crutches.

Venetia sighed contentedly. She was very happy here at the High House, though she'd had to lay down a few ground rules: *The Archers*, for instance, and *Emmerdale*; and the dear old *Daily Mail* for the gossip. The nurse would be in later to make sure all was well; meanwhile she was lucky, very lucky, to have such good friends who were prepared to take care of her.

Pud came wagging in and she smoothed his silky coat very gently with her good hand. He sat beside her chair and she could feel the warmth of him against her leg.

'Tomorrow,' she told him, 'you're going to have a very special guest to lunch. Did you know that? Im

is bringing the puppy and you'll have to teach him
how to behave in company.'

But Pud seemed unmoved by the prospect: he
wagged his tail once or twice and then curled into a
ball and went to sleep.

CHAPTER THIRTY

Nick and Imogen met at The Hunter's Inn late on the Tuesday morning of the Bank Holiday week.

'Alice and the girls are staying in Rock until the weekend,' he'd told her, 'but I have to get back to London. Look, I could just dash straight up the A39 and meet you somewhere along the way. Just for an hour or so. Please, Im . . .'

So she'd suggested The Hunter's Inn and he'd jumped at it. He'd go on to Bossington and spend the night at the High House, he told her, leaving early next morning to travel on to London. She'd been relieved that he hadn't suggested a less public meeting place and tried to persuade herself that this was simply a casual lunch with a very old friend. Nevertheless, she didn't mention it to Jules.

During the drive across the moor she felt nervous and on edge. There were ponies grazing up on the down, sturdy little Exmoor ponies, some of whom were clearly in foal, and she was seized by a longing to be riding over the hills, solitary and free, with the wind in her face and the sun on her back. It was more than a year, much more, since she'd been out on a horse: Rosie had changed all that. Soon, she promised herself, soon she'd go riding again. She slowed the engine, putting down the car window, so as to see the ponies more clearly, and heard the skylark's clear, passionate, bubbling song.

Nick was waiting for her in the lane outside the National Trust shop and she parked her car behind his, climbed out and gave him a quick hug. If he'd been disappointed to see Rosie and the puppy, he gave no sign of it: there was no reproach in his greeting and Im was grateful. Their meeting was much more natural with Rosie clamouring for a drink and the puppy dashing around, excited by the new surroundings.

'Milo found a name for him when we went over for lunch,' Im told Nick as she attached the lead to the puppy's collar. She hoisted Rosie on to her hip and they walked together along the lane and into the garden. 'He kept calling him the artful dodger, so we've settled on The Dodger and it's absolutely right for him. Let's sit outside, shall we? It's really hot. It was wonderful coming over the moor and hearing the skylarks.'

They settled at one of the wooden tables and Nick went to find a highchair for Rosie, and to order a pint for himself and cider for Im. She sat in the sun, watching him disappear into the shadowy doorway of the inn, and wondered what on earth she was doing. A year ago she wouldn't have given it a thought; she'd have told Jules she was having lunch with Nick and there wouldn't have been this sense of disloyalty. Yet nothing had really changed, she reminded herself; nothing had happened. So why this sense of unease?

She sat with her elbows on the table, watching Rosie crawling over the grass, whilst the puppy, tethered by his lead, watched too, whining a little. She could hear the harsh screams of the wild peacocks amongst the trees up on the slopes of the steep coombe, and the voice of the river, placidly murmuring and chuckling on its way through the valley and down to the sea. When Nick came out, holding the glasses, a menu tucked beneath his arm, she felt a rush of warm affection for him: he was so dear, so familiar. He looked relaxed and happy, and she saw, suddenly, how attractive Milo must have been at Nick's age and why Venetia had fallen in love with him. Then she noticed that a much older couple at a nearby table were watching them with benign approval; smiling and nodding at Rosie and

The Dodger, and assuming that this was a happy little family having a day out together.

She thought: They believe that Nick is Rosie's father.

Her pleasure was gone and she looked away from their smiling intrusion, hot with shame and embarrassment. Nick looked at her curiously as he set down his pint and put her glass of cider next to her.

'Cider with Rosie,' he commented. 'Are you OK?'

'Yes, of course.' She moved slightly so that he was blocking the view of the friendly couple. 'Is there a highchair?'

'It's on its way. Come on, Rosie-Posie.' He picked her up and she showed him a stone that she'd found; he bent his head to examine it and admire it. 'But don't eat it,' he warned. 'Look, here's your chair coming. Say "thank you" and you shall have some lunch.'

He was so unconscious of anyone else, so easy and natural, that Im felt ashamed. She dug in her bag and found Rosie's drinking mug and put it on the tray. The Dodger began to whine again and pull at his lead, and Im took out his small leather bone from its plastic bag and gave it to him. At once he began to worry it, to pick it up and toss it and then roll upon it ecstatically, with his paws in the air; and once again she saw the beaming expressions of the older couple, the 'Oh, isn't he sweet?' glances that begged for some kind of response, and she almost hated them for intruding into her own private moment.

She picked up the menu, holding it at an angle so that she couldn't see them. Nick sat down opposite; when he touched her hand she jumped as though she had been burned.

'What are you going to have? I don't want much. I shall have to cook for Jules this evening.' She spoke rapidly, not looking at him, still holding the menu as a shield.

'It's OK, Im.' His voice was reassuring and rather sad. 'Don't worry. I'm not asking for anything except your company. I'm not such a fool as to think that there was anything more to the last couple of months than just a kind of partisan solidarity mixed with a flicker of past passions. I admit that I'd like to go back and start from where we left off ten years ago but I know it's not possible. And I know you and Jules are back on track, and I'm glad for you. I promise I don't want to do anything that would risk our friendship. It's just so good to see you, that's all. Old friends stuff and no pressures, just like before. OK? Look at me. OK, Im?' She nodded wordlessly, biting her lips, and he smiled at her. 'Listen, we'll take Rosie and The Dodger down to the sea after lunch. Has The Dodger seen the sea yet? What about it, Rosie? Shall we go down to the sea after lunch?'

Im took a deep breath; she could feel her muscles relaxing. She was even able to smile at the couple and to see them as kindly people, probably with grandchildren of their own. She sipped some cider and looked again at Nick. His expression was so understanding and so loving that she took his hand.

'Thanks,' she said. 'I didn't mean to mislead you, Nick. It's been so good to have you around just lately, but I want us to go on being friends.'

'So do I,' he said at once. 'Oh God, so do I. It's OK, Im. No harm has been done.'

She was so relieved, so grateful for his intuitive understanding, that the rest of the day was joyful; especially the walk down to the beach and the cream tea at the Inn after the long climb back with Rosie and The Dodger, both exhausted, sharing the buggy.

It wasn't until much later on the way home, when she stopped to text to Jules that she would be late, that she realized that she'd left her mobile at home.

Jules hadn't seen the mobile lying on the table until it began to ring. He was already anxious because

313

there was no sign of Im, and because she hadn't said that she was going out or that she might be late. He was surprised: she was always so conscious of Rosie's tea-time and bedtime, and liked to keep to the routine – and it was certainly unlike her to forget her mobile; it was like a third hand. Now, suddenly, he wondered if it might be Im trying to get in touch with him and, in his anxiety, he picked up the phone just too late. Frustrated, he put it down again; after all, why should Im phone her own mobile? Wouldn't she use the land line or his mobile? Though perhaps she wouldn't remember his mobile number?

These thoughts passed swiftly through his mind; he was too anxious now to be thinking that clearly. Already he could imagine some kind of road accident, or Rosie taken ill . . .

He picked up the mobile again and saw that there was a voicemail message. He pressed the button and listened.

'Hi, sweetie. Just to say that today was so good. Thanks so much for coming all that way. And, look, we know we love each other, Im. That will never change, and I still wish we'd followed our hearts ten years ago, but I know it's too late. Thanks for the last few weeks, you saved my life, and thanks for today. Wasn't it fun? I shall be at the High House in about ten minutes and I'll let you know when I'm back in London. Love you lots.'

It was Nick's voice. Still holding the phone, Jules stared unseeingly at it, conjuring up a vision of Nick and Im together: but where? And was Rosie with them? Fear, jealousy, anger strove together in his heart and the words replayed themselves in his head: *We know we love each other. I wish we'd followed our hearts ten years ago.* What had happened between Im and Nick ten years ago? He suddenly remembered how much Nick had been around recently when Im and he had been at loggerheads over the Summer House, and Nick had been having money problems: *Thanks for the last few weeks, you saved my life.*

And where had she been today, and why hadn't she told him that she was meeting Nick? Common sense told him that if Rosie and The Dodger were with her then no real harm could be done, and hadn't Nick said, *I know it's too late*? So it was already over. Even so, a hot mix of anger and jealousy combined to beat down cool reason and, when Im's car pulled into the yard, Jules' sense of relief that they were safe was quickly replaced by a self-righteous determination to discover the truth.

*   *   *

315

Im, hurrying in with Rosie in her arms and The Dodger galloping at her heels, was brought up against an invisible wall of rejection. In her happiness, springing from the combination of Nick's acceptance of their true relationship and a truly magical day, she assumed that this was just Jules' reaction to his anxiety for their safety. So she simply leaned to kiss him, holding Rosie to one side, apologizing for her lateness and then saying: 'Have you got a kiss for Daddy, Rosie?' and depositing her suddenly in his arms.

Rosie's lavish and unexpected embrace under-mined Jules' icy demeanour and confused him. Rosie was in his arms, chattering unintelligibly about her day, whilst The Dodger began to lap noisily from his water bowl. Im smiled at them all.

'We've been to the sea,' she said happily. 'The Dodger was so funny. He was terrified of the sea. I'm so sorry I'm late but I left my mobile here and I couldn't phone you.'

'I know that,' Jules said coldly, unsuccessfully ducking another of Rosie's hugs. She smothered his head with both arms and then began to wriggle. He set her down upon the floor. 'I think you'll find that you've got a message.'

Im stared at him, beginning to take in the depth of his anger, feeling a trickle of anxiety in the pit of her stomach.

'A message?' she asked lightly. 'How do you know?'

'I listened to it,' he said. His intent, accusing stare dared her to question his right. 'Who were you with today?'

She stared back at him, guessing that Nick had left the message and wondering exactly what he'd said. Answers jumbled together in her head: reasons, excuses, the simple truth. Instinctively she chose the latter.

'Nick phoned this morning,' she said, as casually as she could. 'He's on his way back from Rock to London, via the High House. He asked if we could meet for a drink. I couldn't see any harm in it so we dashed over to The Hunter's Inn and had lunch with him.'

'The Hunter's *Inn*?'

She could see that he was taken aback by her answer; her honesty had cut some of the moral high ground from beneath his feet. She shrugged, trying to look indifferent.

'It's a bit of a drive, I agree, but it's on his route and I wanted Rosie to see the sea. It was a great day out.'

'So he said.'

Im bit her lip. Should she attempt indignation and accuse him of a breach of trust in listening to her private messages? Surely it would be wiser

317

to pretend that no messages could be that private between them, and ignore the rights and wrongs of it for the moment?

'Well, then. If you knew who I was with, why ask?'

She could see that he was slightly disconcerted by her apparent lack of guilt and she moved quickly to seize the advantage.

'Poor old Nick's still having the devil of a time with Alice, and you know very well that he and I have always been close . . .'

'So he said,' Jules repeated with great meaning.

'OK.' She smiled, attempting a calmness she didn't feel. 'Supposing I listen to the message so that I know what you're talking about?'

'He says that he knows you love each other and that he wishes he'd followed his heart ten years ago.'

Im was conscious of a simultaneous reaction: of fury with Nick and compassion for Jules. She knew that her only hope of winning through this was to maintain her air of indifference for anything Nick might have said.

She gave a tiny snort of laughter. 'Poor old Nick,' she said lightly. 'Of course we love each other. Ever since I was a little girl he's been like a big cousin to me, and I was the little sister he never had. I admit that there was a point when it nearly tipped into something else – it was obviously going to happen sooner or later when the hormones clicked in – but it never got off the ground. He likes to believe that I would have been the answer to all his problems. It sort of lets him off the hook when things go wrong. You know the kind of thing: "Oh, if only we'd made a go of it I'd never have been in this state." Alice is a hard-faced cow sometimes so I allow him his little fantasy. It doesn't do any harm. At least . . .' she looked at him, eyebrows raised questioningly, 'it hasn't until now. Come on, Jules! I can't believe you're really making a big deal out of me spending a few hours with Nick in the company of Rosie and The Dodger.'

She could see that he was taken aback by her direct response and she guessed that Nick had said nothing that might get her deeper into trouble. Once again she seized her opportunity.

'Darling, please don't let this foolishness upset you. Heavens! You know Nick. He's mixed-up but he's quite harmless and I should have thought that you know how happy I am with you here and now. It's been so good since we moved, hasn't it? Don't let some silly, sentimental message from Nick spoil it.' She went closer to him, heart thudding, gut churning, and put out her hand. 'I love you,

Jules. If you don't know that by now you never will.'

She allowed just a hint of hurt, even anger, tinge the affection in her voice, and she saw the doubt in his eyes, the relaxing of the muscles around his mouth, and she knew that it was going to be all right. Suddenly she felt exhausted: the long drive and the walk to the beach; the tension earlier with Nick, and now this. She let her hand fall and turned away.

'I think I need a drink,' she said, rather low, rather sad, appealing to his chivalry and sense of guilt. He reacted at once and caught her hand.

'I was worried about you,' he said defensively. 'You didn't say you were going out and then you'd left your phone behind. I wouldn't normally listen to your messages but I was so worried when you were late that I wondered if it was *you* phoning. Oh, I know that sounds crazy, but I was *worried*, Im . . .'

'Oh, darling.' She clasped his hand, put an arm around him. 'I'm so sorry all this has happened. I should have phoned to tell you where I was going but it all happened so quick and I never thought I'd be late back. Rosie and The Dodger were so knackered when we'd got back up from the beach that I stopped to give her some tea. Oh, Jules, you're not really worried about poor old Nick, are you? Surely you trust me?'

He was defeated; unable to resist her reasonable attitude which, after all, chimed with Nick's message. He put his arms around her and she hugged him. Relief flooded her and she felt quite weak.

'I'm sorry,' Jules was saying contritely. 'It was just the way he was talking . . .'

She leaned back in his arms and looked up at him, feeling badly that he should be apologizing. 'I know,' she said. 'Let's just forget it and have that drink. And then I'll have to get Rosie to bed. Look at her; she's knackered. They both are.'

Rosie had climbed on to the sofa and lay sucking her thumb, Bab hugged to her chest; on the floor beside her, The Dodger had curled into a ball and was fast asleep. Im and Jules looked at them and then at each other: both silently acknowledged that there was so much to lose and that neither of them wanted to jeopardize all that they shared. The danger was past and all was well.

CHAPTER THIRTY-ONE

Lottie took the jersey from the knitting bag and laid it out on the sofa. Nick stared at it.

'You've really done it?' he asked, amazed. 'Is it for me?' He reached out to touch its thick warm softness. 'I can't believe you've really done it.'

'Why not?' she asked. 'It was a challenge. I haven't knitted such a big garment for years. It's come out very well, though I admit that it's not the weather for it at the moment.'

Nick was already trying it on; rolling down the sleeves of his blue cotton shirt, pulling the jersey over his head, tugging out his shirt collar.

'It's perfect,' he said. 'What do you think?' He posed, guying it up, turning round. 'Thanks, Lottie. I love it.'

She was looking at it critically, clearly pleased by his reaction.

'It looks very good,' she admitted. 'I got the size right, didn't I? But then you were very patient about being measured. It was great fun to do and I'm glad you like it.'

'I love it,' he repeated. He smoothed the navy, ribbed wool, not wanting to take it off. It gave him an odd sense of comfort, of reassurance, and he sat down beside her again, still wearing it.

'It's good to see you, Nick,' she said. 'We were hoping that we might see Alice and the girls, too. It seems rather a long time since they were here.'

He shrugged, embarrassed. 'You know what it's like when people invite you to stay. There's a timetable, and everyone has to do their bit, so it's tricky saying that you're going off to visit someone else, and it's a bit of a trek up here from Rock. Anyway, Dad's coming up to London very soon, isn't he, so he'll see them all then. And by then I hope that things will have improved. Alice is still a bit . . . well, chilly, if you see what I mean.' He shivered theatrically and grinned at her. 'That's why I'm so glad to have my jersey. But I hope for the best. You know what an optimist I am.'

'Is hope the same thing as optimism?' Lottie asked thoughtfully. 'Optimists have expectations, don't they? That the weather will clear up, or that

323

the political situation will improve. Hope is to do with faith, isn't it? "Hope is the conviction of things unseen." Who said that?'

He shook his head. 'Too complicated for me, Lottie. I think you're splitting hairs.'

'Probably. Have you told Sara that Venetia is here?'

He stared at her anxiously. 'Oh God. I don't think so but I might have done. Would that be a terrible mistake?'

'Probably. She resents Milo using the house as what she calls an orphanage and Venetia will probably be the last straw. We haven't heard from her just lately so you probably haven't told her.'

'But you couldn't do anything else, could you? Poor old Venetia. She couldn't have been left to fend for herself.'

'That's what we thought.'

'Mum's a control freak,' he said. 'Well, you know that, don't you? But honestly, I can't see what business it is of hers.'

'She's afraid that if the High House is full of refugees when Milo dies then you'll have a problem entering into your inheritance, that's all.'

'You're not a refugee, Lottie,' he said, distressed.

'Aren't I?' She smiled at his expression of dismay. 'I told you before that I've always felt an alien in this world and that Milo rescued me. He offered me a refuge. You could say that that makes me a refugee, I suppose.'

'Well, it's not how I see you. Dad needs you. He's not as tough as he seems, is he? He has a few demons lurking. And now, poor Venetia.' He fell silent, making connections, looking bleak. 'Is anyone really happy?' he asked abruptly.

'We're all damaged in one way or another,' she answered. 'Some are more damaged than others, and some are more easily able to manage their disabilities. And some refuse to admit to them at all.'

'Is that bad?'

'Not as long as they don't despise others who do. How was Im?'

He laughed. 'The reason that you feel an alien, Lottie, is simple. You're a witch. How do you know I saw Im?'

'It's nothing to do with magic powers; it's just being able to deduct perfectly obvious things. *Did* you see her?'

'Yes. We had lunch at The Hunter's Inn and then we took Rosie and The Dodger down to the sea. It was great fun; nothing more, I promise. It's all finished, Lottie. Not that there was much to finish. But whatever you feared, it's all over. Do you believe me?'

'Yes,' she answered him. 'Thank goodness. But it was dangerous, Nick.'

'I know, but I can't help thinking that life would be so good with her. Im always loves me, whatever I do, you see.'

'She loves you so unconditionally precisely because she's *not* married to you,' replied Lottie candidly. 'That's your optimism kicking in again. It's not based on anything concrete and requires no effort on your part. Optimism whispers temptingly that, if you and Im were together, the future would somehow be a wonderful cloud-cuckoo-land and you'd live happily ever after. Hope, on the other hand, is implicit in rebuilding your relationship with Alice and your children in a quiet, humdrum, day-to-day reality. Hope tells you that, though you can't see the results, if you have faith and if you are wholehearted, your work will pay off. After all, Alice loves you too, in a realistic, workaday kind of way. Not in a "Let's have a picnic and go to the beach" kind of way. But it's a durable love and she hasn't given up on you just yet. And despite her faults, you love her too.'

'Yes,' he agreed, after a moment. 'Yes, I do. But she's so much harder to love.'

'That's because she's your wife,' said Lottie cheerfully. 'Nobody said it would be easy. Why do you think I never married? And now you have the perfect right to tell me to mind my own business. After all, what do I know? Sorry, Nick. Take no notice of my ramblings.'

He laughed. 'The trouble is, I have a horrid feeling that you might be right.'

'And, anyway,' she said, 'you'd already made up your own mind, hadn't you? So that's great.'

'I've ordered Dad's birthday present.' He changed the subject. 'I stopped off in Porlock and went into the Gallery and had a chat with Marianne about it. I've chosen a painting of Dunster for him by Anthony Avery. The Yarn Market and the castle on a sunny day, with fantastic light and sharp shadows; you can feel the heat. It's almost exactly the view from Venetia's house. I hope he likes it. It's being framed.'

'I'm sure he will. I'm planning a bit of a party so I hope you'll circle the date in your diary in red ink and talk to Alice about it.'

'I will,' he promised. 'It would be good if we could get down for it. How's Matt getting on in the Summer House?'

'He's doing it by degrees. He wants to get it absolutely right and he doesn't want to rush it.'

'Dad says that he's given him some watercolours that some distant rellie painted down there. Judging by Matt's pad in London, I shouldn't have thought Victorian watercolours were much in his line. He's quite stark and modern, isn't he, usually?'

'Well, he is. But I think he's trying to keep with the atmosphere of the Summer House as far as possible, though some of the things he's ordered are quite modern. It'll be an interesting mix.'

'I'm sorry I missed him.' Nick looked down at his jersey again with pleasure. 'I'm really pleased with this, Lottie. Honestly.'

'I'm glad,' she said. 'It was a labour of love. In its truest sense.'

'Thanks,' he said. 'Thanks, Lottie.'

CHAPTER THIRTY-TWO

Matt tried to cry out but he couldn't make a sound; he was shaking Im, shouting at her, yet his arms and legs were heavy and he could barely move. He opened his eyes suddenly and lay in the dawn light; his heartbeat was loud in his ears and he was soaked with perspiration. Breathing slowly, deliberately, he quietened himself, trying to remember the nightmare; reliving it.

He and Im are together on a bus, with Rosie in her stroller. As they stand waiting to get off, a man comes up behind them and begins to talk; all of them join in, laughing. The bus stops and they all climb off and then, at some point, he realizes that Rosie has been left on the bus. His terror is so great he can barely speak but Im won't respond to his fear. She is silent and angry; she pushes him away, growing more and more remote. He shouts at her: 'We've lost Rosie and it's all my fault. We must find her,' and still she stares at him, stony-faced until he seizes her and shakes her.

The dream was fading and his heartbeat was slowing. He pushed back the sheet and climbed out of bed. Apart from the physical reaction to the nightmare he was bitterly disappointed: he had so hoped that the influence of the Summer House was healing him; drawing off the demons. Yet here they were back again; strong as ever. He stood at the window, still feeling the terror and the helplessness. During that glorious period when he'd been writing *Epiphany*, he'd have gone straight to work; using the demons and the nightmares, turning them into shapes and patterns within the story: laying the ghosts by writing them out into something that could be understood, something apart from him, and therefore able to be defeated.

Now he stood in silence staring out. Gently the beauty of the morning was borne in upon him and he opened the window wider and leaned out into the warm, soft air. A thrush was singing; so heavenly was its song that he could barely believe that this was an ordinary garden bird. He listened in silence, whilst the heavy sweet scent of the purple lilac drifted and filled the room. The sound of water, ever present, rippled softly and, quite suddenly, once again he had an inner vision of

Selworthy Church, shining white, standing high on the hill.

Calmer now, he turned back into the room, took his towelling robe, wrapped himself in it and passed out on to the wide landing and down the stairs. He switched on the kettle and went straight to his portfolio of paintings, looking through them whilst the kettle boiled. Presently he sat down with his mug of coffee and examined more closely the paintings he'd selected. Here was a study of the church itself, and here were several sketches of the churchyard with mossy headstones and long shadows, and bluebells and buttercups growing in the long grass. The smallest painting was of a little statue; a cherub holding a stone vase, painted against a shaded, grey-black oval background. There were primroses in the stone vase, their creamy-yellow petals gleaming with an unearthly light. To one side, lightly sketched in and barely visible, was another face; a child's.

As he stared at it, Matt was filled with a strong conviction of a presence close at hand, of something important to be done. He sat quietly, not hurrying his coffee, allowing the idea to form in his mind.

Half an hour later he was driving up the lane towards Allerford; it was not yet six o'clock. He drove slowly, the car window down, gazing in delight at the riot of colour in the hedgerows: rosy patches of pink-red campion; the brilliant golden dazzle of bright buttercups; a little azure pool of bluebells. Creamy cow parsley brushed, thick and powdery, against the car, and the hawthorn flowers were tipped with scarlet. Matt saw all these miracles of colour and design through Helena's eyes now; vivid and entrancing, they drew his gaze again and again.

He approached the A39; pausing at the junction to watch the swallows skimming in the sunshine above the quiet fields, and then driving the short distance to the turning to Selworthy. For the first time since he had been coming here, the church car park was empty. He got out and shut the door, staring across the vale towards Dunkery, rinsed rose and gold with early morning sunshine. He crossed the narrow lane and climbed the steps into the churchyard, turning left and bending his head as he passed beneath low, over-arching branches of the great yew tree. He wandered over the mossy grass amongst the grey headstones, not knowing where to look for the little cherub with his stone vase. He knew where Milo's family was, grouped on the west side, and he paused here and there, reading the names until he saw with a shock her own name: Helena. It was carved beneath the words: 'In Memory of Miles Grenville who died at Bloemfontein 1860–1900 and his beloved wife Helena 1872–1925'.

He stared at it; oddly shocked and confused by this stony manifestation of her existence and paying his own quiet homage. After a while he grew conscious of a bird singing in the trees nearby and he raised his head to glance around for it; he left the grave and walked slowly along the wall where ivy clambered and some young ash trees grew. Behind their twisting roots, beneath the ivy's straggling branches, the cherub lay under the wall: chipped and rubbed, he was barely visible. Matt crouched, staring at him, and then he reached to pick him up, lifting him out gently so as to study him more closely. There was no inscription, no dates or names; only the cherub, his wide, blind eyes looking past Matt's shoulder, his lips curved in a smile.

As he crouched there, an idea presented itself, shadowy at first but becoming clearer. He stood up, still holding the cherub, and walked among the grassy paths: here it was. 'In Memory of George Grenville 1890–1919'. The small blond boy who had played with his toy engine at the Summer House, more than a hundred years ago. Matt stood silently, saluting him across the years, and then made his way back beside the wall, pausing to gather some buttercups. He went once more to Helena's grave, scattered the buttercups over the close-cut grass beneath the headstone and turned away.

He wasn't at all surprised to see Lottie strolling down the drive with Pud running ahead. Matt stopped the car at the turning down the avenue to the Summer House and went to meet them.

'I think I know,' he told her. 'I think I've guessed the truth at last, Lottie.'

He was shivering with emotion and she took his arm. 'Can you tell me?'

'Of course I can, I want to. Can you come back with me now?'

She nodded. 'You go on and we'll catch you up. We shan't be long.'

She was right. He needed to look again at the painting, and to put the chairs on the veranda; even make some coffee. He was aware that he was setting the scene, and marvelled at this detachment that, even in a moment of such overpowering excitement, insisted that he must somehow tell it as a story. He was ready for her when she came round the side of the house. The two high-backed wicker chairs were in place with a table between them holding a pot of coffee, two mugs and the paintings.

'Pud's foraging,' she said, sitting down. 'So tell me.'

He pushed the painting of the cherub towards her and poured some coffee. She lifted it, turning it so as to study it, and then looked at him questioningly. He passed her the two other paintings of the little boy.

'All three of them have something extra,' he said. 'Can you see what it is?'

She looked again, moving the paintings to and fro; then her face changed and she stared up at him, her eyes bright with discovery.

'There's another child,' she said. 'Like a little ghost in the background.'

'Exactly. A little ghost. D'you know what I think? I think this little boy, George, had a twin who died. Helena paints him in with George here at the Summer House and in the garden. See him just there in the shadows of the hedge? I think he was probably stillborn and they simply took his body away and disposed of it. I think the cherub is his memorial.'

He reached down beside his chair and lifted the little stone cherub up. 'He was in the churchyard, down by the wall. I think she put him there in memory of George's twin, hidden under the wall because she couldn't give him a proper grave. But some trees have grown up and their roots had knocked him over. It was only because I was looking for him that I saw him.'

Lottie took the cherub very gently: she touched his stony scars and ran her finger round the chipped rim of the vase.

Matt watched her. 'She couldn't forget him, you see. Like Mum.'

Lottie's hands were stilled; she frowned at him.

'Yes,' he said urgently. 'That's the whole thing. Like Mum, Helena had twins and one died, but she couldn't forget him. She grew reclusive and shut herself up here but little George was a constant reminder of the child she'd lost. Don't you see? That's the connection I can feel. I think I had a twin who died. It explains my sense of loneliness, as if something is missing. And my nightmares and memories where I can feel as if I'm being separated from someone and see my own face in a mirror-image.'

'There was a child,' remembered Lottie, still cradling the cherub. 'When I asked Tom why Helen was so melancholic he said that she'd had a miscarriage.'

'*Did* he, though? Are you certain that those were the words he used?'

'You mean he might have said that she lost a baby and I immediately assumed that it was a miscarriage?'

'It's what we all believed, wasn't it? We grew up

336

remembering some distant mention of Mum losing a baby and, for some reason, imagining that she'd miscarried. And nobody was ever allowed to talk about it. Supposing I'm right, and that I had a twin who died when he was very small and she simply couldn't bear it? And then Dad was killed and she just completely lost it? She wouldn't talk about the past, would she? Her face would go all stony and angry. And I would have been a constant reminder of him, wouldn't I?'

Lottie was frowning thoughtfully. 'Yes, you would. And so the photographs . . . ?'

'Helena painted George's twin into the pictures. He's always there with him. Supposing those photos Mum took of me was her way of remembering my brother? She put me in different clothes, and in different backgrounds, pretending that he was there but in a slightly different world. That was why Im was never there with me. Mum couldn't have pretended so well then, could she? Painting lends itself so much better to the fantasy.'

He drank some coffee, his hand trembling. The solution to this long-carried burden seemed like a miracle; a promise of peace at last. Lottie was watching him compassionately. She set the cherub on the table between them.

'I believe that you're right, that you had a twin—'

He broke in eagerly, 'I just feel it so strongly. As if Helena's here trying to tell me, and to ask me to remember George's twin. We could ask Milo about it, couldn't we? But I don't want anyone else to know about me yet.'

'Not even Im?'

He hesitated. 'Not quite yet. I need to accustom myself to it. Although, to be honest, it seems so right and natural that it's hardly even a surprise. Just a huge relief.'

'You must tell her when it's right for you.' She drank some more coffee whilst he gazed unseeingly across the garden, wrapped in thought. 'I must get back to breakfast. Venetia will be wanting her morning cup of tea.'

They both stood up, and she embraced him, holding him tightly for a moment. He smiled down at her wordlessly, and she gave him a little smiling nod in return, and then went away along the terrace and round the side of the house, calling to Pud. Matt watched her go, then he picked up the little cherub and went into the house. Gently he washed the mud and stains from the rough stone and dried it with a soft cloth. Carrying the cherub he wandered through the house, looking for a suitable place for him.

He climbed the stairs, which turned halfway up

and then led on upwards to the broad landing, and here he paused. He'd set a small sofa before the wide window, with a little table beside it holding books and magazines. Now he placed the cherub on the windowsill, half turned so that his smiling gaze looked out upon the garden, and then he sat down on the sofa and made his own quiet act of remembrance.

CHAPTER THIRTY-THREE

The weather turned chill and wet, and cold winds from the south-east battered the new, delicate blossoms. For two weeks Venetia's outings in the wheelchair were rare but one morning, when the icy wind had shifted to the warm west, Milo took her to Dunster. Inside her little house again, Venetia looked around with pleasure; she'd missed it more than she'd realized. Whilst Milo was bending to pick up some letters from the hall floor, she limped into the sitting room wrapped all about with a warm sense of homecoming. She stood, leaning on her stick, surprised that she should feel quite so strongly. After all, she was very happy at the High House with Lottie and Milo – glad to be safe and to be cared for – and yet, now, she suddenly longed to be home again. She'd missed those little impromptu lunches with her friends; bridge sessions followed by some supper by the fire; watching whatever she chose on the television. Milo was a darling, but he tended to have strong, disapproving views on her favourite soaps, and he always hogged the remote. Lottie didn't seem to care much – she usually had her head in a book – and she'd found it just a tad embarrassing to say that her favourite programmes were the very ones that Milo considered suitable only for the mentally deficient. Thank God he loved *The Archers*. And she'd been rather put out by his tendency to silence at breakfast. She hadn't suspected that he was one of those grumpy types who retired behind the newspaper. Luckily, Lottie was quite prepared to be sociable over the toast and completely ignored Milo's patently paper-rustling irritation at their cheerfulness and bursts of laughter.

Venetia hobbled back into the hall. She could see now that it wasn't all jam living with Milo, though Lottie seemed perfectly happy in her odd, detached kind of way. As for herself, well, it might be very nice to have them both close at hand for company, and in an emergency, but she knew now that she'd be looking forward to coming home again. She followed Milo into the kitchen.

'I've checked everything,' he said. 'No problems. I've left the garden door open. I thought you'd like to look outside.'

'Oh, yes,' she said. 'I would.' Her dear little garden, surrounded by its high stone walls, hardly big enough to grow anything more than the climbers: delicate, purple-flowered *clematis alpina*, white jasmine with its trumpet-shaped flowers and twining stems, and the honeysuckle that scrambled over the roof of the little stone shed, and whose scent she loved.

Today, with the strong westerly wind buffeting the town, the garden remained protected from the wind; warm and sheltered.

'You'll soon be able to come home.' Milo stood at her shoulder. 'No point in trying to rush it, though. You've got to be properly recovered, but you'll want to be here for the summer.'

She looked at him, wondering if he were speaking from his personal viewpoint or if he had sensed her longing to be back amongst her own things. He was looking around the little courtyard with approval, even affection, and she was unexpectedly overwhelmed with love for him. Oh, how confusing the emotions were, swinging first one way, then another.

'It will be nice to be home,' she admitted – trying not to sound too keen lest he should be hurt.

He raised his eyebrows as if surprised by her caution. 'Of course it will. There's nowhere quite like your own patch, is there? I'll be able to help you with your tubs and pots and things. I know you like to make a bit of a show in the summer.'

'Well, I do. There's no space to make a proper border but I like to make a splash once the frosts are over.'

'Well, we can do it together if you'd like that.' He glanced at her sideways. 'I promise I won't interfere. I'll simply take orders.'

She burst out laughing. 'That'll be the day,' she observed caustically. 'But, yes, that would be kind. It'll be a bit tricky, one-handed, though I'm getting better so quickly now.'

They went back into the house and he locked the door. She limped ahead of him down the hall, pausing at the bottom of the stairs where she'd lain in such pain and terror. Panic seized her. Remembering the fear and helplessness of that moment she wondered if, after all, she should opt for safety and stay at the High House. She stood, gripping her stick, fighting down the panic: reminding herself that the little suite of rooms at the High House would be waiting for her if she were to need help or company. Her courage gradually reasserted itself and she straightened her shoulders: she wasn't quite ready yet to give up her independence.

'I shan't attempt the stairs,' she said. 'Have you got my letters, Milo?'

'In my pocket,' he said. 'Shall we go and have a drink in the Lutts?'

She considered his suggestion; a drink in The Luttrell Arms would be very pleasant, and perhaps lunch too. Milo had promised her a day out and she was determined to make the most of it.

The Dodger was watching Pud with great caution. Each time the older dog twitched in his sleep, The Dodger's tail would thump anxiously. Pud, meanwhile, continued to slumber and presently The Dodger relaxed and he began to quarter the floor of the garden room, one eye on Pud's recumbent form.

Im and Lottie watched, amused.

'It's so good for The Dodger to have Pud to teach him how to behave,' Im said. 'I think they really enjoyed the walk, didn't they? Poor old Pud. The Dodger's a bit of a pain but he's very patient with him most of the time.'

'He's coming on very well,' agreed Lottie. 'It's always useful to have an older dog to show a puppy the ropes, and it's good for Pud too. The Dodger's livened him up no end. How's Jules?'

'Fine. Listen, I've got some good news. The Websters have offered to let us buy the barn.'

'Really? Oh, that's fantastic. But how odd that

they didn't suggest you buy it at the start. Why now?'

'I don't know. I think that they'd got into the mindset of having a permanent tenant rather than holiday lets when they first suggested it to Jules, but probably, like most farmers at the moment, they're a bit short of cash and so they've decided to sell it. I think they know that we wanted to buy, really, and they seem to like having us as neighbours. It's just so brilliant because we love it so much but we never imagined they'd sell. It's quite small, but that's OK. I love where it is, and the views.'

'So no regrets about the Summer House?'

'None. The barn is just right for all of us, and I'm beginning to get my project going. You know? Sourcing Exmoor holidays for young families. There's a lot to research but I'm really enjoying it. Hope it works.'

'I think it's a great idea. I imagine that you'll be checking all the riding stables personally?'

'You're so right. I can't wait to get on a horse again. I think I'm ready now. I had to get through that bit of being terrified of taking any kind of risk after Rosie was born but I'm over it now. Is Matt joining us for lunch?'

'Yes, he is. He'll be here any minute, I should think.'

The Dodger had found Pud's ball. He butted it and it rolled away; he dashed after it and cannoned into Pud, who started up, alarmed, with a sharp bark. Rosie, who had been deeply asleep in her stroller, jerked into wakefulness, and Im sighed.

'Our five minutes of peace and quiet are over. Can I help with the lunch?'

Im bent over the paintings, studying each one carefully. Beyond her, through the window, Matt could see Lottie and Rosie playing in the garden with the dogs. The garden room was full of birdsong and sunshine, though the westerly winds still roared overhead.

'And you really believe this?' She raised her head to stare at him, shocked. 'You think you had a twin who died?'

He nodded. 'It all fits, if you think about it. It explains how Mum behaved with us; you and me, I mean. I could remember, you see, how she used to be happy. I had memories of her playing with me and someone else and laughing, and then I realized that it was before you were born, so there must have been another child around. And it explains that feeling I've always had of being separated from someone.'

'And how long have you suspected this?'

He shook his head, shrugged. 'Not long. And yet I feel that I've always known it now. The fact that nobody ever talked about him didn't help, of course. Memory needs feeding when you're very small, doesn't it? Anyway, a couple of weeks ago I found the paintings and I saw the little ghost-figure and that's when I began to have this strong feeling that I identified in some way with it. I think George's twin was stillborn, which is why there's no record of him anywhere, apart from the cherub. Milo can't remember ever hearing about him. But Helena would never have forgotten, would she?'

Im shivered; she wrapped her arms around herself and stared out of the window where Rosie was staggering, holding tightly to Lottie's hand, and screaming with delight.

'Of course she wouldn't. Oh, Matt. How awful. Poor Helena. And poor Mum. But you think your twin lived?'

He nodded. 'I remember him, you see. I remember watching her lifting him and swinging him up high, and I remember looking at him sitting opposite, in the bath or in the pram, perhaps, and it was as if I were looking at myself. Just glimpses, that's all, but I'm sure of it now.'

She was silent for a moment. 'But what would have happened to him?'

'I guess that he died of some illness out in Afghanistan and she just couldn't bear it afterwards. You know? Leaving him out there when we came home. I think that Dad asked people not to talk about it because it upset her so badly. And then he died out there too, and it was the last straw.'

'Oh God, how sad it is.' There were tears in her eyes. 'How awful for you, Matt.'

'Well, it is in a way, but in another it's a huge relief. It explains all these weird feelings I have. I just wish we had some proof but it's all so long ago and there's nobody left to ask. Do you believe that it's true?'

She stared at him. 'I believe it if you do. It would explain why Mum was so unhappy. I can understand how terrible it would be to lose a child; and in a foreign country, too. And then Dad as well. And if it makes sense to you and you think you can remember him . . . Why do you think it was a him?'

He frowned, thinking about it. 'It just feels right. And I think it explains the photographs.'

'Photographs? Oh, those ones of you but not me. Where you don't recognize the clothes and things?'

'Mmm. I wonder if she did that to try to pretend he was around somewhere. Rather like the ghost in the paintings. A remembrance.'

She shivered again. 'I think that's a bit creepy. But if you're OK with it . . . It's just so awful to think we had a brother and don't even know what his name was or anything. There must be something. What about a birth certificate?'

'I've looked through everything we've got and I suppose any evidence must have been very thoroughly destroyed.'

'Well, I think it's wrong, if you want to know.' Im stared out of the window again. 'I feel we had a right to know the truth.'

'It depends how desperate she was, I suppose. Try to look at it like that.'

'I am trying to,' said Im, her eyes on her daughter. 'It's OK, I just need to get used to it. You've had a few weeks to accustom yourself to it, remember.'

'And it wasn't really a shock,' he said. 'I think I was almost expecting something like it, somehow. It explains things, and that helps. I'm sorry to upset you, Im, but I wanted you to know.'

She turned back to him, the tears still shining in her eyes. 'Of course you had to tell me. I'll be fine with it. What does Lottie say? She never guessed, either?'

Matt shook his head. 'It was clearly a very well-kept secret.' He paused, put an arm about her shoulder, and they stood for a moment, staring out into the garden. 'Shall we go out and join them?' he asked at last.

She nodded, and they went out into the sun and wind together.

CHAPTER THIRTY-FOUR

Matt sat on the veranda of the Summer House: he was puzzled and disappointed. He'd really believed that his discovery would begin to unlock his creative powers, that the lifting of his lifelong burden would free up all sorts of ideas. Yet still the block remained, and along with it the insistent suspicion that there was something more to be revealed. Some memory nagged at the back of his mind, preventing true release. But what was it? So certain was he that his long period of frustration was over he'd agreed to Annabel's suggestion that she should come down for another visit. Now, surely, he'd be able to cast off the shadows and be normal and free with her; that's what he'd told himself in the new exciting light of his discovery.

'I'm not ready yet to have Annabel at the Summer House,' he'd told Lottie, praying she'd understand. 'I know it sounds weird but I really don't want to make that kind of statement yet. If ever. Can I move back into the attic for a few days and have her to stay here again? I'm really sorry, Lottie. I know it sounds pathetic but I don't want to give her any false impressions. And, anyway, the Summer House is still only half furnished. We'd be on top of each other, if you know what I mean. It would be different if we were . . .'

He'd stopped, feeling wretched and inadequate, but Lottie had quite grasped the situation.

'I agree that it could give off all sorts of messages,' she'd replied. 'Of course she can come here. And you don't have to ask for yourself. You know that.'

If only he could make up his mind about Annabel: he knew that she wouldn't be the kind of girl to take any gesture lightly, and that any move beyond their present friendship would definitely be a commitment – and he certainly didn't feel ready for it.

He sat quite still, emptying his mind, waiting for some creative movement; a fragment of an idea or the ghost of a character. Birdsong and the sound of the brook were his only rewards, and he opened his eyes still feeling confused and frustrated. There was a sudden movement amongst the roots underneath the lilac tree, a little flurry of leaves, and he leaned forward to see what it was. The creature was larger than a bird, pale in colour, striped and patched with sunshine and shadows. The kitten came out on to the grass; it patted a leaf with its paw and then sat back on its haunches. Matt saw its mouth open in a brief pink yawn.

Watching, he was reminded of two things: the marmalade cat in the paintings – and something else, which just at the moment eluded him. The kitten came forward, and Matt got up and went down to meet it. It was so pretty, so sweet; he crouched on his haunches and held out a hand to it. The kitten pressed itself into Matt's hand, miaowing piteously, and Matt picked it up, stroking it with a finger, speaking to it quietly. A quick check showed that it was male and he carried it back towards the house, still talking: 'Poor little fellow. Where have you sprung from? Are you hungry?' and all the while he was thinking about the cat in the painting – and the other thing that remained just out of range.

In the kitchen he broke some bread into a bowl with some milk, put it down on the floor and watched the kitten eat gratefully. He had no idea what other nourishment he could offer but the kitten seemed satisfied at the end of his meal and began to examine his surroundings. Matt hunted through his portfolio of paintings until he found the cat in the chair; marmalade just like this one. He looked at it, wondering if there were some clue that might somehow trigger the memory. There were several more paintings featuring the cat and he looked for them, hoping that they might show something important. Here he was, sitting with his tail curled around him, watching George playing; and here was another of him crossing the lawn, tail held high; another showed him sitting in a patch of sun-barred shadow, which gave his coat a stripy, tigerish look, and his satisfied expression appeared rather like a wicked smile.

The pang of recognition startled Matt, but he couldn't place it. The kitten was back, winding himself around Matt's ankles, his purring the sound of a boiling kettle. Matt bent to pick him up and held him for a moment against his cheek, still puzzling over this mystery.

'Come on,' he told the kitten. 'We're going for a little walk.'

Milo was in the garden trying to decide whether the grass was dry enough to cut. He greeted Matt absent-mindedly but peered into the hessian shopping bag that Matt held out to him.

'What is it? Good grief; a kitten. Didn't know you were going into livestock.'

'It wasn't my intention. He turned up just now and I don't quite know what to do with him.'

'Do you have to do anything? Maybe he belongs to someone in the village and he's just taking a stroll through your garden.'

'Well, you might be right.' Matt was surprised at how disappointed he felt. 'Do kittens do that?'

'My dear fellow, how should I know? Never been a cat man. Maybe Venetia knows. She had cats at one time. She's around somewhere. Now, what d'you think about this grass?'

'I think your sit-on mower will simply tear the ground to pieces,' Matt said. 'It's pretty wet.'

Milo made a disgruntled face. 'You're probably right. Don't let Pud see that kitten. He might think it's lunch.'

Matt laughed. 'Pud wouldn't be so ungentlemanly. Come on, kitty. Let's find Venetia.'

She was pacing the paved terrace outside the open french windows of the parlour.

'Look,' she cried gleefully. 'No stick! But I can't do it for very long without tiring. It's too frustrating for words. The trouble is that when you get old it takes so much longer to heal.'

'I think you're doing wonderfully well,' he told her. 'Best not to rush it, isn't it? I need your help, Venetia.' And he held out the bag.

'Ooooh,' she said softly. 'But he's so sweet. I didn't know you had a kitten, Matt.'

355

'He just turned up this morning and I don't quite know what to do with him. I've given him some bread and milk.'

'Wait,' she said. 'Let me sit down so that I can see him properly. Come on into the parlour.'

She sat down on the sofa and Matt put the bag on to her lap. The kitten walked out cautiously, enquiringly, and Venetia laughed.

'He's beautiful, and perfectly well cared for. Where has he come from, d'you think?'

Matt shrugged. 'Milo thinks he's wandered in from the village.'

Venetia frowned. 'Unlikely, I should think. It's quite a long way from even your nearest neighbour and he's not old enough to go so far from home. How odd. Still, Milo might be right. You'll have to put a notice up in the village and one in the post office at Allerford. He's a beautiful little fellow and someone must be missing him.'

The kitten jumped on to Venetia's shoulder and walked along the back of the chair. Matt watched him.

'D'you think he might have been dumped?'

Venetia's eyebrows arched in surprise. 'In Bossington? Unlikely, isn't it? Don't people usually do that on motorways?'

'Well, it might not always be that easy to get to

a motorway. Perhaps he was a present to someone who simply couldn't cope with him but dumped him in a village in the hope that someone would find him quickly and look after him.'

She looked at him, smiling. 'That's a very plausible story. Anyone might think you were a writer. I believe you've lost your hard heart at last, Matt. You want to keep him, don't you?'

He chuckled. 'My heart isn't that hard. And yes, I do rather like him.'

She caught the kitten and held the little, wriggling body. 'I confess I do, too. Much better than that rather tiresome Annabel.'

Matt managed to resist pointing out that Annabel was none of her business; after all, deep down he agreed with her.

'She's coming down again tomorrow,' he said, 'so I hope you won't tell her so.'

'Much better for everyone if I did,' answered Venetia sharply. 'Finish it once and for all. And don't tell me to mind my own business. You're simply dithering, Matt. You know you are.'

Matt sat down beside her and took the kitten into his own hands. 'How can you be so sure of anything to do with the heart?' he asked. 'You said just now that I have a hard heart because I don't fall in and out of love or have messy affairs. I hate emotional mess. How can you tell if someone is really right for you, Venetia?'

She sighed. 'My mother had a good answer to that one. And to making other decisions, too. She used to say, "If in doubt, don't." You're clinging to Annabel because you're afraid you might be missing out on something if you tell her to go, but meanwhile you're not growing any fonder of her, are you? Well, love doesn't work like that. It doesn't have to be love at first sight, but if it *is* love then there's always some evidence of it. Do you remember the old rule? "Do you want to see her? Do you want to touch her?" And if you don't, then it isn't love.'

'To be honest,' he said, letting the kitten climb on to his shoulder, 'I don't think about her for days at a time. I just feel guilty because I think I ought to be able to respond in some way to her.'

'Oh, don't be foolish,' Venetia said impatiently. 'And anyway, she simply isn't right for you. Take my word for it.'

She smiled blindingly at him and he began to laugh. 'How simple you make it sound.'

'It *is* simple. Make up your mind to it and do it. Now, much more interesting, what are you going to do about this little chap?'

*   *   *

358

Later, Lottie appeared at the Summer House carrying a small cage.

'Milo wonders if this would be any good?' she asked. 'Pud used to travel in it in the car when he was a puppy. You could go and see Richard in Antlers and get a litter tray and some proper food. Where is he?'

Matt led her into the sitting room and pointed. The kitten was curled on the velvet seat of the wooden chair, fast asleep. They stood together, watching him.

'Odd, isn't it?' Matt said at last. 'It's just like the painting.'

'You think there's something else.' It was a statement. 'Something you still don't know.'

He nodded. 'It's so frustrating. I thought it was all over, you see. And though it was tragic I was getting used to it because at some level I'd already known about it, if you see what I mean.'

'And why do you think it isn't all over?'

'Oh, I don't know.' He turned away and wandered out on to the veranda. 'Because I thought that all the nightmare stuff was bound up in it, I suppose, and that, once I knew, I'd be able to write again. And I still feel as desperate as I did before any of this happened. If I can't write now I never will.'

'But that's not quite logical, is it?' she asked gently.

'After all, you wrote *Epiphany* without knowing any of this, didn't you? In fact, it sprang out of all the things that you call the "nightmare stuff". You're beginning to understand your past; things are being revealed to you. Maybe the new book will follow when you've had time to assimilate all these things thoroughly.'

'I still feel there's something else.' He sat down on the edge of the veranda steps. 'Something more. The kitten reminded me of it, and I looked at the paintings again.'

'And?'

'And nothing.'

He sat disconsolately, his arms on his knees, staring down the garden, and she felt a great wave of compassion for him.

'It's not over yet.' She spoke without thinking, and saw the muscles beneath his shirt tense. 'Try not to strain towards whatever it is. It will come to you. I know it will. Give it time and try to enjoy Annabel's stay.'

He snorted. 'Venetia thinks I should finish it.'

'It's not Venetia's business. Are you very fond of Annabel, Matt?'

'I've no idea,' he answered moodily. 'I feel like Prince Charles when he said: "Whatever love means." I just can't concentrate on anything, that's the trouble. I feel like this whole business is crippling me emotionally and I don't want to live this way. Why am I like this, Lottie?'

She spoke strongly to him. 'I think that you had a twin, and that something traumatic happened when you lost him. Clearly it affected Helen very badly but because you were so small nobody understood quite the effect it might have on you. Your "nightmare stuff" is a direct result of that trauma, but simply knowing the truth might not be quite enough to put an immediate end to it or to result in a sudden burst of creativity. Give yourself a chance to adjust properly to knowing rather than just suspecting. And perhaps you're right, and there's one more piece of the puzzle to unravel. You've waited over thirty years, Matt. You must be patient for just a little longer.'

She paused for a moment, but he didn't respond, and she cast around for some lighter topic.

'I have a feeling that you've got this kitten for life, you know. We'll ask around in the village, just as a formality, but meanwhile shall we go into Porlock and get some food and stuff from Richard?'

He nodded, turning and smiling at her, trying to cast off the weight that pressed upon him, and her heart went out to him.

'Isn't it lucky that the Moretons were cat lovers

and there's a flap in the back door? What will you do with him whilst Annabel's here?'

Matt stood up. 'I've thought about that,' he said, 'and I've decided to make a test out of it. I shall put food down for him in the kitchen for the next two days but I shan't make him come up to the High House. I'm hoping that between us all we can keep an eye on him. If he's still here when I get back then I'll know he's meant to be here. What d'you think?'

'It seems reasonable to me.' Lottie thought about it. 'It would be better for him not to be too confused about where he lives right at the start, and cats are very independent, aren't they? We'll check with Venetia. She'll know. It'll be interesting to see if he's still here when we get back from Porlock, or are you going to lock him in?'

'No. He came of his own free will, and he can go again if he wants to. I feel very fatalistic about this.'

She nodded but, despite his determination to give the kitten his freedom, she could see that Matt was hoping that the kitten would still be there when he came home.

CHAPTER THIRTY-FIVE

It was very sunny; very hot. No breath of wind stirred the young, green herringbone bracken. A fuzzy, black and gold bee hung, heavy laden, in the mouth of the foxglove's bell, and the soft warm air was thick with the nutty scent of the gorse-flower. Out in the Channel two container ships hovered on a glassy sea that was all one with the white sky: a shuddering, shimmering wall of heat.

Across the vale, on Hurlstone Point, a shining arc of light dazzled and gleamed. The curved, silken wing of the hang-glider lifted gently, turning and drifting high above the cliff. Magically, other wings – green and scarlet and silver – joined the first; gently, slowly, they soared and swooped in an aerial dance.

Matt had raised himself on his elbow, watching through the binoculars. He was lying on a rug beside the car on which were the remains of a picnic. A few feet away, Annabel was trying to tempt a robin with some crumbs.

'He's quite tame,' she was saying, kneeling up on her heels, pushing back her hair. 'Isn't he sweet?'

Matt felt as if his mouth were full of dough; or of some substance that prevented him from speaking naturally. Ever since they'd left the High House she'd been acting a role; she was determined that he should see her as The Helpmeet. The conversation at breakfast had turned on the subject of writers, the difficulties of living with someone who inhabits another world, and Matt had come in for a great deal of good-humoured teasing.

'Self-absorption,' Milo had declared, tempted from his newspaper for a bit of the action, 'is the phrase that leaps to mind. No good talking to him when he's got his head full of a story. Ever since a child he's been the same. The eyes glaze over; the attention wanders. Might as well talk to yourself.'

And Lottie had told the story about the writer she'd met at a wedding. He'd talked about himself right through the wedding breakfast and then he'd said: 'Well, that's enough about me. Let's talk about my book.'

It had been clear that Annabel had been torn between joining in with her own amusing experiences about writers, and defending Matt.

'It's all worth it, though, isn't it?' she'd asked. 'Look at the terrific success Matt's had.'

She'd smiled understandingly at him, a kind of 'I'm on your side' smile that had been excruciatingly embarrassing, and the other three had been silent for a moment before one of them had changed the subject. Ever since, she'd been determined to show that, however antisocial, tiresome or peculiar writers were, *she* was made of the stuff that could support and encourage them: and him in particular.

Now, she looked over her shoulder at him and he made himself smile at her.

'I love your little house,' she said. 'And it's such a romantic story, isn't it? Milo's great-grandmother having it built specially so that she could paint.'

'Lots of people have had follies built,' he answered idly. 'That's what it was, I suppose.'

He'd realized right away that he didn't want to talk in any depth about the Summer House, though he'd been obliged to show it to her. She'd been thrilled with everything, even the kitten.

'Oh, Matt, he's so sweet,' she'd cried. 'I didn't know you were a cat person.'

'Neither did I,' he'd said, pretending indifference. 'He just appeared from nowhere and I'm waiting to see if someone in the village is going to claim him.'

He'd known then: he hadn't wanted her to know

about the kitten, or Helena, or George and his ghost twin. And he certainly didn't want her to know about his own history. There on the veranda of the Summer House he'd taken the decision, and now it only remained to tell Annabel.

'Perhaps we'd better get a move on,' he suggested, 'if we're going to have tea with Im.' He got up and began to pack the hamper, to shake out the rug. He glanced back towards Hurlstone Point, but the dance was over and the silken wings were folded.

Annabel helped to pack up the picnic feeling furious. Whatever she did or said, she got nowhere, and she simply dreaded getting back to London and having to tell her friends that she and Matt were no further on. Whilst she collected the plates, she brooded on the last twenty-four hours. For a start, she hadn't been prepared for the ghastly Venetia to be a fixture at the High House; the old witch made her feel nervous, as if she could see right through her, though Lottie and Milo were quite sweet and made her very welcome, though not exactly as Matt's girlfriend; not as though she were *special* to him.

And then, it had been something of a shock, and not a good one, when she'd discovered that Matt's little house was right next door, so to speak, and that the gardens connected, and that there was all this matey to-and-fro stuff going on. Of course, it was a very, very nice little house, and definitely worth having to put up with the communal bit to have it *plus* the swish London pad. It was perfect for the bolt hole; the weekend retreat. But there was still this block where Matt was concerned. He treated her like a friend but nothing more; nothing personal, nothing intimate. Apparently, he'd had a couple of relationships, neither of them very long-lived, and she'd heard that both girls had been very sad when he'd finished with them. Perhaps, since *Epiphany*, he was wary that any woman would be after his loot.

Annabel gave a mental shrug: if that was the case she'd simply hang around until she'd won his confidence. She was good at waiting. And now they were off to see the sister and the tiresome child, and, if that weren't enough, a puppy as well. She wasn't really an animal person, to tell the truth, but she could put on a good show with them if she had to; like she'd had to with Pud and that wretched kitten. There was nothing worse than the smell of cats in a house, unless it was dog hair everywhere. She might have to do something about the kitten if things moved on a bit. She wished Matt would come back to London. It was so much more her scene, and she so loved his flat.

The packing-up was done, and the car bumped down the track and into the lane. The robin hopped out from the sheltering gorse and began to peck up the last of the crumbs.

'It's been a bit odd,' Im said. 'I can't help thinking about Mum and wishing I'd been a bit, well, kinder. If anything happened to Rosie I'd be out of my mind and when you think about it, Matt, he must have been about her age, mustn't he?'

They stood together at the big doors that led into the garden, watching Annabel playing with Rosie and The Dodger.

'Why do you say that?' asked Matt. He didn't question who the 'he' was; he knew that.

'Because you were at the age where you could remember some things but not others. You can't remember his name but you can remember watching Mum playing and laughing with you both. And, of course, nobody ever referred to him afterwards so he never entered into a collective family history. Your memory is bound to be very patchy under those circumstances. I think you can't have been more than eighteen months at the very most. An awful lot of our earliest memories are bound up with what other people tell us. Received wisdom underlines things we can recall and puts the flesh on the bare bones, so to speak, and builds up pictures for us. You didn't have any of that. Poor Mum. I just thought that it was all about Dad and that she should have been able to pull herself together a bit for our sakes. After all, think of all those young army widows. And I know they lost their sons too, and still coped without drinking themselves to death, but I still wish that I'd *known*.'

'The thing is,' Matt said after a moment, 'that we still might not have been that patient about it. Perhaps you have to have a child yourself to truly understand what she was going through.'

'Perhaps.'

Im stood in silence. In her hands she held a toy: a garishly painted Russian doll which she turned and turned about, smoothing it with her fingers, her eyes still fixed on Rosie. He watched her, something teasing at his memory, and then Rosie called to them and Annabel waved.

'I still don't think she's right for you,' Im murmured.

'Neither do I,' he agreed. 'Sad, isn't it?'

'Then tell her,' she said sharply. 'Don't drag it out.'

'I'm not going to,' he said crossly. 'I decided this morning and I'm waiting for the right moment, that's all. She's going back to London tomorrow morning.'

'Well, as long as you don't do it by text or email,' she said, and she put the doll on the table and went out into the garden.

Matt hesitated, picking up the doll, unscrewing it and seeing the smaller doll inside: and two thoughts clashed in his mind. One was a mental picture of the painted, wooden cat that had been kept in his mother's rosewood box but the second was a much more profound shock. If his mother had taken the photographs in order to act out a fantasy, then who had taken and sent that last photograph? He'd almost forgotten about it – but who had taken it, and why send it to the agency with no message or explanation? Had he been wrong about the photographs?

The group in the garden were calling out to him, and, making a great effort to control his shock, he went out to them.

CHAPTER THIRTY-SIX

The journey to Taunton had been a difficult one. Luckily, Annabel had needed to catch the first London train so as to arrive at the office by lunchtime, and this had meant an early start. Matt had explained, on the way to the station, that he wouldn't be seeing her again; not like this, anyway: that he didn't want to be giving her the wrong idea. She'd sat silently, biting her lips, her hands wringing and twining, as she stared ahead. He'd told her that it was not fair to allow her to believe that their friendship was anything more than simply that. She'd broken in then, saying that she didn't want anything more just yet, but that surely they could go on seeing each other, that they had fun together.

Desperately, he'd agreed that they'd had fun, of course they had, but it was best that she shouldn't be misled; that he had lots of women friends and that he wasn't ready for any kind of commitment;

371

that he had a book to write. He'd hated the sound of himself but all his self-preservation instincts were warning him that he mustn't give an inch here and that it was cruel to give her any kind of hope.

She'd climbed out of the car in stony silence and taken her bag. 'Please don't wait,' she'd said icily; and he'd merely checked that the train was due on time and driven home.

He'd felt such relief as he'd let himself into the Summer House and the kitten had come to meet him, purring and winding round his ankles. He'd made coffee and taken it out on to the veranda. The garden was soaked in heat, and, some way off, he could hear the cuckoo. He sat in silence allowing the peace to fill him, opening his mind and emptying it; the gentle presence was close at hand, comforting him, preparing him. Visions filled his head: the kitten, stripy and tigerish under the lilac tree; Im turning the Russian doll in her hands; the last photograph.

Matt opened his eyes. He sat quite still, puzzling over these images, and then got up and went inside. The rosewood box, which he'd fetched from London on his last visit, stood on a shelf in the sitting room. He picked it up and took it back to the veranda. Opening the lid he was instantly transported back in time; running to his mother with treasures: 'Shall we put them in the box, Mummy?' and then the ceremonial fetching of the key, which he'd left in its tiny lock.

The envelope containing the letter from his father was still there, and the suede pochette with his grandmother's silk handkerchief. The small treasures that he'd been allowed to put in the box were long withered and gone, but the carved and painted wooden cat was there. He took the striped, tigerish-looking object into his hands remembering how his biggest treat had been to play with it. Like Im's Russian doll it separated into two halves, though in this case it would reveal a smaller cat, and then another, until the final, delightful surprise: a tiny mouse. Gently, Matt twisted the two halves of the cat but it remained firm and he was obliged to use more pressure in order to separate them. As soon as he managed it he could see why. Around the next cat a piece of paper had been wrapped: a very thin, blue sheet of airmail writing paper.

Matt unwrapped the sheet and smoothed it out on his knee: he stared at the words, hardly able to take them in.

Forgive me. Your son David is here with us. He is safe. No harm will come to him. Knowing that I am barren and unhappy because I long for a child, Taji brought him to me. She is my niece and she will stay with us as his nurse. She has done wrong, great wrong, but she loves him too, and she says you have a son and another child to be soon born. My husband is high up in the government and believes that David is Taji's love child. He will give him a good, happy home. He will want for nothing. Already we love him but I think of your pain and fear. I can do nothing. No scandal must touch my husband. But I will send proof of David's safety and happiness through your husband's news agency. We love him so much and we call him Vladimir. Forgive me.

Twice, unbelieving, Matt read the letter. He dropped it and snatched up the packet of photographs from the box: one sent every year to assure his mother of David's continuing existence and his happiness. Again and again he picked up one, and then another; not his own face, after all, but David's face: smiling, laughing, looking away at something distant; a happy, confident face. At first he experienced a shock of anger. He'd readily believed in a dead twin, but the proof of this live boy, mirroring so exactly his own face and expressions, filled him with a deep, atavistic anger, as though his identity had been stolen; as though he were no longer unique. Very slowly, as the anger subsided and he studied the photos again, the tight, familiar knot of loneliness in his heart began to uncoil; slowly he allowed himself to reach out towards the boy who gazed back at him with such openness and trust.

'David,' he murmured – and remembered his mother's anguish when he'd named his own fictional child's alter ego 'David'.

'Why did you call him that?' she'd cried, and he'd imagined that it was because it had been his father's second name that she'd been so distressed. At some subconscious level he'd remembered his twin's name and used it innocently. How she must have suffered: every time she'd looked at him she would have seen David at his shoulder, like the little ghost in the paintings. He tried to imagine her horror when she'd received the letter; the anguish she and his father had suffered, knowing that David was still somewhere in the world and that they might never see him again. They must have tried to track him down but, in such a country as Afghanistan, with its miles of borders into Russia, they would have had little chance of finding him; and the Cold War was still in its last stages, hindering any easy communication, refusing to allow any damaging information to escape. So at last, when hope was gone, they'd come home and tried to start afresh. Nobody at home would have known much about it; back then, a child's disappearance in a distant country would not have made the front pages as it might now. And those who had known had kept silence at Helen's request.

And David was alive: he was alive now. The continuing shock of this fact struck again at his heart. That photograph he'd received a few weeks ago was the latest assurance that David was a strong, happy young man. Matt remembered it, wondering if it had been taken on one of his own book-signing tours abroad. He remembered the cheerful face, half-turned over his shoulder, laughing into the camera. David was alive.

And then another name – 'Taji'. He repeated it, and instantly memories stirred and shifted: a smiling face bending down to him; small, strong hands lifting him; a pretty singing voice. And now he saw his nightmare's vision: David being lifted from the other end of the pram by those same small, strong hands and whirled away, whilst he, Matt, remained alone, strapped in the pram, crying until people came running; and then the screams and cries and anguish of the discovery of David, gone.

The kitten jumped up on to his knee and head-butted his hand, curling into the crook of Matt's arm. He settled, blinking out at the bright sunshine, and Matt stroked him absent-mindedly, yet taking comfort from the warmth and companionship. What now? He must tell them all, Im, Lottie, Milo, about this new discovery; but not quite yet. He needed time to adjust to the shock, to come to terms with this new information.

He smoothed the letter, read it again and folded it. His mother had left it for him to find; she'd left the box to him hoping that he'd open the packet of photographs first, because it was new to him, and then be led onwards to discover the truth. He put the letter back into the box with the photographs and took out his father's letter. It was a short one and he could remember it almost word for word. A letter from a father, far away, telling his son to be a good boy and to look after his mother and little sister; it had made him feel proud and strong. He took it out, with its familiar photograph of his father standing in a dry, dusty, arid place, holding his camera in his hand.

And here was another heart-stopping shock: now there was a second photograph. His father smiled at him, a child sitting on each arm; twin boys staring into the lens, puzzled and alert. Helen stood beside them, her face turned lovingly towards her boys and Tom. Matt stared at it. This must be the only record to exist of all of them together. The others would have been destroyed before they returned to England lest questions were asked and curiosity roused. Yet she'd kept this one secretly all her life, in hope and faith and love, and passed it on to him at the end.

Matt held the photograph on his knee, staring into the sunny garden; and at last he wept, painfully, agonizingly, for his mother and for his father; and for himself.

CHAPTER THIRTY-SEVEN

They sat around the table in the breakfast room – Matt, Lottie and Milo. The photographs were scattered between them, the two letters lying side by side. Earlier, Venetia had been picked up by a friend and taken out to lunch, and now the three of them sat contemplating the photos and the letters. The words of Matt's extraordinary story and their shocked response to it seemed to echo in the silence.

'So this Taji,' Milo broke the silence at last, 'she was your nurse?'

'As far as I can remember anything, I think she was. The name, when I read it in that letter, gave me an immediate memory jolt. That's the trouble, you see. I can only see flashes of things. Everything is so fragmented.'

'Well, that's fair enough. You can't have been two. And she was in a prime position to take David, wasn't she?'

Matt was still finding it odd to hear David referred to so naturally but Milo had grasped Matt's story with an acuity that had surprised him, and was now working it out for himself.

'It would have been carefully planned,' he was saying. 'Taji would have had some help. She'd have wheeled you somewhere away from home in your big pram where she knew you'd be safe. Then she'd have taken David out, hurried down some little side street and probably into a waiting car, and then she'd have been away and over the border into Russia. Calling David "Vladimir" is the clue there, isn't it? Vladimir is Russian for David, if I remember rightly. I wonder where it all happened. In the bazaar? Somewhere it was safe to leave Matt but that gave her long enough to get some distance away before the alarm was raised.'

Matt nodded; that sounded perfectly reasonable. He could tell that Lottie was anxious lest he was finding Milo's down-to-earth approach painful, and he smiled reassuringly at her.

'I've always remembered it,' he said. 'The heat, and the exotic scents, and the babble of foreign voices. It could easily have been a marketplace. I have this vision of being lifted and whirled away, and yet at the same time I was watching myself being carried off. And then the sense of terrible loss. It's such an odd sensation that I'm surprised I didn't guess the truth or remember him more clearly. I suppose that it was because nobody ever talked of him or mentioned him again. At eighteen months you can't verbalize it, can you? Eventually there's nothing to feed your memory. Just this terrible sense of traumatic loss. I wonder if he's suffered from that, too.'

Lottie moved the photos around, looking at them.

'He looks happy, doesn't he?' she ventured. 'Maybe he's had his demons too, but on a day-to-day level he looks a balanced, happy sort of fellow. Thank goodness he had Taji as a kind of continuity.'

'I keep wondering how I might trace him,' Matt said. 'Knowing he's out there somewhere is wonderful in one way, but terrible in another.'

'But how could you do that without bringing his whole life tumbling down?' asked Milo sharply. 'Clearly he has no idea of his past. You'd have to tell him that the person that he thinks is his mother has been party to his kidnapping. His father knows nothing about that, either. He thinks that David is her niece's child. It might destroy them all.'

Matt sat staring at him. 'I hadn't thought it through,' he muttered at last. 'You mean we can never meet? I can never go and look for him?'

He saw Lottie's swift warning glance at Milo, who sat back in his chair and crossed his arms. There was a little silence.

'There is a way that one day might bring David to *you*,' she said. 'I'm surprised you haven't thought of it.'

He stared at her, puzzled, and she got up and went swiftly out of the room. When she returned she was carrying two copies of *Epiphany*: one hardback, one paperback. She showed him the photograph on the back of the dust cover of the hardback, and the author photo on the inside cover of the paperback.

'You're an international bestselling author, Matt. Don't you think that one day David might see this and then, maybe, *his* memories might begin to make connections?'

Hope rose in his heart but he crushed it down. 'But, like Milo said, that could cause huge problems, couldn't it?'

Milo remained silent, staring at the photographs on the table, but Lottie shook her head. She looked calm, even happy.

'I think there will be a moment when it will all come together and the time will be good for it. I have a strong feeling, Matt, that one day you and David will meet again in the right circumstances.'

He wanted so desperately to believe her that he could hardly bear to think about it, but Milo's warning was a real one.

'Both your parents are dead,' Lottie was saying. 'Who knows whether David's stepfather is still alive? Clearly his stepmother is, since you had the photograph only a few weeks ago, but there will come a time when David will be able to meet you without quite the disaster that Milo describes. I feel certain of it. You'll simply have to go on waiting, Matt, but now, at least, you know the truth. That must be some comfort.'

'Yes, it is.' He shuffled the photographs together, picked up the letters, paused to look again at the most recent photograph; Milo and Lottie watched him. 'I wonder what he's like,' he said. 'Whether he's a doctor, or a teacher, or a musician. He might even be a writer.'

'Whatever he does,' Lottie said after a moment, 'he looks as though he enjoys it.'

'When will you tell Im?' asked Milo. 'How will she take it, d'you think?'

'I think she'll be emotional about it for all the obvious reasons, but especially because of Rosie. It was bad enough thinking that David had died of some kind of disease. To hear that he was snatched will probably really upset her.'

He got up, and they rose too, watching him with anxiety and love.

'I'm fine,' he said, as if in answer to some unspoken question. 'It's a relief because I really know it all, at last. I'm going to see Im as soon as I can. I think she should know too. Thanks for, well, for being around.'

When he'd gone they looked at one another.

'It hardly seems possible,' Milo said. 'What an extraordinary story. I wish I could believe that he won't be knocked off balance by it. It's one hell of a shock, isn't it?'

'Except that Matt always suspected that there was something missing; he's always been lonely for David though he didn't know what or who it was until he saw Helena's paintings and began to guess, but deep down he knew that there had been some traumatic event way back in his childhood. Even as a small boy he was trying to write the fear of it out of his system and finally it all came together in *Epiphany*, though none of us quite recognized it. It's much better that he knows the truth. Actually, it will be harder for Im.'

'But why should it be? It wasn't her twin that was taken. She didn't even know David.'

'But she knows now what it's like to fear for your

384

child. Matt's quite right. It will be Im who will really need support. If I know Matt he's already beginning to think of how he can use all this material. Oh, not consciously in a cold-blooded way. He simply can't help himself. His creative spirit will take it and set it apart from him and he'll turn it into a story that he can tell himself. That's how he'll manage it and understand it and gradually come to terms with it. Im can't do that. She might imagine it happening to Rosie or be afraid to leave her alone. Things like that. She'll need a great deal of reassurance.'

They stood together; Milo put his hand on her shoulder.

'Do you wish that she and Jules were at the Summer House, after all, so that they were close to us?'

Lottie shook her head. 'They'll deal with this together. It's exactly what they needed after all the fuss with Nick.'

'With Nick? What about Nick?'

Lottie bit her lip. 'I simply mean the fuss about Nick needing the money, and you offering Im the Summer House and then Jules not wanting it and it causing a lot of problems between him and Im, that's all. They know now that it would have been wrong for them and they're back on an even keel, but this news will bring them even closer. Much better that Im is depending on Jules for comfort than on us. We'll be here, of course, but it's Jules she'll need now.'

He sighed. 'I'm sure you're right. I'm going to do some work in the garden. It'll settle me down after all that.' His hand tightened reassuringly on her shoulder. 'We'll get through this,' he said.

She smiled gratefully up at him. 'I know we will.'

He went out, Pud at his heels, and she watched him go, puzzled as always that other people couldn't see quite obvious things so easily as she could. Clearly Milo had not suspected that Nick's recent spate of visits had been anything other than filial; but why should he? Nick had now accepted that his place was with Alice and his children, however uncomfortable it might be to begin with, and his visits would drop back to a more usual rate.

The telephone rang: it was Sara.

'I hear that Milo's turning the place into a hospital,' she said in her abrupt way. 'Nick says that Venetia managed to fall down the stairs and break nearly every bone in her body and that she's taken refuge with you. Drunk, I suppose?'

Lottie began to laugh. 'No, not drunk. Just not terribly well. A tiny stroke is suspected, so they're going to keep an eye on her, but it was just her ankle and her arm that were broken, luckily.'

'A stroke?'

Lottie detected a tremor of fear in her sister's voice. 'Difficult to believe, isn't it? Venetia seems indestructible,' she said. 'But she's much better. Going home soon, so don't worry.'

A short silence. 'I'm glad to hear it.'

'I knew you would be,' Lottie said cheerfully. 'You sound in good form and thank you, yes, we're all well here in La-la Land. I'm coming up to London to see some friends next week and staying a couple of nights. Could you get up for lunch, say, Wednesday?'

'I suppose I could,' said Sara ungraciously.

'Good. I'll give you a buzz when I'm in town and arrange to meet. We'll exchange all the news then. 'Bye.'

She put the phone down and took a deep breath. She walked out to the parlour and on to the terrace. David. It was as if someone near had spoken his name. In her mind's eye she saw again the photograph of the little family: Tom holding his babies, and Helen, standing easily and relaxed, smiling happily and lovingly at them all. Pain sliced into her heart. How different was the Helen she'd known; her face rigid with control; the blank eyes always looking back at the past; the nervous, uncontrolled gestures. Oh, there had been happy moments when, briefly, she'd been able to forget the anguish, but then memory would snake back, coiling round her heart, and there would be the hasty exit, the quick tilt of the bottle.

Lottie put her hands to her own heart. She'd imagined that Helen's pain had been for Tom, and of course some of it had been; but how could one forget, even for a minute, the loss of a beloved child? And in such a way.

And Tom? She remembered his determined perseverance in his effort to appear normal and how she'd sometimes been irritated by Helen's excessive grieving over a miscarriage whilst she had two beautiful children and a devoted husband. She'd felt sorry for Tom, and glad that he'd known a kind of respite in her company. Like Matt, he'd hidden his feelings in his writing, immersed himself in work; how like his father Matt was; and David looked just like him, too.

David. The name echoed again in her mind but now it came with a sudden uplift of joy; a reassurance that all would be well, and a promise for the future.

CHAPTER THIRTY-EIGHT

'The trouble is,' Im said, 'that I keep going over it in my mind. And then I want to rush and find Rosie, wherever she is, and hug her and not let her out of my sight. I wake up in the night and want to go and make sure she's still there.' She and Jules sat close together on the sofa with The Dodger fast asleep at their feet. She was holding Jules' hand tightly.

'And do you?' asked Jules. 'Do you actually do that?'

'No,' said Im firmly. 'No, I don't. I've been thinking about it really carefully, you see, now the first shock is over. I thought about Mum and how her whole life was destroyed by horror and fear. And I feel an absolute cow, now I know the truth, because I could never relate to her, you see. It was so difficult living with this buttoned-up, silent person but, at the same time, it was what I'd always been used to, and we had Lottie, thank God. Lottie wasn't actually

389

maternal in the usual kind of way but she was *there*, and she enabled us to be normal children, so it was OK. But as I grew up I became more resentful of Mum's silences, and the never-actually-drunk but never-quite-sober kind of state she lived in, and in the end I just kind of gave up on her. Matt never did. He was always so patient. But then he could remember Mum from before, you see, and he went on hoping that some miracle would happen and she'd be her old self again. I can understand why she was like that now, of course, and I feel so guilty that I didn't make more allowances, and it's ghastly what she went through. She couldn't ever have forgotten David for a moment. Every time she looked at Matt she would have seen David. And the torment would have been that she'd have felt that nobody else could ever cherish David or understand him like she did and she'd have felt so helpless. And then there would be the grinding guilt and all those "if only" conversations with Dad. Poor, poor Mum.'

Jules waited whilst the storm of tears passed, and Im blew her nose.

'But you say you're not going to let yourself worry about Rosie?'

'No,' Im said fiercely. 'I won't let her grow up in an atmosphere of paranoia. Looking back, I guess that it was Lottie who unwittingly saved us from a crushing straitjacket of care; who made sure that we went out and about like other ordinary children. And I've seen where fear takes you: straight to the bottle. I don't want to be like that, Jules.' She shuddered. 'I've decided that the only way is simply to stamp on it right from the beginning and not let it get a grip. Rosie's in no more danger now than she was last week. I shall take all the usual sensible precautions but I won't allow myself to become paranoid. I mustn't for her sake.'

Her face crumpled, and she sobbed again, and Jules held her tightly.

'You are absolutely right,' he said. 'I'm with you all the way.'

'I've decided something else.' Im wiped her cheeks. 'Something Lottie said about fear made me feel that it would be right.'

She hesitated, and Jules asked: 'What did she say?'

'She said that it didn't take much to push people into a climate of fear. That one act of terrorism could almost paralyse the entire world and create suspicion and hatred where there had been none. She was talking about faith in humanity and hope for the future, and I suddenly knew that I wanted another baby, Jules. Our baby, as a kind of symbol.'

He smiled. 'A kind of two-fingers-to-fear baby?'

391

She smiled too, a rather watery smile. 'Exactly that. It's all so terrifying if you allow yourself to think about it. And one fearful thought quickly lets in others, and then you're just sliding all the way down into a kind of hell of images and horror. I won't go there, Jules. I have a choice. Mum had reasons for her dependency on alcohol: David disappearing, and then Dad being killed. I don't judge her at all. But, actually, nothing's changed for us, has it? At least we know David is alive and looks happy, and he hasn't really known anything else or, at least, he probably can't remember anything else. I suppose, as far as he's concerned, it's no different from being adopted into a loving family. Except that being a twin, he's probably had those odd feelings and flashes of memory that Matt's had.' She shook her head. 'I probably sound callous, or I'm oversimplifying it, but we have to survive this news and go on making a happy world for Rosie. So this is my way.'

They held each other tightly. Jules knew that this conversation would be repeated in many different forms, and on many occasions, and that it was necessary for Im's mental health that she should be allowed to talk about it as often as she needed. Recently, since the move to Exmoor and the new job, it had been her courage and warmth that had sustained him through unconfident and fearful moments. Now it was his turn to support her.

'I like the idea of this baby,' he said now. 'I have a strong feeling it'll be a boy and we'll call him Jack.'

She raised her head curiously. 'Why Jack?'

'Jack-the-giant-killer,' he answered cheerfully. 'He'll triumph over the fear and darkness. He'll be our stake in the future.'

'Oh, Jules.' She put her head back on his shoulder, hugging him. 'I do love you.'

'Not puppy love this time,' he said teasingly. 'Baby love. Oh dear. Here we go again.'

She laughed, and hit him with a cushion. 'You'll do your duty like a man,' she said. 'And you'll enjoy it. This is not a subject for negotiation,' and she kissed him.

The azaleas and rhododendrons were in full flower. The small lawn was held in an encircling embrace of white and purple and crimson blossom. On the bank beside the brook, yellow and blue flag irises in their green sheaths stood straight as swords, their vivid colours reflected, broken and refracted, in the fast-flowing water. A blackbird swooped, beak filled with food for her babies sheltering in the hedge, and sunshine filtered through the tender, green beech leaves, casting ever-changing patterns on the grass. The kitten pounced upon them and stared in amazement to find nothing beneath his paw but sunbeams.

From the veranda, Matt watched, amused.

'I shall call him Pickles,' he'd said to Milo and Lottie. 'He makes me think of all the Beatrix Potter books that Milo used to read to me, and all those cats and kittens. I know . . .' he held up his hands in defence as Milo began to protest, 'I know that Pickles was a terrier and that Ginger was the cat's name, but it suits him.'

He wondered what name the cat in the painting had had, and wished that he possessed Helena's talent for painting. Helen and Helena: in his consciousness the two seemed to be merging, to be with him in the house and in the garden, a kindly, gentle presence; enfolding and healing. He sat quite still, listening to the summer sounds: the breeze murmuring amongst the leaves; the singing brook; the trill and call of birdsong. Beside him on the table was his laptop and a notebook. Early that morning, wakening in the silvery dawn light, listening to the thrush's song, he'd known with certainty that he was ready to enter once again into the parallel universe of the imagination. Relief and joy had sent him down, barefoot, into the cool, dew-drenched garden, to wander by the brook and to allow his thoughts to flow free. He'd glanced up at the landing window, saluting the little cherub, and then he'd gone inside to make coffee. He'd dragged the chair out on to the veranda, and put his work things on the table; and now he waited confidently.

Visions and ideas swarmed in his mind; he could see the beginnings of a story about two boys, twins; separated early in their lives, and growing up on separate continents, yet still mysteriously connected. It wouldn't be quite his story, nor yet David's, but the essence of both their stories; distilled, changed, recreated. Matt was filled with energy and excitement. Now, at last, he knew what he would write – and how he would begin: he would begin with the photographs.

THE END

THE CHRISTMAS ANGEL
Marcia Willett

'We're all pilgrims,' he said thoughtfully.
'One way or another, aren't we? Always
searching for something.'

Twelfth night – time to put away the Christmas angel. A
new year dawns and everything seems to be falling into
place for Dossie. Her son Clem and his adorable five-year-
old son Jakey have moved to Cornwall to be closer to her.
She runs a successful catering business. All she needs
now is some better luck in her romantic life.

Complementing Dossie's rather unconventional
family set-up is the wonderfully eccentric Janna: a
warm-hearted, generous woman who looks after the
quirky nuns of the local convent – and little Jakey.
With humour, kindness and the support of
friendship, they form a tight bond.

But the Sisters' life as they know it is thrown into doubt
when an avaricious property developer starts prowling
around their beautiful, historic home. Will this close-knit
unit who so depend on each other still be together
next Christmas? And what will they have learnt
about the true meaning of family, and about
having somewhere you really belong?

**MARCIA WILLETT'S WONDERFUL NEW NOVEL
IS AVAILABLE NOVEMBER 2011**

READ ON FOR A SNEAK PREVIEW . . .

EPIPHANY

The Holy Family live in an old linen shoebag. The bag is dark brown, with a name-tape sewn just below its gathered neck where a stout cord pulls it tight, and each year on Christmas Eve the bag is opened and the Family, along with its attendant Wise Men, shepherds, an angel with a broken halo and various animals, are set out on a table beside the Christmas tree. They have their own stable, a wooden, open-fronted building, which has once been part of a smart toy farm, and they fit perfectly into it: the golden angel standing devoutly behind the small manger in which the tiny Holy Child lies, swaddled in white. His mother, all in blue, kneels at the head, opposite a shepherd who has fallen to his knees at the foot of the crib, his arms stretched wide in joyful worship. Joseph, in his red cloak, with a second shepherd – carrying a lamb around his neck as if it were a fur collar – stand slightly to one side, watching. A black and white cow is curled sleepily in one corner near to the grey donkey, which stands with its head slightly bowed. And here, just outside this homely scene, come the Wise Men in gaudy flowing robes, pacing in file, reverentially bearing gifts: gold, frankincense and myrrh.

Jakey stands close to the table, gazing at the figures, his eyes just level with them. Occasionally he might pick up one of the figures in order to study it more closely: the angel's broken halo; the lamb curled so peacefully around the shepherd's neck; the tiny caskets carried by the Wise Men. Once he'd dropped the Holy Child, who rolled under the sofa. Oh, the terror of the moment: lying flat on his face, scrabbling beneath the heavy chair, hot with the frustration of being unable to move it – and the huge relief when his fingers had closed over the little figure, and he'd drawn out the Baby unharmed and placed Him back in His blue-lined crib.

Now, as he stands by the crib, Jakey grows slowly aware of the sounds around him: the clock ticking weightily, its pendulum a crossly wagging finger; the sigh and rustle of ashy logs collapsing together in the grate; his father talking on the telephone next door in the kitchen and the monotonous quacking of the radio turned down low. Today the decorations must be taken down because it is Twelfth Night: the last day of Christmas.

Jakey begins to sing softly to himself: '"Five go-hold *lings*. Fo-ur calling birds, thlee Flench hens, two-hoo turtle doves, and a partdlige in a pear-*tlee*."'

He feels restless; sad that the tiny, sparkling lights and the pretty tree will no longer be there to brighten the short dark winter days. Still singing just below his breath, he climbs onto the sofa and tries to balance on his head on the cushions, his legs propped against its back, until he falls sideways and tips slowly onto the floor. He lies with his feet still on the sofa, his head turned sideways on the rug, and regards Auntie Gabriel, who stands on the bookcase presiding over the Christmas festivities. The angel is nearly two foot tall, with clumsy wooden shoes, a white papier-mâché dress and golden padded wings. Her hair is made of string, her scarlet, uptilted thread of a smile is compassionate; joyful. The clumpy feet might be set square and firm on the ground but when the golden wire crown is placed upon the tow-coloured head then there is something unearthly about her. Held lightly between her hands is a red satin heart: a symbol of love, perhaps?

There are several other, smaller, angels strung from convenient hooks about the room; but none has the status of Auntie Gabriel. Not as fierce and cold and glorious as the Archangel himself, flying in from heaven in all his power and majesty, and trailing clouds of glory; she is, nevertheless, a distant relation: the human, fallible face of love.

With a mighty heave, Jakey rolls head over heels and stands up. He goes over to the bookcase and stares up at Auntie Gabriel, who beams sweetly at him with her lop-sided silk-thread smile. He doesn't want her to be packed away in the soft roll of material that protects her fragile dress and padded wings, her gold crown wrapped separately, before they are all put into a large carrier bag and tucked into the drawer in the old merchant's chest. He doesn't want Christmas to be over. Jakey is utterly miserable. Deliberately he kicks out and stubs his toe in its soft leather slipper against the corner of the bookcase, hurting himself, and his mouth turns down at the corners. He decides to let himself cry; he's just going to, even though he knows that he's a big boy now; that next birthday he will be five. He experiments with a sob, listens to it with interest, and squeezes his eyes shut to force out a tear.

Clem watches his small son from the doorway, his heart twisting with a mix of compassion and amusement.

'Listen,' he says. 'Guess who that was on the phone.' And at the sound of his voice, Jakey jumps and turns quickly. 'It was Dossie,' Clem says. 'She's on her way over and she's bringing something special with her.'

Jakey hesitates, head down, his lower lip still protruding, not quite willing yet to be jollied out of his self-pity.

'What?' he asks, pretending not to care much. 'What is she blinging?'

'It's a secret.' Clem sits down and scoops a long-eared, long-legged brightly knitted rabbit onto his knee. 'Isn't it, Stripey Bunny? It's a Twelfth Night present. Something you have when all the decorations have been taken down.'

Jakey looks around the room: at the Holy Family; at the glittering tree; at Auntie Gabriel. He hesitates, debating with himself, but Clem senses signs of weakness and blesses his mother for the idea.

'He's utterly miserable,' he told her on the phone. 'He can't bear the thought of Christmas being over and I can't really explain to him why we have to take all the decorations down. It's going to be a bad evening.'

'Poor darling,' she said. 'I couldn't sympathize more. I hate it too. Now here's a plan. Why don't I bring over the chocolate cake I made this morning and something out of my present drawer. I've got one of those *Thomas the Tank Engine* thingies. James, I think it is. Or is it Edward? Jakey will know. We were reading a story about them all.'

Clem hesitated. 'He's had so much for Christmas, Dossie. I don't want to spoil him.'

'Oh, darling. One little truck. Remember how you used to feel? Anyway, we couldn't spoil Jakey. He's much too balanced. A Twelfth Night present. What d'you think?'

'OK. Why not? Do I get one too?'

'Certainly not. You're not nearly as balanced as Jakey is and I can't risk spoiling you at this late date. But you shall have some cake. See you soon.'

Now, Jakey wanders over and leans against Clem's knee. He twiddles Stripey Bunny's long soft ears and allows himself to give in.

'When will Dossie be here?'

'Soon.' Clem glances up at the clock: the drive from St Endellion to Peneglos should take about half an hour. 'Let's have a quick walk before it gets dark and you can ride your new bike. Stripey Bunny can go in the back.'

Jakey runs shouting to the door, high spirits restored.

'Boots on,' calls Clem. 'And your coat. Wait, Jakey. I said, *wait* . . .'

Presently they go out together into the wintry sunset.

READ THE COMPLETE BOOK – COMING SOON